Sex and
Murder.com

By Mark Richard Zubro

The Tom and Scott Mysteries

A Simple Suburban Murder
Why Isn't Becky Twitchell Dead?
The Only Good Priest
The Principal Cause of Death
An Echo of Death
Rust on the Razor
Are you Nuts?
One Dead Drag Queen

The Paul Turner Mysteries

Sorry Now?
Political Poison
Another Dead Teenager
The Truth Can Get you Killed
Drop Dead
Sex and Murder.com

Sex and Murder.com

Mark Richard Zubro

St. Martin's Minotaur
New York

www.minotaurbooks.com

Library of Congress Cataloging-in-Publication Data

Zubro, Mark Richard.
    Sex and murder.com : a Paul Turner mystery / Mark Richard Zubro.
        p.   cm.
    ISBN 0-312-26683-9
    1. Turner, Paul (Fictitious character)—Fiction.   2. Police—Illinois—
Chicago—Fiction.   3. Computer software industry—Fiction.   4. Chicago
(Ill.)—Fiction.   5. Gay police—Fiction.   6. Gay men—Fiction.   I. Title:
Sex and murder dot com.   II. Title.

PS3576.U225 S4 2001
813'.54—dc21
                                                              2001031629

First Edition: August 2001

10   9   8   7   6   5   4   3   2   1

To
Cal and Marilyn Sustachek

Thanks to
Barb, Hugh, Kathy, Rick

Sex and
Murder.com

⊾ 1 ⊿

It is surprisingly easy to pick a victim. The real problem is waiting for the one you've chosen to be sufficiently frightened before killing them. The waiting can be a pain in the ass.

Standing in the bedroom doorway, Detectives Paul Turner and Buck Fenwick gazed at the dead body. Neither of them had gaped at a murder scene in years, but Turner thought that if he was going to gape at one, this was it. He could see blood covering or splashed on or flecked over every surface. The man who had become a pincushion for the killer lay in the middle of the floor. He had bled copiously from stab wounds on his face, neck, chest, arms, stomach, thighs, and calves.

Fenwick said, "I hate to go too far out on a limb here, but my guess is that we have a very, very, very, very, very angry killer."

"That's so like you," Turner said, "always jumping to wild conclusions."

"I feel philosophical angst when I don't jump to conclusions."

"I hope that isn't catching. Anybody been in here?"

Fenwick wrinkled up his nose. "It smells like piss."

The dead man's wet and stained boxer shorts were the only clothing he wore. They were soaked, but they weren't red. Turner knew it wasn't blood.

Tommy Quiroz, one of the beat cops, said, "I know my training. I didn't touch anything. I waited for you guys."

"How'd you get in?" Fenwick asked.

"The gate was open. We found the entire security system completely shut down."

"What kind of system?" Turner asked.

"As far as we could tell, he had alarms on all the doors and windows, even those on the second floor. A surveillance camera on the street entrance."

Fenwick said, "Did the victim shut it down, and if so why? Although my money is on the killer shutting it down."

All of them moved aside for the personnel from the medical examiner's office and the evidence techs to enter the room.

Continuing to be careful not to step in any of the smears of blood, the three cops retreated to the hallway to wait for the experts to finish their work.

"Who is this guy?" Turner asked.

Tommy Quiroz flipped open his notebook. "I assume it's Craig Lenzati, the owner. We found a wallet in one of the other rooms. My partner says he was rich. Place is sure big enough for it to be true. I think I read something in the papers about this guy owning half the Loop."

"I always wondered who owned the other half," Fenwick said.

"It's nice of you to be willing to share," Turner said.

The mansion was south and east of the Loop, the Prairie Avenue District. These homes had been spared by the Great

Chicago Fire back in 1871. The fire had traveled north and east from its origins on the site of the current Fire Academy between Jefferson and Clinton Streets just south of Taylor. Turner found it intriguing that they had decided to build the academy on the site of the conflagration's beginning.

All the rooms on the ground floor had high ceilings with windows close to the ground. Each room they'd seen had been crammed with antiques.

"Supposedly he owned a lot of real estate, businesses, and politicians." Quiroz leaned closer. "The rumor is the call reporting the crime came in from the police superintendent's office."

"As in Devin Nelson superintendent of police in Chicago?" Turner asked.

"Himself."

"How's old Devin?" Fenwick asked.

"I don't know if he asked for you specifically," Quiroz said.

"He doesn't call me much anymore," Fenwick said.

"The superintendent found the body?" Turner asked. "Was it someone in his office or the superintendent himself who called?"

"I don't know."

Fenwick said, "We need to find out the sequence of events and who was involved in them, even if it includes everyone in the superintendent's office, which would be no bad thing. Locking up bureaucrats should earn me several merit badges."

"I never knew you were a Boy Scout," Turner said.

"I have many secrets," Fenwick replied. "What pisses me off is top police brass being involved in anything I am connected with. I was depressed enough already when I got to work."

"About what?" Turner asked.

"Life," Fenwick replied.

"You've been testy since before roll call. I know you haven't been to court to get steamed at the judicial system lately. You haven't seen any of the higher-ups all day. Something wrong at home?"

"No."

Fenwick was taciturn and not forthcoming, which was unusual but not unheard of. Turner knew to let him be when this happened. Eventually his partner would tell him what was bothering him. For now his reticence was not interfering with their jobs and might lead to a slackening in Fenwick's output of ghastly humor, though Turner doubted he'd be that lucky.

Fenwick continued, "If I see too many idiots from downtown, I'm not sure I'll be up to making death scene, cutecorpse comments."

"I'm not sure that's all bad," Turner said.

Fenwick said, "I live to make cute-corpse comments. It's my métier."

Everyone present, the medical examiner, the crime lab and evidence technicians, the photographers, and the beat cops, all stared at Fenwick. He saw the attention and smiled, "What?"

"Buck," Turner said, "why don't you go back to making cute-corpse comments. It fills a need in your soul, and it might keep you from spouting out-of-character clichés. Philosophical angst? Métier?"

"You don't like my grim cop humor? Instead of philosophical angst, you want me to talk about hemorrhoids?"

"Specifically or generically?" the ME asked.

"Hell of a choice," an evidence tech said. "If we're voting, I vote for neither."

Turner said, "Buck, we've been partners for years. I've

4

heard more of your trenchant comments, gotten more information about your physical oddities, and heard more of your jokes than anyone except your wife."

"More. She cuts me off from sex if I keep it up."

Turner guffawed loud enough for beat cops in the living room to enter the hall and stare at him wonderingly. When Turner stopped chuckling, he said, "I certainly hope that was an inadvertent choice of words rather than a description of reality."

The ME said, "Did I hear right? Somebody's cutting off Fenwick's dick? I want to be there for that."

"That's not what he said," a crime scene tech said, "however, we could make that a threat to keep him from telling any more jokes. And we could offer to make it a complicated, painful operation using only a spoon and a fork."

"Count me out," Turner said. "The sight of blood makes me want to interrogate people."

An evidence tech said, "Maybe the killer heard one of Fenwick's jokes and went berserk."

"Can we get out of here?" Quiroz asked. "It's painful when you guys stand around trying to be funny. I don't get paid for listening to that crap."

"Let's cut off *his* nuts," Fenwick suggested.

The beat cops in the past few years had become less inclined to put up with Fenwick's jeers and sneers. One of them muttered in a stage whisper, "If we're lucky, he'll be next."

"I heard that," Fenwick snapped. "It's not funny."

The reference to being "next" was to a report in that morning's *Chicago Tribune* claiming that there was a serial killer on the loose who was targeting police detectives. The reporter had drawn a line from Boston to Gary, Indiana, with five stops in between, where police detectives had been killed. All had been in cities through which Interstate 90 ran. Starting in Boston and preceding west through Albany and Buffalo, New York; Cleveland and Toledo, Ohio; South Bend and Gary, Indiana, one cop in each city had been stabbed multiple times. The murders had occurred once every six months over the past three years. If the killer was on schedule, according to the report, he or she would strike within the next week to ten days and the next major city west on the Interstate was Chicago. While the cop profiles in each city had not matched perfectly, the parallels the reporter had drawn between the descriptions and lives of the victims had been numerous and unsettling. Few cops might admit it, but Turner guessed most detectives in Chicago had checked to see if they matched the profile of the victims. Turner and Fenwick had each met some of the criteria.

Unfortunately, no one could be certain what the discrepancies might portend. The reporter's analysis could be inaccurate, or incomplete, or dead wrong. Cops could hope they weren't in danger, but no one could be sure. Turner knew that if there was a serial killer, this doubt was one of the things he or she could prey upon.

2

I like it best when they're complacent. When they don't believe it could happen to them. Detectives have huge egos. I want to deflate them. Their indifference to real human problems causes pain and suffering. I'm going to make them pay for all the indifference, and all the pain, and all the suffering.

Vinnie Girote, the mayor's press secretary, and Alex Yerson, the director of news affairs for the police department, showed up fifteen minutes after the evidence techs. Fenwick spotted the unwanted intruders. He asked, "Why are we being inundated with those fools?"

Turner said, "A desire to work on the side of truth and light? The politicians are frightened about the impact of the killing? One of our prominent fair citizens committed the murder? Hysterical overreaction? Damage control? I don't know, Buck. How many more guesses do I get?"

Fenwick said, "You can be Mister Question Man, and I'll be Mister Wisdom."

"How come you always get to be Mister Wisdom?"

"I'm better at making cute-corpse comments."

"That's getting just a trifle stale today." Turner knew that Fenwick was always one to beat a good joke to death.

Girote was a short, bald man in his late sixties, whose clothes never seemed to fit him quite right. They might be the most expensive, but he always looked like he'd just lost or gained fifteen pounds, so his clothes either clung too tight or billowed out too far. He had one characteristic Turner found most annoying. The detective had seen the type before: those who believed that if you were shouting, you were being effective.

Turner had seen Girote on the news and in person. His role as cheerleader seldom got in the way of his avoiding giving out information that was helpful or informative. The press corps, however, seemed to like him. He always made sure they had copious amounts of food at press buffets at major events and his sound bites resonated perfectly for the evening news. The reporters got plenty of advance notice of hot stories, which might be mostly geared to shed favorable light on the mayor and his administration, but it also made the reporters' jobs easier. Girote was also fantastic at doling out perks. If a writer needed tickets for their kids to an important sports event, they got them. If a reporter wanted front row seats at a hot theater opening, the tickets would miraculously appear.

Girote bulled past the beat cop stationed at the hallway entrance. He attempted the same maneuver on Fenwick.

"Going somewhere?" Fenwick asked. He moved his bulk to block Girote's progress. Fenwick's heft was legendary. His ability to pack away food second to none. His ability to devour chocolate unrivaled. His size, as much as his determination, effectively blocked the way.

"I need to see the body," Girote said. "I'm Vinnie Girote,

the mayor's press secretary." Turner wished he had a volume control knob so he could bring the guy down several decibels.

"No." Fenwick's voice matched Girote's in volume, but Fenwick's tone also gave the syllable enough finality to impress a hardened gangbanger. Girote, at the moment immune to Fenwick's best, tried to push past him again.

"How would you know where the body was?" Turner asked.

Girote ignored him and attempted to surge forward for the third time.

Fenwick put a large fist on the man's chest. He said, "You are not going to disturb my crime scene. You are not going any farther. You are going to turn around and march out of this house faster than you came in."

Girote drew in more than his full share of oxygen and resumed shouting, "I told you who I am. You're only a cop. I represent the most important politician in this city. That makes what I want to know important." He began rocking from foot to foot, a prize fighter out of his element, or a case of nerves in someone unable to conceal his emotions.

Turner liked it when press people were nearly out of control. They were actually easier to handle at such moments and far more likely to blurt out something indiscreet.

Fenwick laughed. He asked, "Are you the pope or a close relative of his? Wouldn't matter. He wouldn't get in there either."

"Why are you here?" Turner asked. "And why do you need to see the body?"

"The mayor is very concerned."

Turner said, "How does him being concerned have anything to do with you seeing the body or the crime scene? I see no connection. What is it exactly he is concerned about?"

"I don't answer to you," Girote said.

Fenwick gave his lowest grumble, before which crazed, heroin-addicted triple murderers had quailed. He said, "This is a murder investigation. If necessary, you will answer to me." He took a step forward.

Girote stopped talking and moving. He eyed both detectives carefully.

Turner said, "I asked you once already. How did you know which direction to go in to look for the body?"

"Am I a suspect?" Girote demanded.

"Not if you have a good alibi," Turner said.

"Would you like to be?" Fenwick asked.

The man continued to breathe heavily. His eyes bugged out like a fish on a cold slab waiting to be grilled. His mouth gaped like a nozzle on a vacuum cleaner hose.

Finally Fenwick said, "I'll get someone to escort you out." He took the man's elbow in one massive paw.

Girote tried to yank his arm away from the grip. "Let me go!"

Turner said, "Buck, wait a second. Mr. Girote, if you give us some useful background about Craig Lenzati, perhaps we can accommodate you in some way."

"Well, I suppose," Girote said.

Fenwick let him go. They repaired to the kitchen, out of the way of any technicians. The director of news affairs for the police department followed silently.

Fenwick asked, "Why are the politicians so concerned about this murder?"

"It's obvious. He's a prominent citizen. One of the richest in the city. He was thinking of buying a professional sports team and bringing it to Chicago. He's brought a lot of high tech jobs to this town. His loss will be severely felt. The mayor wanted to make sure the investigation was being pursued with all vigor."

"Why not just call our boss and apply pressure?" Fenwick asked. "Why send you?"

"Is that really germane to solving the case?" Girote asked. "I think the mayor's concern is natural."

Without discounting this explanation, Turner remained highly suspicious of this level of direct personal concern.

"Tell us more about Lenzati," Turner said. "What's his background?"

"I thought everyone knew about Craig Lenzati. Don't you detectives read Kup's column or the INC column or anything?"

"Humor me," Turner said.

"Well, he and a friend started one of those Internet businesses in their garage while they were still in college at Northwestern. They were very rich before they were twenty-five. They sold their company for over a billion dollars. Now they have an experimental technology company that's making even more money. The original company employs several thousand people in this area. The new company is expanding very fast. They are on the cutting edge. It is only a slight exaggeration to say that he and his company were responsible for the technological renaissance in the city. Before them, it was moribund. Forget Motorola. They were pikers compared to these guys. He has also invested heavily in real estate in cities around the world, but nowhere more so than in Chicago."

"What kind of guy was he?"

"Great. Smart, a genius. A big tipper. A big contributor to charitable causes. He always had a big smile for everyone, but shy. A computer nerd, after all. Socially okay, in a if-I-don't-make-a-move-I-won't-make-a-faux-pas kind of way."

"Did he live alone?" Turner asked.

"As far as I know, he did. He came to many functions with eligible young women. One more beautiful than the last. I don't know if he was serious about any of them."

Fenwick said, "I hate it when they have mostly frivolous relationships with women."

Girote gave him a puzzled look.

"Gritty cop humor," Fenwick said. "Not important to solving the case."

"Do you think you should be approaching this with a flippant attitude? Maybe the mayor should get someone else on this case."

Fenwick said, "You're the one who wants to look at a dead body for no discernible reason, unless you've got a corpse fetish."

They glared at each other.

"Who's his partner?" Turner asked.

"You really don't know?"

Turner said, "If I know the answer to a question, I promise not to ask it."

"Brooks Werberg."

"You know these guys personally?" Turner asked.

"Yes, I've met them on numerous occasions."

"Have you ever been invited to their homes for dinner?" Turner asked.

"I've attended many events."

Fenwick asked, "You've never gone over to watch a football game, just the two or three of you, or had them over for dinner at your house?"

"Well, no."

Turner asked, "Do you have any names of people he was close to?"

"No."

Turner asked, "How did Werberg and Lenzati get along?"

"Great. They've been best friends since they were kids. They lived together in college."

"Where can we find Werberg?" Turner asked.

"I can give you his business and home addresses and phone numbers, but I don't know where he is."

"Has he been told about his friend's death?"

"I'm not sure. Someone else was trying to contact him."

Turner said, "We were told the superintendent himself called in the report. Who called him? Or was the mayor's office called first? We need the sequence of the calls and who made them. The name of the original caller is the most important."

"I don't know who called."

"Who would know?" Turner asked.

"I'm not sure."

"We're going to know that for sure before we're done," Fenwick said.

"Is that a threat?"

"I hope you take it as one," Fenwick said.

"I don't know who called."

"We'll have to ask the mayor," Fenwick said.

"He can't be involved in a murder investigation," Girote insisted.

Fenwick asked, "Why? Doesn't he have a get-out-of-jail-free card?"

"You can't run around asking him questions. You can't come to the fifth floor of city hall and accost the mayor."

"Bull pizzle," Fenwick stated.

"Fine," Turner said. "All you have to do is show up with the information on who called the mayor, and we don't bother him."

Girote looked shocked. "Are you trying to bully me?"

Turner said, "You can call it a threat, bullying, blackmail, or making a deal, the life blood of politics anywhere. We need that name. We may need more information than that. You are going to provide it for us." Turner doubted if the mayor had committed murder, but he also knew he and Fenwick would follow any clues no matter where or to whom they led. If they pointed to the mayor, the problems for the case and their careers would be more than monumental.

Girote said, "I'll have to talk to some people, including your bosses."

"I smell a deal," Fenwick said. "Either that or we're going to be tattled on."

"Again?" Turner asked, then said, "Tell us more about Werberg."

"The two of them are the toast of the town. They go to all the openings. They give a lot of money to a lot of politicians. They could buy and sell the state legislature several times over."

Fenwick said, "I hear bribing all the legislators and the Chicago City Council wouldn't take much. Aren't half of the former aldermen in prison for over-feeding at the public trough?"

"Not that many," Girote said.

"Close enough," Fenwick said.

Turner said, "Lenzati and Werberg had significant political connections. I got that part. Were they smooth operators? Did they know the ropes? Did people like them?"

"They were a trifle naive early in their careers."

"How so?" Turner asked.

"There's a correct way to approach a legislator."

"Bribery etiquette," Fenwick said, "an area Miss Manners has yet to delve into. Perhaps the selection and use of the proper fork to skewer your opponent could become an art form."

Girote said, "They learned quickly. That they were rich helped, but people genuinely liked them. In the beginning they were the usual computer nerds, mole-eyed dweebs hunched over machines and screens. But these guys were able to change. They had decent hygiene. They would listen to advice. They learned to socialize. Their businesses were well run. The employees were well taken care of with some of the highest salaries and best benefits in the computer industry. They were extremely popular. Everyone liked them."

"Everybody but one," Fenwick said.

Turner asked, "Where were you this morning, Mr. Girote?

"Is that another threat or a very sick joke?"

"It's an easy question," Turner responded.

"I was in the press office at City Hall by five. I'll fax you my schedule and a list of eyewitnesses."

"Fine," Turner said.

"Can I see the body now?" Girote asked.

"No," Fenwick said.

Girote pointed at Turner. "You said I could."

"He said we'd try to accommodate you somehow," Fenwick said. "We're not about to define 'somehow' as letting you screw up a crime scene."

Girote glared at them. "That's a politician's way of weaseling out."

"Then you should be used to it," Turner said.

Girote huffed and puffed, but it was obvious that the detectives were not going to give in. "I'm going to report this to your superiors," was Girote's parting shout as he swept out the door.

Fenwick called after him, "Parting shots are for cowards."

Yerson stepped forward. The department director of news affairs, he had held back during this discussion. "Do you think you handled him correctly?" he asked.

"You want second guessing, try a Republican who hates Bill Clinton," Fenwick said. "We're not wasting our time with you. We've got real police work to do. Go away." He turned his back.

Yerson, who had been chosen more for his telegenic looks than any reportorial skills or press credentials Turner was aware of, said quietly, "Are you really sure this is a good way to deal with the mayor's and department's public relations offices?"

Fenwick didn't skip a beat as he said, "Yes."

Turner asked, "Do you know anything about Lenzati and Werberg?"

"I was told to come over here. I was working in an office full of people since very early this morning."

"I didn't suspect you," Turner said.

"I don't know anything more than Girote told you. In fact a great deal less."

⌐ 3 ⌐

At crime scenes I like to watch from the assembled onlookers.
The detectives always look so official in sport coats, or some-
times even suits. The techs usually look like they just got done
mopping somebody's floor. I'd like to get close to all these cops.
I'd like to be able to tell if they wear expensive cologne or
cheap deodorant. I want to know them. I want to know them
while they don't know me and don't know that I'm watching or
that I'm learning about them. I like being silent and unseen. If I
were invisible, it would be perfect.

The evidence technicians and ME people entered the kitchen. "You guys can go in now," the ME announced.

"He still dead?" Fenwick asked.

The assistant ME said, "He was when we left him."

"Any way to tell what happened?" Fenwick asked.

An assistant ME said, "Yeah, he got stabbed a lot of
times."

"I was looking for something a little more specific," Fenwick said.

The ME said, "This is not a contest for who can say the most cryptic one liners. As far as I can tell at the moment, about half of the stab wounds were inflicted after he was dead. The obvious is true. He was stabbed to death. It probably started in the bathroom, continued across the hall and into the bedroom. I can let you know more later this afternoon, although tomorrow morning you'd get more details and possibly more helpful information. I'm not sure when he died. Certainly within the last couple hours."

"What was the liquid around his thighs?" Turner asked.

"We'll know more in the morning. He probably pissed himself as he died," the ME said. He left.

Examining the corpse, the room it was in, the bathroom, and the hall took less than an hour. Flecks of blood stained bits of the walls and floor in the bathroom and hallway. By far the vast majority of the bleeding had been done in the bedroom. They noted the placement of every object in all three areas. The photographers might catch details, but the detectives were trained to rely on their notes and sketches. After the body was removed, they gravitated to the area of the hall beyond the blood stains.

Fenwick closed his blue notebook. "I don't see evidence of a struggle," he said.

"Me neither. Our guy is nearly naked. It's early. Did he have a guest for the night, and he never got dressed? Or maybe he always walked around his house and answered the door in his underwear?"

"The techs took the bedsheets. We'll get DNA results on everything they find."

They'd examined the entire downstairs of the sprawling mansion. There was no evidence of any crime throughout the rest of the antique-encrusted ground floor.

"Struggle," Turner said. "There has to have been some

kind of struggle." He looked in the hall. He pointed. "We've got what looks like a handprint on the wall. So he propped himself up at least once as he was going this way? Was he running? Why was he heading for the bedroom? Why not the front door? Was the killer taunting him? Waiting for him to bleed some more before striking again? Or maybe it's the killer's handprint?"

Fenwick said, "Or the killer cleaned up all the disarranged furniture because he thought it would be a dead give away." Fenwick groaned at his own humor.

"An anal-retentive killer is your friend," Turner commented.

Fenwick said, "He or she figured if he cleaned well, everybody would ignore a dead body and gobs of blood all over. Have to be a very dumb killer."

"We've run into our share of those. This strikes me as a guest bedroom. There aren't many clothes in the closet, and just a lot of sweaters in the dresser drawers. In fact, no personal items down here at all. I bet he didn't sleep down here."

Fenwick said, "We'll get the techs to take the sheets from upstairs as well."

In the entryway, Turner summed up. "We know he was rich. We are fairly sure he was straight. He probably let the killer in, which means he probably knew him or her."

"There could have been more than one," Fenwick said.

"I like it," Turner said. "It would account for the lack of struggle. One or more of them holds the guy and the other stabs him. Maybe they enjoyed his suffering. Stab him a few times, let him run, and stab him a few more. We've got to get the tech reports. We've got no proof of more than one person, from what I can tell. I didn't see any signs of restraint on the body."

Fenwick said, "I'm fascinated with the concept of the

killer tootling on out of here covered in blood. We've got nobody outside shouting he or she saw anything."

"Had to have had a car handy. Or they changed into clothes here, which the killer either brought with him, or borrowed from Lenzati."

"Where's the murder weapon?" Fenwick asked. "Why the hell can't the criminals of the world learn to leave the murder weapon where we can find it easily?"

"It'll put out a memo reminding them of your needs," Turner said. "So, he comes home with the killer or lets the killer in. That doesn't tell us much."

"I don't see any evidence of forced entry," Fenwick added. "I agree. He knew his killer and let him or her in. Why does the confrontation start in the bathroom? He didn't like the way he shaved? The killer got pissed when he pissed?"

Turner said, "We're not going to go there."

"Did the killer bring the knife with him or her?" Fenwick asked.

Turner said, "We found nothing broken or disturbed. Did he just stand there and let himself be stabbed? I find that hard to believe. Did the killer get stabbed? Is any of this blood the killer's?"

"I think we ask the very best questions," Fenwick said.

"Self-referential analysis is all the rage," Turner said.

"And I'm good at it," Fenwick said.

"Is there anything you're not good at?" Turner asked.

Fenwick thought a moment, then said, "I shall pass over the inherently hostile nature of that question and proceed to the simple answer. No."

"I was afraid of that," Turner said. "Stupid question."

"I'm not the only one who's a little surly today."

Turner was irritated because he'd agreed to go to a cop poetry reading that evening. He'd tried to put the obligation out of his mind. After being out all day dealing with criminals, he'd rather stay home in the evenings with his family. He was not about to tell Fenwick where he was going or why. If Fenwick knew Turner was going to a cop poetry reading, Fenwick would tease him mercilessly.

Turner said, "Surly to bed, surly to rise."

"This is getting out of hand," Fenwick said.

Turner said, "We've got a lot of questions, and I doubt that the ME is going to be able to answer as many as we need."

"As many as they always do," Fenwick said. "I don't know about you, but I'm getting a craving for suspects and witnesses."

"Is that craving as in vampire-/cannibal-lets-have-them-for-dinner, or craving as in you're addicted to police work and you need a fix, or craving as in need for more cheap humor?"

Fenwick said, "You'll notice that in that article about dead detectives east of us, not a one of the murdered cops had the funniest-cop-comedian in their city as part of their profile. I'm sure I'm safe."

"Not if the killer hears any of your jokes. Although, maybe if all the criminals knew part of their sentence was listening to continuous tapes of your collected jokes, they'd stop committing crimes. Maybe even sue for mercy or beg for the death penalty."

"Cruel but all possibly true. All I know is, it's getting tougher and tougher to do grim-cop-humor in this town. I think I'm going to join a twelve-step program."

"You've made that threat before and you never do. For now let's go over the rest of the house."

In an electronics room they found three computers, one printer, and rows of disks and shelves filled with technical manuals. Papers covered three large tables against one wall. In this room there wasn't an antique in sight. The decor ran to stainless steel stem lamps, stark white walls, and an absence of that which would make it warm or personal.

There was a bank of smaller monitors tucked in one corner. "This must be the security system," Fenwick said.

All the monitors were dark. A small shelf contained tapes. "These must be the monitor's records," Turner said. "We'll have to check them out."

"Want to bet the ones from last night are missing?" Fenwick asked.

"No," Turner said. "Although, if he knew the killer, and let him in voluntarily, all the security in the world wouldn't have helped much."

After they'd hunted through a drawer jammed with bills, checkbooks, and personal correspondence, Turner said, "I don't see an address book." Nothing they found revealed anything significant. Turner discovered a pile of postcards without messages or stamps. They were from cities throughout the world.

"He didn't bank electronically?" Turner asked.

"You'd think a computer guy would," Fenwick said.

"A guy this wealthy must employ a team of accountants. We need to talk to them. We'll have to get some of the department computer people in here and go over everything carefully." Turner gazed at all the papers. "Not something I'm looking forward to quite yet."

"You and me both," Fenwick said. They decided to leave the papers for that afternoon when the computer expert could be present. He would be able to tell them what was safe to touch, or what could be secret diagrams to technological marvels that could rule the world, or what could possibly be a clue in a murder investigation.

In a walk-in closet off the electronics room they found an entire wall that held a library of DVD recordings, thousands of alphabetized movie tapes, and thousands of CDs. Numerous shelves were filled with pornographic videos.

As he examined the outer coverings of these last, Turner said, "My guess is, he was straight." Fenwick checked several of the box covers. Many featured naked women wearing spike heels and enough makeup to fill yards of counter space in the cosmetics section of a major department store. Most were sprawled in fantastic contortions displaying as much flesh as possible.

"Are these poses supposed to be enticing?" Turner asked, holding up one with a woman leaning backward while straddling the largest watermelon Turner had ever seen. She wore only a pair of red spike heels and the requisite gobs of makeup.

Fenwick examined the proffered box for a moment and then said, "To the fourteen-year-old boy inside of every adult, straight male, they are."

"No real woman has breasts that big," Turner asked, "do they?"

"I haven't made a study, although I'd be willing to volunteer to do the research if my wife were on a trip to Mars and wouldn't be back for ten years, and that radar she has for knowing what I'm up to was turned off."

"Is there any significance to the fact that he had all these tapes?" Turner asked.

"He whacked off a lot?"

"Maybe he was into making them. I haven't seen any apparatus for that yet. These sure look like regular commercial tapes. You don't make highly glossy boxes for your own self-filmed collection, do you?"

"I never have," Fenwick said.

Turner said, "I like the newspaper articles where, when a criminal is arrested, they include the porn tapes in a list of things found. As if by their very presence, they revealed something sinister about the owner."

Fenwick waved his hand at the assembled tapes. "Having this many is a little unusual. Maybe he was just rich and could afford to indulge his tastes. We'll have to ask around to see if there is any significance. Adding a highly sexual element to a gritty murder always perks me right up."

"I thought we disposed of the problem of you being perky and up earlier today."

"Not hardly."

"Ouch."

Just off a second floor bedroom they found another large walk-in closet. They checked each dresser drawer. All the boxer shorts were silk. All the shirts were hand-tailored. A receipt was attached to several of them, each with the address of a dry cleaner two blocks away. Lenzati had a line of suits unlike any Turner had ever seen on racks in a store. They found another large closet tending to jeans and T-shirts. Turner counted the pairs of athletic shoes and then asked, "Who needs thirty pairs of gym shoes?"

"One for each day of the month?" Fenwick offered.

Lenzati also had warm-up outfits and athletic clothes, titanium tennis rackets and titanium golf clubs. When he saw the clubs, Turner said, "If we didn't have those tapes, I could still tell he was straight."

"How's that?"

"He played golf. No gay men play golf."

"There must be some who do."

"Nope. In the gay gene there is no golf strand."

"I thought there wasn't a gay gene."

"No one knows for sure, but if there is, trust me, it does not include playing golf. It's just one of those little oddities of the universe. Gay men play in all sports except golf."

24

"Even hockey?" Fenwick asked.

"I hope they play hockey, and I want to meet them."

"Good for you," Fenwick said. "Next question. Did he live with someone? I see lots of expensive clothes, but I don't see evidence of two sets of clothes, or any feminine apparel. I don't see personal items that would indicate cohabitation. There was only one toothbrush in the john, one stick of deodorant, a razor, and shaving cream. My guess is he was single. Unless he kept wives and mistresses in mansions throughout the world."

"Speaking of mistresses," Turner said, "where's the hired help? He must have had servants of some kind, but we haven't seen any. I wonder why not?"

"How many guesses do I get?" Fenwick asked.

"Not enough."

Fenwick said, "Girote claimed Lenzati dated, but it doesn't look like anyone was sharing this place at the moment."

"A safe enough conclusion."

The king size bed in the master bedroom was covered with a quilt made of alternating red and black squares. The abstract paintings on the walls continued the red and black color scheme. On the top of glass cube endtables, they found several arrangements of toy rubber ducks and pink flamingoes in sexual congress with each other.

Fenwick said, "If we were looking for sexual perversity, I think we found it."

"My definition of sexual perversity is a little raunchier than this. More colorful too."

"Care to tell me about it?" Fenwick asked.

"Not in this life time," Turner said. They checked all the dresser drawers. "I don't see evidence of someone else. No underwear of a different size."

"Either two males of exactly the same size lived here, or he was living alone. Or, he was dating a woman who wore the exact same clothes as he did."

"I'm voting for alone," Turner said.

They went back downstairs. Fenwick grumbled, "Where the fuck is the murder weapon?"

"It's Carruthers' fault," Turner said. "He's talked to all the potential murderers in town and warned them not to help you in the slightest way." Randy Carruthers was the most maligned officer on the Area Ten detective squad.

"Why is the world all of a sudden paying so much attention to Carruthers?" Fenwick asked.

"If you can't trust someone who is dangerously stupid, who can you trust?" Turner asked.

The front door swung open. Tommy Quiroz said, "I've got a guy out here who says he has to talk to whoever is in charge. Says his name is Brooks Werberg. Claims he was the corpse's business partner."

, 4 ,

I like it when famous people show up. I love publicity and out-
rage and upset. I like it when they have news conferences over
something I've done. It's best when some reporter asks why a
killer would be doing such a thing. Everybody always wants to
know why. Well, sometimes there isn't a why. Sometimes peo-
ple are just mean sons of bitches.

Turner remembered Werberg's name from what the mayor's
press secretary had told them. They let him in. Brooks Werberg was in his mid-thirties. He wore a Prada suit that Turner
knew to cost several thousand dollars. Turner recognized its
sleek, lean lines, three buttons, and notched collar. He knew
what it was because his older son Brian had been campaigning to buy one for the prom in the spring. Turner had told his
son he could buy it with money from his job at the neighborhood deli. Any money, that is, that was not earmarked for
college.

Turner thought Werberg might attend a gym for several
hours every day of the week. He was about five foot eight

with enormous shoulders, a thick neck, a very narrow waist, and muscles that the suit highlighted perfectly. His hair was evenly brush-cut all around. Turner noticed his red-rimmed eyes and believed that they indicated bouts of recent tears.

"What's happened to Craig?" Werberg asked. "I was called from the mayor's office. They said Craig was dead, but I didn't believe them." He began to walk farther into the house. "Where is he?"

Turner stood in his way. "This is a crime scene, Mr. Werberg. We need to talk. We can't let you farther into the house at this time."

"Is Craig here? Is the body here?"

"No," Turner said.

Werberg began to cry. After several minutes he took out a hanky, blew his nose, and wiped his tears. He whispered, "He can't be dead. I saw him just last night. We had dinner. We've been best friends forever. My god, he can't be dead." His suit might be expensive, but his tie was askew and his shirt collar was crumpled on the left side. Werberg's unshaven blue beard-shadow showed starkly against his pale skin. Turner guessed that he hadn't shaved that morning.

Turner said, "We're very sorry for your loss. We know this is a difficult time, but it would help us if we could ask you a few questions. The early hours in a murder investigation are the most valuable in trying to catch the killer."

Werberg snuffled. "I can try."

Fenwick said, "We understand that you were his business partner."

"Yes, for many years. We—"

Turner interrupted, "Mr. Werberg, when you found the body, why didn't you call the police? Why did you call the mayor's office?"

Werberg's face went from pale to ashen to greenish. "It wasn't me!" he gasped.

"We're going down to the mayor's office," Turner said. "Even he cannot conceal evidence in a murder investigation. If necessary, we'll subpoena phone records. My guess is the call came in either from this house or from a cell phone registered to your name."

"With computers you can erase records," Werberg said.

"I have no doubt you have that ability," Turner said. "Did you take the time to do it already? It can't be done that quickly, can it? I doubt it. Did you?"

Werberg hunkered down on an eighteenth century settee, which was far too small to be a real couch, but too large to be a comfy chair. Turner always wondered if people actually sat in such things when they were first built centuries ago. In his ultra-modern suit, Werberg looked out of place on the maroon antique.

Werberg began to sob, great wracking gusts of emotion that went on and on.

Fenwick pulled up a straight back chair. Turner sat next to Werberg. He said, "Mr. Werberg, you need to tell us what happened." He had a fleeting thought of having someone confess to a murder within seconds of being questioned. His sense of reality and knowledge of human nature prevented that thought from becoming more than a passing fancy.

Finally, Werberg drew a deep breath. He used his now sodden linen hanky and said, "We were supposed to meet at seven for breakfast and then go to work at our offices on the west side. I called earlier to confirm a few things he needed to bring along to a business meeting, but no one answered. I have the private number that bypasses the caller ID locks and the privacy manager. When he didn't answer, I became concerned."

"Why?" Turner asked.

"He was always at home very early in the morning."

"Maybe he ran to the grocery store."

"He was rich. He didn't need to run to the store. In all the years I'd known him he'd never been late for an appointment. If he was supposed to be here, he would be here.

"I came over. I have a key." He ran his hanky across his forehead. Turner didn't know if he should tell him he just smeared snot on his eyebrow. The detective touched his own forehead, nodded toward Werberg, and said, "You might want to wipe that again."

Finished with hygiene, Werberg resumed. "I opened the door. It was nearly seven. The house was very quiet. He always listens to jazz music when he's home. Always. He claimed he owned every jazz CD ever manufactured. He'd even hired a woman who did nothing but hunt for obscure jazz CDs."

The perks of being rich, Turner thought.

"Since there was no music, I figured he might be out. I thought I'd go up to his office, and see if he'd left a message on the computer. Sometimes he did that."

"I thought you said he was never late."

"I'm talking about a habit of leaving messages, not his ability to be on time."

Turner said, "If he was thinking of going out, why not just e-mail you on your computer at home and save you the trip?"

"Well, he didn't and normally he would have. It was kind of odd, but I wasn't really, really worried. I certainly didn't imagine anything horrible had happened. I began to walk through the house. The lack of noise seemed unnatural. I saw the blood in the hallway. I stopped to listen. I began to get scared. I don't know how long I stood still. Not long, I don't think. I don't know why I didn't just run away. I don't know why I didn't call the cops. Anyway, I looked in the bathroom, then followed the trail of blood." Tears began to flow again, but he retained enough composure to continue his narrative. He whispered. "I called his name and approached his body. He wasn't breathing. I touched his finger tip. He felt so still. I'd never been in the presence of a dead body. I didn't know what to do. Finally, I just ran."

"Why didn't you call nine-one-one?" Fenwick asked.

"I didn't, okay? I know that was wrong. I didn't kill him; I ran. I called a friend."

"Who?" Turner asked.

"A friend who suggested I call someone official and not report it directly to the police myself. It didn't matter. I came down here anyway. I couldn't stay away."

Turner stated, "You have no witnesses that you were home at the time of the murder."

"I didn't kill him."

Although lack of an alibi didn't prove guilt, Werberg was high on Turner's suspect list. The man had made one mistake in not directly phoning the cops, but that didn't qualify him for handcuffs yet.

"Did he have any enemies?" Turner asked.

"When you are rich and successful, there is always someone coming out of the woodwork to cause you trouble, but there was no one who was a personal, get even, you're-an-evil-bastard enemy."

"How about your company?" Turner asked. "We heard you sold one and started another? Any problems there?"

"Years ago we started with an Apple IIe computer. For a work table we had a door propped up by two filing cabinets. Less than ten years later, we sold that business for a billion dollars. We made a *staggering* profit. Who could be unhappy?"

"Your competitors?" Fenwick said. "People who were envious of you or who felt you stepped on them on your way to the top?"

"We were creators and engineers first, businessmen second. We were totally honest. It took imagination, drive, and hard work to get where we are. You can't steal imagination."

"What about your new company?" Turner inquired. "Any rivals there?"

"We were on the cutting edge of technology. Everyone is trying to share information and create new things. Of course, there is rivalry, but no one kills over computer software."

Fenwick said, "We had a woman last week who killed her husband because he watched too much ESPN. Murder for millions or billions makes a strong motive."

"Oh."

"What kind of guy was Mr. Lenzati?" Turner asked.

"What do you mean?"

"Did he have a lot of friends? Was he quiet and reserved, or outgoing and boisterous?"

"Sometimes a little of each, but mostly quiet. We grew up together on the north side of Chicago. We were in all the bright and accelerated programs in every grade, attended magnet schools. Neither one of us dated much. We went to Northwestern on full scholarships. During college we worked on our computer business in a little garage we rented just outside downtown Evanston. We managed to create some desirable software and Internet connectors. It grew from there to something international and vastly profitable."

"What was his routine every day?"

"It varied, like today, but mostly, we both worked at home in the mornings. We'd usually meet early in the afternoon to go over whatever projects we were working on. Then we'd go to the office to meet with project managers.

Who we met with depended on what people were working on or how close they were to completion, or if they were having particular problems. The company was fiscally sound; among the best. We hired the top computer management people in the country to work for us. We even created a computer program that helped manage our money, but we liked to have humans to consult with on the business end."

"What particular computer things was your company involved with?" Turner asked.

"Almost anything from the simple to the vastly complex. We designed Web sites, or worked on operating systems for big and small corporations, experimented with new software or game systems. The last few years we've done a lot with computer security. We did just about anything some of the best computer geniuses in the country could think of. We are a research and development company of the highest order. No project is rejected because it isn't possible now. Who knows what could be possible in the future?"

Turner asked, "Any particular projects that someone might think you stole or a rival might be angry about? Maybe they were coming out with the same thing, and they didn't like what you were doing or thought you were copying theirs?"

"No. We created. We had no need to steal ideas from anyone."

"We'd like you to go over some of the items in his computer lab with us," Turner said. "Maybe explain a few things. That would be after our computer expert has gone over the room. We'd want to have him there with us."

"There are business secrets that I can't reveal to you."

Fenwick said, "This is a murder investigation. I'm afraid you don't have much say in what we look at of Mr. Lenzati's. This is a crime scene. We could get a warrant if we had to."

"We have no business secrets that someone would kill for."

"But we don't know that, do we?" Fenwick said. "You guys deal with millions, even billions of dollars. That's plenty of money for someone to want to get their hands on, even little bits of it. Plenty enough to kill for."

"We had no rivals. We were the smartest creators around."

Turner wondered at the man's ego. Of course, someone somewhere was probably the smartest computer person in the world. He just had a hard time believing he was in the presence of the very best.

Fenwick said, "Maybe whoever's in second place got jealous."

Werberg looked frustrated. "I don't know how many more questions I can deal with. The man who has been my best friend for thirty years is dead."

"Just a few more," Turner said. "Did you have business rivals? Problems with competitors?"

"Bill Gates had nothing to fear from us. We've met with him numerous times and worked on a few projects with him. He has a lot of money, and we are very skilled."

Tommy Quiroz entered with a portly gentleman in a dark blue suit, Burberry overcoat, white shirt, and dark blue tie. He introduced himself, "I'm Claud Vinkers, one of Mr. Lenzati's and Mr. Werberg's lawyers. It's on the newscasts that Mr. Lenzati is dead."

"Did Mr. Werberg call you before he came down here?" Fenwick asked.

"That, of course, is privileged information. My client is willing to cooperate in any way possible in solving this awful crime."

Turner suspected they'd have to wait for another time to

probe into Werberg's exact movements that morning. Cops generally hated lawyers showing up, and this was a prime example. Turner guessed Werberg knew more than he was admitting, but he doubted if they'd find anything out with the lawyer hanging around.

Turner asked, "Do you know who Mr. Lenzati's next of kin are, and how we might get hold of them?"

Werberg said, "His parents live in a castle Mr. Lenzati bought for them in the south of France. I know them, and I called them before I left. They are making plane reservations and coming to this country as quickly as possible."

"We'll need a list of his friends and acquaintances."

Werberg said, "I can put something together and get it to you tomorrow."

"Did he have a maid, a cook, or hired help of any kind?"

"He had a cleaning service in two days a week," Vinkers said. "He hired a cook for any special occasions."

"Who inherits all his money?" Turner asked.

The lawyer said, "He had no direct descendants. The will is quite complex. His parents will be more than comfortably well off. The bulk of his estate goes to a number of charities or back into his current company. There are a few specific beneficiaries. I can get you a list. None of those last is over a hundred thousand dollars."

"How about Mr. Werberg here?" Fenwick asked. "Is he in the will?"

"My client had no need for anything from Mr. Lenzati. He had nothing to gain from his death."

Turner said, "If the money goes back into the company, as co-owner he stands to gain a great deal."

"I did not kill him," Werberg insisted.

"How about any enemies?" Turner asked. "Do you know of any?"

Vinkers said, "I'm not aware of any enemies. He was a great man with a successful business."

Werberg added, "Our dreams all came true. Why would he be dead?" He wiped more tears from his eyes.

After Werberg composed himself, Turner said, "We'd like you to come down to the station to sign a statement."

"Now?" Werberg asked.

"That would be best for us," Turner said. He didn't want to risk arresting the guy. They'd never get away with an accusation based on what they had so far. With any suspect, rich or poor, he didn't want to try to get away with anything. He wanted solid forensic evidence tying a very good suspect to the crime.

A beat cop led the lawyer and Werberg away.

"How did you know he was the one who called?" Fenwick asked.

"I didn't, but it seemed logical. First, he was close to the victim. Second, to get someone to call the mayor and then the superintendent, and to get him to go outside channels means someone with lots of clout, which means bunches of money. Werberg has money. He shows up at the crime scene, a habit some killers have. He hadn't shaved today. His shirt and tie were a mess. If he's busy discovering a body, or upset about the body, would he have time to shave? None of that makes him a murderer, but taken together they add up to a bit more than an insight, but less than an arrest."

"Maybe he was up all night, or he never shaves on Fridays?"

"I realize there's all kind of possibilities, but why wouldn't he be the one? It was worth a shot, and it got us information and frankly, I think a very good suspect."

"He should be watched," Fenwick said. "Their company apparently benefits in a big way from Lenzati's death. We'll have to dig into the company's finances."

Turner said, "There's something odd about his movements this morning. There's more there."

"I agree," Fenwick said. "The part I like the best is him being able to get in. We get a fingerprint or two of him in all that blood, and we're in great shape."

"He already admitted being in there," Turner pointed out. "I don't see how proving the accuracy of his own statement is going to help us much."

"I also like Girote as a suspect," Fenwick said.

Turner said, "I don't think he did it."

"Why not?"

"He struck me as the kind of guy who would be confessing loudly and often."

"The loudly part I can believe. I'm not ruling him out."

Turner said, "We need to find people who knew Lenzati. Let's try the neighbors and then his office."

The mid-morning was cool and crisp as they began the canvass of the neighborhood. Turner knew their best hope was to find the neighborhood gossip or a shut-in.

Judy Wilson and Joe Roosevelt, two other detectives from the squad, joined them. Roosevelt was red-nosed and short, with brush-cut gray hair and bad teeth. Judy was a fiercely competitive African-American woman. They had a well-deserved reputation as one of the most successful pairs of detectives on the force. When Turner and Fenwick met them on the sidewalk, the other two detectives were arguing over what was the proper way to hang the toilet paper roll in a bathroom.

Turner had heard Roosevelt and Wilson raising their voices to each other about everything from the most appropriate caliber of gun a cop should keep in reserve, to the politics in the Streets and Sanitation Department in the city, to the proper method for sharpening a pencil. He figured they must take delight in disagreeing. Over the years neither had ever requested a transfer. Turner forestalled a resumption in this latest round of debates between them by diverting their attention to the case at hand.

Turner knew the appearance of extra detectives to help with the canvass was a sure sign that the case was of major concern to the higher-ups in the city bureaucracy. A detective was lucky to have a partner to do the canvass with him, much less extra help. Pressure on the case would only continue to build with each hour they didn't make an arrest.

"What have you guys got so far?" Roosevelt asked.

"A lot of blood," Fenwick said.

"We heard you got a no brainer late yesterday," Wilson said.

Turner said, "A killer confessing to everything except the Lindbergh kidnapping and taking a shot at JFK."

Fenwick said, "I could have kissed her."

Roosevelt chanted, "Fenwick and a suspect sitting in a tree, k-i-s—"

"Cop humor," Turner interrupted. "Some of the finest and most sophisticated wit on the planet."

"Let's get this done," Fenwick said.

But the neighbors on either side of the house north and south were not at home. At a mansion across the street they found three housekeepers who had seen nothing. At the fourth house, catty-corner from Lenzati's, they had better luck. A decidedly pregnant woman in her mid-twenties answered the door. She held a child of about three. The detectives introduced themselves and showed their identification.

"I'm Amanda Veldon. Is it true that Craig Lenzati is . . ." She glanced at the child in her arms. "Is he?"

Turner said, "We'd like to ask you a few questions, about your neighbor."

"I didn't really know him."

"Any little bit would be helpful."

She led them into the house. She placed the child on the floor amid a scattering of toys. She and the detectives sat in comfortable chairs a few feet away.

"Mr. Lenzati is dead," Turner spoke softly so the child would not hear the news.

"How awful. What happened?"

"We're trying to build a profile of the victim," Turner said. "That often helps in solving these cases. What can you tell us?"

"Not much, I'm afraid. We just moved in a month ago. My husband was transferred here from Puerto Rico."

"Does he work in the computer business?" Fenwick asked.

"No. He's in sales for a satellite dish company. He might make vice president in just three years."

"Did you know Mr. Lenzati?" Turner asked.

"We knew *of* him. We'd never actually met. This is a pretty quiet neighborhood and pretty exclusive. You don't expect neighbors to bring pies across the street."

"Did you see him coming and going?"

"Every once in a while. I take Todd"—she pointed at the child—"out for strolls quite often. He likes to get out and see things and explore."

"Anyone in particular show up, or one particular car that you noticed?"

"No one, really. Except that famous partner of his in that computer business. They made all that money."

"Anything at all unusual that you ever noticed?"

"Well, I'm not sure, but with this pregnancy, I've been up late a lot. Mike, my husband, has been so sweet . . ."

Turner let her ramble for several moments before bringing her back. "You were talking about late nights?"

"Yes. It was odd. A few times he had late visitors around two, three, even four in the morning."

"Did you see anyone last night?" Turner asked.

"No, I'm sorry. I'm just grateful when I do sleep through the night."

"Any regulars?" Turner asked. "Anyone you recognized, or would recognize again?"

"His partner. I think I saw him once. I didn't recognize anyone else."

"Were these men or women?"

"Women. Usually young women who seemed happy."

"Happy?" Turner asked.

"Well, that kind of giggly drunk, that so often sounds more like fake happiness."

"Were these individuals or groups?" Turner asked.

"Once it was a group. The other times, just one."

She knew no more. They left.

"He had intimate little parties," Fenwick said. "Not a big motive for murder."

Turner said, "I thought not being invited to parties was the big problem."

"Maybe the rich are different. We'll have to ask Werberg about parties."

Continuing along the block, they found two more not-at-homes for which they would have to return. At three homes farther down the block no one had noticed anything. Apparently in this wealthy enclave you often drove through your security gate and then ignored the rest of the world. Turner and Fenwick rendezvoused with Roosevelt and Wilson, who hadn't learned anything helpful either. They returned to their car.

5

Technology makes it so much easier to find and kill victims. I love gathering information about people I don't know. I love knowing that which they think is secret about their lives. Computers are wonderful in the way they let anybody intrude, and I am more "anybody" than anyone they are ever going to have to deal with.

"Let's try his company," Turner said.

"A secret computer cabal," Fenwick said, "doing mystical things with machines that Bill Gates hasn't even dreamed about. I like that as background and even more if it lends us a motive."

"I still think Bill is innocent. I doubt if he came to town and committed murder, and he probably wouldn't like you mentioning his name."

"When he talked to me last night, he said I should tell you hello."

"Don't applaud, just send money," Turner said.

"What does that mean?"

"That what you're telling me is a crock, but I'm too polite to mention it. Or that you've told that type of joke so many times that it's too stale to trigger an intelligent response."

"You ask me if I've got problems, and here you are disparaging my jokes."

"I always disparage your jokes. You're just depressed enough today to notice."

Fenwick thought about that a moment. "Oh."

As they waited for the light at Balbo and Lake Shore Drive, Turner said, "You were kind of touchy about that reporter's article. I thought you said you were going to ignore it."

"It was crap. I hate useless speculation. A cop serial killer? Bullshit."

Turner said, "Seven killings? That's an awful long string to simply be a set of coincidences. He seemed to have a lot of data. Is it that you don't believe it's possible, or you don't want it to be possible?"

"How much choice do I really have?" Fenwick replied.

"He drew some logical conclusions."

"Then how come no cop anywhere has noticed?" Fenwick asked. "They can't all be that stupid."

"We didn't notice it," Turner said.

"We don't live in those cities."

"Neither did they, before there was a killing in one," Turner pointed out. "I think I know why they didn't notice. The reason is simple. How many cops in this country die in the line of duty every year?"

"An average of one hundred fifty-nine in the last five years, and half of those because of high-speed chases or being hit by cars, stuff like that."

"Where do you get those statistics?" Turner asked.

"I like to know my odds."

Turner said, "We only read about the deaths here. I only know a few cops in other cities. No one we know has died. Even if we did, we'd know about deaths in one city and not the others. Relating them from city to city and presuming they are a connected string is probably a stretch of the imagination. The operative word is probably."

"I know that. I just didn't want to be reminded about it."

Turner and Fenwick dined on take-out burgers from the Area Ten cops' new favorite take-out burger place, Beef on the Hoof, just south of Roosevelt Road on Canal Street. The burgers were three quarters of a pound and mounded with cholesterol-infested extras. Fenwick claimed the fried onion rings were the best in the city. Certainly they gave a larger glop of them than any Turner had ever seen.

After grabbing the burgers and eating on the run, they headed for Lenzati and Werberg's company.

Fenwick said, "I can't stay that late today. I've got places to be."

"Any place special?"

"Places."

Turner let it go. Fenwick would tell him whatever it was eventually.

Turner used his cell phone to call the local police district and arrange for officers to help with some of the interviews. The address they had for the offices of Lenzati and Werberg, Incorporated was on Austin Avenue just inside the city limits from Oak Park. A gargantuan Victorian mansion, housing the executive offices, was linked to an immense array of ultramodern buildings constructed with vast quantities of glass and gray steel. Carved wooden beams made a canopy over the entrance to the mansion. A red and yellow, hand-painted sign on the solid oak door read,

THE BELL WORKS, BUT EVERYBODY'S WORKING REAL HARD
AND WON'T HEAR YOU, SO COME ON IN ANYWAY.

Fenwick pointed to the sign. "Not a very prosy bunch."

"Trying to be down home, realistic, and fanciful at the same time. It just doesn't ring or scan."

"You a poetry critic?" Fenwick asked.

"Nope, just a cop."

The interior looked more like a frat house inhabited by a herd of particularly messy buffaloes than the entrance to a multi-million or billion dollar company. From out-sized sheets to piles of confetti, paper was strewn over everything. Numerous computers flashed dazzling screen-saver graphics. Against the walls from floor to ceiling was more chaos—stacks of printouts, stacks of paper, shelves filled with office supplies in original packets, mostly unopened cardboard boxes, and enough wiring scattered about to run a cable to Europe and back. Occasional breaks in the mess revealed floors of solid oak, walls of burnished walnut, and paintings that Turner thought might be authentic Picassos. He wondered at the nerve or stupidity of having such valuable artwork in an area where anyone could walk off with it. What kind of security did they have?

No one sat at what could be assumed to be a reception desk. They heard a murmur of voices emanating from down a wainscoted hallway.

Turner and Fenwick followed the sound. In a room thirty feet down the hall, four men and two women were gathered around a computer screen. They were arguing. The detectives stopped to listen.

"Just pick up the phone and call." It was a woman's voice.

"Call who?" a male voice.

"We can find all we need to know on the Internet," another male voice.

"All we're getting is nutty rumors. Each one crazier than the last. The Internet is bullshit."

"They all agree he's dead."

This silenced them for several moments until another one asked, "Where is Brooks? Is he okay?"

"The reports are mixed."

"Our stock is plummeting."

"How can you think of a thing like that at a time like this?"

"*I'm* not dead."

"How *dare* you?"

"Excuse me," Turner said.

They all turned from the computer screen. Turner said, "I'm Detective Paul Turner. This is my partner, Buck Fenwick." They held out their identification. Several of those in the room moved closer to inspect the IDs. Turner said, "We need to talk to whoever's in charge."

The crowd looked at a skinny guy in glasses. He stepped forward. "I'm Terry Waldron, the CEO. What's happened?" He wore faded blue jeans that fit poorly on his lanky frame. His rumpled flannel shirt was frayed at the elbows, and the buttons at the end of the sleeves were unbuttoned. He wore heavy work boots, a narrow black tie, and a grim smile.

Turner said, "Mr. Lenzati is dead. Mr. Werberg is fine. We need to speak with everyone who worked directly with Mr. Lenzati. We'll need a list."

Stunned silence enveloped the assemblage. Turner saw pale faces, several fighting back tears, several more not bothering to fight them back.

Interviewing strangers was one of the oddest parts of the

job of a cop. Often you were talking to people at one of the most emotionally critical moments of their lives. The ability to talk to people was an unmentioned but stunningly vital part of a detective's job. Most of the time you had to speak with frightened or hostile people before you got to a killer. Empathizing with the emotionally overwrought was difficult. Knowing how to handle all of them in any kind of situation was tricky at best, dangerous at worst. You never knew which of the emotionally charged might turn on you. A bad cop presumed he knew how to handle all such situations. A good cop knew you never stopped learning.

The very oddest part of the job to Turner was still the viewing of the dead bodies. Turner assumed it would always affect him. He hoped he'd realize when it didn't and quit.

"Hold on, now, hold on," a woman in her early twenties said. There were only two women in the group. This one wore a faded denim skirt, a white blouse, and white walking shoes. "We knew and worked with Craig Lenzati. You come barging in here uninvited and now you're demanding information. We're all grieving. We're all . . ." She drew several deep breaths. "We were all close to him. We cared about him. This is impossible. This is . . ." She stopped.

"We know it's tough," Turner said.

"He was murdered?" Waldron asked.

"Yes," Turner said.

The woman who spoke said, "How could we possibly know anything about murder?"

Turner said, "Statistics prove that a person is most likely to be killed by someone they knew. When we interview everyone, we begin to get a sense of his life, who he knew, who didn't like him, who might have wanted to kill him."

"Everybody liked him," Waldron said.

"Everybody but one," Fenwick said.

48

"None of us is a killer," the woman said.

Turner said, "We'd like to begin the interviews with those who worked most closely with him. We'll have uniformed officers conduct preliminary interrogations of anyone he came into contact with at other levels in the company. Mr. Waldron, we can start with you. We'd like everyone to stay until we say it is okay to leave."

There were nods in the group. Turner and Fenwick arranged for beat cops to begin the interviews with the other employees.

First, they asked to be shown Lenzati's office. It was a surprisingly small cubicle with little more than a cheap metal desk, a folding chair, a monitor, computer, and a keyboard.

"For a rich boss, his office is kind of a big nothing," Fenwick observed.

Waldron said, "He and Brooks worked mostly at home. Here they used any computer that was handy. They worked with individuals and groups at their stations. All of them are connected to the main server. You can do anything from just about any computer. They felt it was a more personal touch that way."

Next, Waldron led them down another hall to a conference room with an oval, solid oak table that Turner thought might look at home in a castle in Europe. Dark stains overspread and deep gouges scored the well-polished surface. On top of the table at each place setting was a laptop computer. A large display screen hung on the far wall of the narrow room, and a computer projector hung from the ceiling. As they talked, Waldron idly toyed with the keys on the computer in front of him. Turner wondered if the old masters that hung on the wall were originals or reproductions. You sell your company for over a billion, you could buy a lot of expensive artwork. They sat near a window in a room that looked out on a courtyard. Periodically, Waldron used a tissue from a box on a small work table in an alcove.

Fenwick said, "You seem awfully young to be the CEO of a company."

"Craig and Brooks learned from the mistakes a lot of engineers and creative people made in other computer companies. I had much less power than most CEOs. They kept control of the company securely in their own hands. They hated people in suits who just wanted to sit on boards of directors. They called me their real, live, hands-on CEO."

"What did you do?" Turner asked.

"I was just a numbers cruncher. In essence I do the day-to-day running of the operation. I oversee bookkeeping, receiving, accounting. All major departments not connected to creativity report to me. I'm in charge of making sure the research operation gets hassled as little as possible. I know how to run a business."

Turner thought the man might be in his late twenties, if that. It was a little hard for him to believe the guy was in charge of millions or possibly billions of dollars. Of course, Lenzati and Werberg each were worth half a billion when they sold off their first company when they were in their mid-twenties.

"How often did you see him?" Turner asked.

"I had contact with Craig every day, either in person or on the phone."

"How's the company doing?"

"Great. One of the most solid in the computer industry. The dot-com crash has barely touched us."

"How did you wind up working here?" Fenwick asked.

"In business school I created a new software program for businesses to keep track of inventory, profit, loss, product development, delivery; all facets of a business reported and analyzed in one continuous flow. No duplication was necessary. With my program you could tell how many items you sold in Newton, Iowa, in the past hour. It was the perfect melding of needs of the customers and product delivery. It limited the amount of merchandise you had sitting on a shelf taking up space. It even made selling on the Internet more efficient. Its key, though, was identifying an area where a new product was needed and projecting how much revenue the new software or program was likely to generate."

"What kind of man was Mr. Lenzati to work for?" Turner asked.

"Great. A creative genius. Sometimes he was shy and awkward with people. He never confronted anyone directly. He had this quiet, soothing voice. He would explain things very gently and at great length. At critical moments he did have an instinct for knowing exactly when to give encouragement and back off or when to step in and give direction himself. His leadership was always aloof but surprisingly effective. Everybody liked him and Brooks. They were great guys to work for. The salaries here are high. The benefits are terrific."

"Who fired people?" Turner asked. "Who dealt with company problems?"

"I didn't work on hiring and firing, but these were good people."

"Not one disgruntled employee, ever?" Fenwick asked.

"This is a cooperative group working on the cutting edge of technology. This is a place people were eager to come to work. There's a waiting line just for accepting applications. This is paradise. Sure, everybody's got an ego, probably some pretty big ones, but not big enough to kill for."

"Who has the biggest egos?"

"Craig and Brooks. When you're as bright as they are, you've earned the right to a big ego."

"Do you know of any clashes of any kind Lenzati might have had?"

"No. I never did. My department deals with numbers."

"What do you guys actually make?" Fenwick asked.

"We provide goods and services," Waldron said. "Computer games, operating systems, network security—anything on the cutting edge of technology."

"What kind of life did Mr. Lenzati live outside of the office?" Turner asked.

"I have no idea. He and Brooks worked from sixteen to twenty hours a day. I've been with them since the old company. I left with them when they started this new venture. I finished my first advanced computer degree from college at nineteen. We weren't close outside of business hour: I'm not sure they had much of a life outside of business."

Turner said "We've been told about late night parties at Mr. Lenzati's. You know anything about them?"

Waldron looked genuinely mystified. "That's the first I've heard of it."

"You never stepped out for a night with the boss?"

"No. There might be social events here, but they were very subdued—like cakes for birthdays kinds of things. Those were just interdepartmental, small lunchtime events."

Fenwick said, "They had millions to spend on luxury yachts, vacations, trips to exotic locales. They never did any of those?"

"They might have bought entire exotic locales for that matter. For all I know, they did. I dealt strictly with the business. For their personal stuff you'd have to look elsewhere."

"Where?" Turner asked.

"I don't know."

"Isn't that kind of odd?" Turner asked.

"It's the way they did business. Their paychecks and profits went into electronic accounts controlled by them."

"Who did their taxes?" Fenwick asked.

"You'd have to ask Brooks."

Turner said, "We were told that sometimes Mr. Lenzati dated women, brought them to functions."

"Yes, Craig did. They were usually bright and funny women."

"Do you remember any of their names?" Turner asked.

"I vaguely remember a few first names, but no addresses or anything. He never brought the same one around more than a few times. I'm not very social. None of us really is. I'm not good at it and I'm not sure Craig was either."

"Were there business problems?" Turner asked. "Did the firm have any trouble with industrial sabotage or computer hackers?"

"You mean crackers, of course," Waldron said. "By strict definition a hacker is somebody who develops programs and makes them better. Crackers break into computer systems."

"Whichever it is," Fenwick said. "Was there a problem?"

"They were always on the alert. Complete checks of all equipment are done on a weekly basis. If there are possible problems, sometimes the checks are daily."

"Were there problems?" Turner asked.

"I don't know. You'd have to speak with the engineers."

Turner said, "Mr. Werberg said they had no rivals."

"I'd put it that they had no equals. Aren't there always others who wish they have what you have? Although in this case, I have no idea who that would be specifically."

"Who would know?"

"Rian Davis, the head of the creativity division."

"Where were you early this morning?"

Waldron looked pained. "I got up like I do every morning. I shaved, showered, dressed, stopped for coffee, and came in. I was here before seven. I have no witnesses. Although, I stop at the same coffee shop every day. The clerk might recognize me."

Rian Davis was the woman who had not spoken in the first group they'd met. She wore black jeans, a highly starched, pink cotton shirt, covered by a black silk vest, which was buttoned in a bustier effect. She spoke quietly, calmly, and authoritatively. "Waldron hasn't got an ounce of creativity in his body. He can crunch billions of numbers, good for him. My division was the heart and soul of this company. We were engineers, creators. The real lifeblood of the operation."

Turner said, "He mentioned problems with people getting into your systems."

"Sabotage? Hackers! Crackers!" She snorted in derision. "We were the company everybody turned to for preventing just such problems. Only we could develop systems faster than crackers could break into them. We were the ones governments from around the globe turned to. The security area is a gold mine. Spending on security is up to five percent of corporate operating budgets now. It used to be around one percent."

"If you specialized in it, didn't they try and break into your computers?" Turner asked.

"Sure, crackers and hackers targeted us. They'd try every trick to best us. They never could. Brooks and Craig were too smart and too clever. We spent innumerable hours on it. Every computer company has to. Unfortunately, Brooks believed it was good for the company to hire the most successful crackers. I told him he'd be sorry. It's like hiring the criminals to police the streets. It's a pleasantly liberal notion, until it goes very wrong."

"And did it go wrong here?" Turner asked.

"No one ever got into our files from the outside. We were just too good for that, but we hired a cracker a couple years ago, Eddie Homan. About ten years back he broke into the Pentagon computers and supposedly was three clicks away from starting a thermonuclear war."

"Is that true?" Turner asked.

"True enough that he got a seven-year prison sentence. Against my advice, we hired him. No question, he was good—very, very good. I warned them about internal sabotage. Craig and Brooks could be very arrogant about their abilities. They wouldn't listen to me. Homan ended up trying to sabotage everything we were working on."

"Why?"

"Perversity? He's nuts? That he was a brilliant nut case made it very difficult for us to figure out what was going on. One day a teenage intern accidentally came upon an anomaly in one of our programs. He reported it to me. It took me an hour or so to realize we had a major problem. I immediately notified Craig and Brooks. We worked forty-eight straight hours to find out where the problem originated from. Homan was aware of us from the first. He and his files were long gone by the time we went to confront him."

"Did the company lose much because of him?" Fenwick asked.

"Time, energy—but nothing monetarily. At least Brooks learned a lesson about hiring known felons."

"When was this?" Turner asked.

"A few months ago."

"And where is Eddie Homan now?"

"He's disappeared into the Internet ozone. He has no known address. Every once in a while when we get a nibble trying to get into our computers, we assume it's him. We had to change all the codes very fast when he left."

Turner asked, "Who fires employees?"

"We didn't fire Eddie. He just walked out and never came back."

"Who fires people who are not Eddie?" Fenwick asked.

"Each department head is in charge of their own personnel. Frankly, I don't remember anyone having to be let go. The screening process for hiring is pretty thorough."

"Are there business rivals?" Turner asked.

"None who would be willing to kill. At least none that I know of. I can't imagine it. This is a civilized business."

Fenwick said, "Capitalism can lead to greed and murder as well as fame and riches."

Turner asked, "Among the employees in your department, were there arguments, fights, even any minor disagreements that lingered?"

"I don't want to single anyone out. Not anyone who's here. Eddie was the one big problem."

"How'd you get started here?" Turner asked.

"I was particularly grateful to Craig and Brooks. My little computer start-up company did not make millions. My husband and I were working out of our home. We were going broke and Craig and Brooks bailed us out. They paid a lot more for our company than it was really worth and put me in charge of the creative division here. My husband does consulting work for this computer company and many others. We owe Craig and Brooks a great deal. They rescued a number of businesses. A lot of us didn't have MBAs, didn't have a sense of the possible or the practical. They did the same for

Justin Franki, the head of the research and development department."

"Where were you early this morning?"

"With my husband, having breakfast and getting ready for work, as we always do."

Justin Franki looked like he had just parked his surfboard on the nearest beach and come in off the waves. His blond hair was wet and slicked back. He wore khaki pants molded to his hips and a light brown T-shirt that clung to broad shoulder muscles and stretched taut across beer-can abs. He looked tan, healthy, and energetic. Turner realized most of the others they'd seen looked like they spent every minute of every day indoors. This guy had either just been vacationing somewhere much warmer than Chicago in winter, or he was the best customer a tanning salon ever had.

Justin might have been over thirty, but if he was it was just barely. "Yeah," he said in answer to their inquiries, "Craig and Brooks saved my ass. I was way in debt. I tried to take my company public. I did take it public. The stock soared. Then it plummeted. They don't talk much about the tech stocks that drop out of sight."

"What happened?"

"Most of these dot-com companies are a lot more promise than product. Eventually people are going to demand to see a profit. I never even got off the ground floor. The software I was developing had nothing but glitches, and I could never get it to work right. Everybody in the industry knew I was about to lose everything. Craig and Brooks offered to have me come work here, where I could continue to work on my product while doing other things for them. It got me out of a deep hole." Franki paused. "These guys were great."

"What about this Eddie Homan guy?" Turner asked.

"You always get malcontents. Security and crackers are a problem with almost every computer company. I never got big enough to have any problems. I wish I had been."

"Did you know Eddie personally?"

"Sure. We worked in offices next to each other for a year or two."

"Was he angry enough to kill Mr. Lenzati?"

"Eddie wasn't the confrontational type. He fit the wimpy nerd stereotype pretty well. If he was angry, he'd just go back to his machine and try and think of elaborate schemes to get even with people."

"What were those?"

"He never told me much. I don't think he ever gave up hacking into other people's stuff, but I think the time in prison made him so careful that he really couldn't be effective."

"Do you know of anything specific Eddie might have been working on when he quit?"

"No, either Craig or Brooks would be the ones to ask, maybe Warren Fortesque."

In response to their questions about his whereabouts that morning he said, "I went to the gym for an hour at five, like I do every weekday. I had breakfast at Healthy Mornings restaurant like I do every day. Frederico, my regular waiter, would recognize me. Then I went to work."

The head engineer was Warren Fortesque. He was young like all the others. He wore a brown sweater vest over a white shirt and faded blue jeans. He was maybe five-foot-six, and might have weighed one hundred and twenty-five pounds.

"This is a great place to work," he said. "A fabulous place. No computer company anywhere is working on so many different aspects of the future. You hear about the big egos and huge fights at other companies—here we work together. If you have an idea, you go with it. You don't have to worry about getting start up money. Lots of these companies have engineers who dream fantastic dreams, but those people have no sense of what something is going to cost or if anyone really wants the stuff they make. Here, it doesn't matter. The goal is to create, to always be on the next cutting edge of technology."

"Any problems?" Turner asked.

"Never. This place is paradise."

"What about Eddie Homan?"

"A complete twit. I wish he'd stayed around long enough to get fired."

"What was he working on before he left?" Turner asked.

"Lots of security programs. Many programs computer users buy contain bugs that affect security. He was an expert at finding hidden viruses and eliminating them."

Turner asked, "If he was good at getting rid of them, wouldn't he also be good at inserting them?"

"Sure, but not here. We took too much care. Craig and Brooks were way too smart to trust him with anything vital to the company. Craig and Brooks might be young, but they knew to be careful."

For the next fifteen minutes, they got nothing further from him but cheery pabulum.

Finally, Turner asked where he'd been this morning. Fortesque claimed to have had an ordinary morning, as he and his wife got ready to go to their respective jobs. She was a school teacher in the north suburbs.

They interviewed six of the other top employees of the firm. Not one was over thirty-five. All said basically the same thing. Lenzati was a very nice man with an awkward way of handling people. But he had a gift for unleashing genius and getting the best out of an employee. Each worked in their creative niche and either knew of no one with whom Lenzati fought, or were unwilling to point to a coworker as a possible killer.

When Turner and Fenwick finished with the interviews, they compared notes.

"What I've got," Fenwick said, "is that this guy was a reasonably nice dweeb and a decent employer who paid well, and who had a pornographic collection which he supplemented with a topping of late night visitors that nobody knew anything about. Can anybody be that ordinary?"

"Besides you?"

"Just remember, when you get your ballot for saint of the millennium, I'll be on it."

"You're going to have a tough campaign."

"I'm not campaigning. The selection is obvious. Mother Theresa had nothing on me."

"I always wondered who had something on Mother Theresa," Turner said, "but if we could leave celestial politics aside for a moment. These people liked the boss, which is not a crime. There's got to be a few places on the planet where that happens. We just happened to run into the only one on this continent."

"We need to find an enemy. We need to find someone who knew these people in their personal lives. If we track down this Eddie Homan, I may kiss him. I feel like I'm drowning in a vat of candy with all this saccharine sweetness and light. No one is as good as they all claim Lenzati was."

6

I like watching people and thinking about what their last moment alive is going to be like. I want to be the one in charge of that moment. I want power over them. I want the cops to be the ones without the power for the first time. I like to watch their eyes as they realize they are going to die.

Back at Lenzati's home in his electronics room, they met with the computer tech from the department. To Turner the guy looked younger than his son Brian. He had brush-cut hair, which was slicked down and pulled forward. He kept a tuft of hair growing under his lower lip. He was as pale as someone just getting the flu. He wore baggy pants, a white T-shirt, and a leather jacket that looked several sizes too big for him.

"You're the computer guy?" Fenwick asked, his voice soaked with an ocean of doubt.

The kid glared at him. Without speaking he held out his ID. "You want my driver's license for proof of age of admittance?" Turner saw the guy's name was Dylan Micetic, aged twenty-four. Micetic said, "What is it you guys want?"

"We didn't mean to give offense," Turner said, "but you do look awfully young."

"Yeah, well, I've been that way all my life."

Turner said, "We need to inventory everything in here with someone who has knowledge of what we're looking at. We also need to find any evidence of computer hackers and/or sabotage."

"You mean crackers. Don't they train you guys in any of this stuff? The big thing here with the monitor on top is a computer." He pointed and began naming objects. "That's a printer, a chair, a desk—"

Fenwick interrupted, "Listen, you snot-nosed twerp—"

The kid held up a hand. "Abuse someone else on my time. I have knowledge you need. I'm paid to give it to you, but not to put up with you." He pointed at Fenwick. "And I've heard all about you."

Fenwick grinned. "I hope you heard nothing but the worst."

Turner said, "I'm willing to call a truce. We'll promise not to disparage you for your age if you'll promise not to look down on us for our lack of computer sophistication."

Everybody nodded, although if it was possible to give a surly nod, Fenwick did so.

Turner continued, "What we're looking for is something that might give a hint as to who killed Lenzati. What we want to concentrate on is any kind of fraud or double dealing."

"You think he'd have that out in the open?" the kid asked.

Turner said, "I'm not sure what he'd have, how he'd have it protected, or what its value might be. I suspect we'll find nothing. I'm not an expert on this stuff. I'd settle for an anomaly that will lead to who killed him."

In fact, Turner had taken several computer classes and seminars through the department. All of the detectives had taken at least a word processing class. But he wasn't about to claim vast knowledge, especially in the face of the department's supposed expert.

While Micetic worked, Turner and Fenwick checked with the neighbors who hadn't been home on the first canvass. They also interviewed the members of the cleaning service. None of them knew anything that was helpful.

Back in the electronics room, the work was tedious. The room had been photographed already. They had to take each piece of electronics equipment, software, and disk, note where they found it, what was next to it, what they did with it, and where they placed it when they were done. The trail of evidence had to be clear, and they couldn't know at this point what might be important in their search.

It was nearly four o'clock and they'd been searching for half an hour, when Fenwick said, "Screw it. We've got a million other things to do. We're not going to find anything here. I've got to get home."

"Big case," Turner said. "We're not going to be able to leave it like this. At the least, we've got to get back, report, and write up what we've got."

"They're all big cases," Fenwick said. "They're also all dead bodies. They aren't going anywhere."

"We should stay a while longer," Turner said.

"I've got something," Micetic said. "I think I found out what the main project was that they were working on in their business. The latest cutting edge technology is artificial intelligence. They've done a lot of work with it. No one is close to creating what I consider real intelligence. Essentially computers are still just a series of on and off switches. Today they just go faster than anybody ever dreamed of. An infinitely fast calculator does not add up to intelligence."

"You a Luddite?" Fenwick asked.

"Skeptical is all," Micetic responded. "It's easy to oversell what computers are going to be able to do. Instead of looking through a catalogue that comes in the mail or running to the mall, you make some clicks and buy stuff. You may have convenience, but I'm not sure you've got a revolution. You can talk about vast technology, but if you've got machines that wear out in less time than an average car lasts, I'm not sure you've got much."

Turner thought he might like the guy. He peered over Micetic's shoulder at the screen. It was filled with calculations that made no sense to him.

"What is all that?" Turner asked.

"Formulas. I recognized some of the basic ones. These guys were far ahead of me. I don't pretend to understand all this stuff, and I've got three different computer degrees. I've got an IBM AS400 at home, which I think is the best computer on the market. This stuff makes that look like an abacus."

"What's so important about working on artificial intelligence?" Fenwick asked.

"It's cutting edge. They would have rivals. That kind of project would be ripe for industrial sabotage, international intrigue, double dealing, anything. The closer computers get to what they call artificial intelligence, the more efficient they would be. Build the better mouse trap, etcetera."

"Which companies would be interested?" Turner asked.

"All of them."

"That's not helpful," Fenwick said.

"It's the truth."

"We'll have to talk to their business rivals," Fenwick said.

"Many of them will be out of state," Micetic said.

"I think I knew that," Turner said. He assayed their work so far. "Are you almost done with what's on the computer?"

"I have to get into its innards to try and discover any hidden programs."

"If he hid them, how will you find them?" Turner asked.

"I've had a lot of training. I'll look very carefully. The guy was a computer genius. So far I've beaten all his codes and tricks, but they were fairly simple. There are more, I don't know how many. I cannot guarantee omniscience. I can guarantee I'll do a better job than anybody else you could possibly hire."

"I like confidence," Fenwick said.

Micetic said, "You're going to have to get Werberg in here with me to go over some of these."

"Probably tomorrow," Turner said.

"Whenever," the kid replied. He pointed to the screen. "This next bit is the only thing I haven't been able to crack yet."

Turner and Fenwick gazed at the monitor. "It's gibberish," Fenwick said.

"Precisely," Micetic said. "It is also very organized gibberish."

"It's a code," Turner said.

"Encryption, yep," Micetic said.

"I'm old fashioned," Fenwick said, "to me it's a secret code."

"Can you break it?" Turner asked.

"I've tried a few simple things, but I'd need an encryption breaking program from my office. I should be able to."

"Print us a copy of that," Turner said. "We can add it to the inventory."

Fenwick asked, "Why isn't there an address book anywhere?"

Micetic said, "They don't have address books anymore. They have Palm Pilots."

Fenwick gave him a quizzical look.

Micetic said, "Those hand held computers that you write on?"

"Whatever the hell you call it, where is it?"

"I have no idea. It's a physical object that you would need to look for, not me."

For the next half hour, Fenwick's impatience grew. Finally, he threw down his pen and said, "Let's leave this until the morning. It's nearly five. We can get back to the station, suck up to as many superiors as we need to, and go home."

Micetic promised to keep trying to uncover any secrets. Before leaving, they called Werberg and set up an appointment with him so that the three police officers and he could meet at nine in the morning and go over all the computer materials.

.7.

Sometimes I get lucky and there's a murder or an attack that I've had nothing to do with. They get all confused because they think that's part of what I'm up to. Those are some of the fun times, and I don't have to do a thing to make it happen.

Turner and Fenwick drove back to Area Ten headquarters. Fenwick handled their unmarked car with his usual maniacal glee. The pedestrians of the near north side survived the experience—some of the less attentive, just barely. They pulled into the Area Ten parking lot and headed to their desks on the third floor.

The building housing Area Ten was south of the River City complex on Wells Street on the southwest rim of Chicago's Loop. Many years ago, the department purchased a four-story warehouse scheduled for demolition and designated it as the new Area Ten headquarters. Turner was convinced that soon the grandchildren of some of the original rehabbers would be working on the site. Over many years in fits and starts the building had changed from an empty hulking wreck to a people-filled hulking wreck. For years, construction debris had accumulated in nooks and crannies throughout the building.

In the past few months someone had gotten the insane idea that mid-winter was a good time to replace all the windows in a four story building. No question, the windows needed replacing. The cops who inhabited the place used vast quantities of torn and tattered T-shirts, bits of old rags, and duct tape to block the cold wind that whipped in through the multitude of cracks and crevices. The rehabbers had gotten three-quarters done with the window project and then simply stopped showing up.

Adding to his usual high level of annoyance, the window nearest Fenwick had been accidentally broken by a youthful workman. The wind constantly snapped at the plastic covering they'd used to block it up and the cold oozed relentlessly through the ersatz opening. Numerous promises had been made that the workers would return by the following Monday. No one believed this the first time they were told it. Four weeks later, with no construction workers evident on the horizon, it was long past the point of a running joke. Supposedly the city was thinking of filing suit against the rehabbers. Turner figured the turn of the next millennium would come before the legal system would be of any help. Fenwick disagreed. He thought they should arrest the whole crew. He figured that would shake them up enough to get the work done. Turner wasn't so sure.

Area Ten ran from Fullerton Avenue on the north to Lake Michigan on the east, south to Fifty-ninth Street, and west to Halsted. It included the wealth of downtown Chicago and North Michigan Avenue, some of the nastiest slums in the city, and numerous upscale developments. It incorporated four police Districts. The cops in the Areas in Chicago handled homicides and any major non-lethal violent crimes. The police Districts mostly took care of neighborhood patrols and initial responses to incidents.

When they arrived at their desks, Turner found a box wrapped in a pink ribbon on top of a pile of papers. A label said Nutty Chocolates, Fenwick's favorite purveyor of confections. "You lose this?" Turner asked.

"It's got your name on it."

"Who put it here?"

"Maybe you have a secret admirer."

"I hope not."

Turner called down to the front desk. Dan Bokin, the cop on duty, said the package had come in the mail.

Stunningly enough, the Chicago Police Department had no security measures or policies in place to deal with packages sent to the District and Area stations.

Fenwick said, "You want to call Bomb and Arson?"

Turner examined it carefully. The package was barely larger than a matchbox. It would be hard to conceive that it could be an explosive. The printing of his name and the address of the station was tiny and precise.

"Maybe it's from Ben," Turner said.

"He would send you something like that here without putting his name on it?"

"I'd prefer to think it was him. I'm sending it to be analyzed." Even if it simply contained a piece of chocolate, he was not about to eat a piece of food that mysteriously appeared on his desk.

While Turner was on the phone, Fenwick made several calls to get pictures of Lenzati and Werberg that he and Turner could use as they interrogated those connected with the dead man.

Turner flipped on the computer on his desk. He actually

seldom used it. Mostly he left it in the sleep mode. A message on the screen said HOW MANY INNOCENT PEOPLE HAVE YOU KILLED TODAY?

"What the hell?" he muttered.

"What's up?" Fenwick asked.

Turner moved the screen so Fenwick could read the message.

"What the hell?" Fenwick said.

"Exactly my words," Turner said. He could find no one who would admit to being at his desk or using his computer. Nor had anyone seen a stranger at his desk.

"Could someone have turned this on from another location?" Turner asked.

"We'll have to get Micetic up here and ask him. Don't erase the message."

They called Micetic and asked him to stop by.

Fenwick and Turner methodically began working through mounds of paperwork. They would be in the next day on a Saturday, probably for more hours than either cared to admit.

As Fenwick finished writing in his Daily Major Incident Log, Randy Carruthers entered the squad room. Turner knew that Carruther's partner, Harold Rodriguez, had taken to working by himself in an unused and unheated cubicle on the fourth floor. Rodriguez claimed the cold was better than putting up with his partner. No one doubted this. No one had told Carruthers of this secret location. With the warren of rooms throughout the old building, it was easy to get lost or stay out of sight.

Rodriguez had made a deal, which Turner understood involved large quantities of pastries from a nearby restaurant, with the clerk nearest to the stairs on the fourth floor. The clerk would signal Rodriguez of Carruther's possible approach, and Rodriguez would quietly slip out. The porcine and unpopular young detective was forced to wait long intervals for his partner to appear. As he saw him less and less often, Carruthers became more and more frustrated and upset. Rodriguez was pleased with this, and turned a deaf ear to his partner's requests to disclose his whereabouts.

The rest of the cops on the shift were getting annoyed by Rodriguez's ploy. The less time Rodriguez had to put up with Carruthers, the more time the rest of them had to. Carruthers always seemed to need to find somebody to talk to, check a fact with, compare a sports anecdote with, tell a boring story about his personal life to—in short, to share. Normal conversational give and take, which others found so natural, Carruthers found forced. Turner thought this sad, but not sad enough to feel more than a trifle sorry for the guy, and not sorry enough to pay a lot of attention to him.

Carruthers marched up to Turner's and Fenwick's desks. "Have you guys heard the news?"

Turner did his best to show polite disinterest. Without looking up and while reaching for more forms to fill out, Fenwick said, "We saw the story. A bunch of cops dead around the country. A vast conspiracy to do in the best detectives in each city. Not a shred of concrete evidence to back up the reporter's suspicions. It sounds like all in a day's work for the newspapers in this town. You don't need to worry, Carruthers. No one would confuse you with someone who was competent."

"I'm talking about the pool downstairs among the beat cops."

Turner and Fenwick actually looked up. If there was a sporting event, Fenwick was the one in the building who put together the pool. Almost everybody from the commander to the newest beat cop got in on them. Someone else doing a pool was unprecedented.

"What pool?" Turner asked.

"They tried to keep it a secret. Based on the detectives who work in this building, they're taking odds on which of them is most likely to be murdered by this serial killer."

"Isn't that a little premature?" Turner said. "If not downright macabre."

"Who's the betting favorite?" Fenwick asked.

"You," Carruthers said.

"I'm honored. This must mean they think I'm the best detective on the squad."

"Turner has much worse odds. Only a few guys are taking bets on him."

Turner said, "It could mean they don't like you, Buck."

"Kindly, little old me?" Fenwick asked. "I'm sweet. I'm friendly. I bring them chocolate for Christmas. I'm the best at making cute-corpse comments. What's not to like?"

"It's the jokes," Turner said. "The serial killer is actually a saint who wants to eliminate hideous puns from the face of the earth. Can this be a completely bad thing?"

"No one appreciates a true *artiste* of humor."

"Perhaps we haven't met one," Turner said.

Fenwick pronounced his most recent, favorite, oft-repeated malediction. "May the next corpse we meet piss in your fur-lined jockstrap."

Carruthers said, "I don't think it's the humor. I think they don't like you because you push too hard. You're too mean to them. You ignore them. You make too many demands. You criticize them too much. You—"

Fenwick interrupted. "Is this their opinion or yours?"

Carruthers paused in his declamation. He licked his lips and glanced around the room. His insecurity in the face of Fenwick's blatantly aggressive personality was palpable. Finally he said, "I'm just telling you what I've heard them say."

"You mean they confide in you?" Fenwick asked.

"I'm the one who knew you were their odds-on favorite to be the one the killer picked as the next victim."

Fenwick looked at Turner. His partner shrugged.

Carruthers said, "If you wanted, I think they'd let you guys get in on the pool."

Fenwick said, "I wonder if I dare bet against myself."

"Thanks for the news, Randy," Turner said. "We'll check it out when we get time." The attempted dismissal didn't work.

Carruthers leaned closer to their desks. He whispered, "There's real news." His voice had lost its usual timbre, that of a nose whistle being abused. "Rumor is the police board is going to fire Devonshire and Smythe."

Ashley Devonshire and Dwayne Smythe were the newest detectives in Area Ten. They'd started as superior know-it-alls, moved on to spiteful envy as most of the others in the squad got more arrests and convictions, and finally graduated to murky scandal blending into abject horror. Late on a dank and foggy night, they had encountered what they had thought was an armed rapist. Both had fired their guns. It turned out they were confronting a twelve-year-old in a wheelchair. They claimed a gleam from the metal on the chair arm had looked like the barrel of a gun. As usual, an immediate investigation had taken place. Rumors of a cover-up persisted. Debate on cable television and talk-show radio continued as to responsibility and blame. Protests in the community, the newspapers, and on every newscast covering the Devonshire/Smythe shooting had been loud, insistent, and incessant.

There is always an immediate investigation whenever a Chicago police officer discharges a firearm. Immediate, as in before the officer goes home. Representatives of the superintendent's office, the District, and Area officials, all converge to make a report within hours. Turner had heard of some commanders who insisted that the police look good on any report but he'd never run into the problem.

Devonshire and Smythe were disliked differently than Carruthers. The cops in Area Ten had worked with Carruthers for years. It was like the old Bob Hope line to Dorothy Lamour in one of the *On the Road* pictures, "I want you, I need you, I'm used to you." Carruthers might be a fool, but he was a familiar fool.

Turner didn't believe that Devonshire and Smythe would deliberately kill or harm a kid. He did believe that their misplaced aggressiveness and overzealous ambition had led to a lapse in judgment. Turner knew police work involved a lot of quick thinking. Those who were best at juggling the needs of the community, the law, and their own conscience were generally the best cops. At some point, most cops pushed the limits of their job.

Fenwick was an excellent example of the delicate balance policework often involved. He might be able to do a "bad cop" routine better than anyone else, but he never went over the line to abuse. His decisions were always considered. Devonshire and Smythe were foolishly ambitious and willing to push any situation for any advantage for themselves: either with coworkers, superiors, or their reputations on the streets. It had caught up with them in a dramatic, career threatening, and possibly criminal way. Turner thought maybe the two detectives should lose their jobs.

If the boy died, Turner knew the situation could turn from a nightmare to a disaster. His sympathy lay with the parents. Turner's son Jeff was confined to a wheelchair, so he knew the problems of a disabled child first hand.

The newest rumor Turner and Fenwick had heard that morning, from a far more reliable source than Carruthers, had been that several of the arrests that Devonshire and Smythe had made in a high profile drug bust were under review. There was suspicion that they had doctored their paperwork on the case. Another rumor, from a less reliable source, claimed that all their arrest records were under review. Turner knew for sure that the lieutenant in charge of signing off on their cases was furious at them, and over the past few months had continuously sent back paperwork and even refused to approve several of the arrests. Devonshire and Smythe had made the monumentally stupid mistake of trying to bypass him in the chain of command. Besides the inherent impossibility of this leading to anything positive for them, it was an extremely poor choice of behavior in any bureaucracy, especially the Chicago Police Department.

"You gossip central around here now?" Fenwick asked.

"I know what I know," Carruthers said.

"You've spread plenty of rumors in the past that turned out to be bullshit," Fenwick said. "Even more often you have what you claim to be facts that turn out to be crap later on."

"I do not."

"Yeah, you do. You're stupid. What about the time you claimed for sure there was going to be a change in the pension law for cops? There was no change. There was never any plan for a change. Did you just make it up, or did you take a stupid pill that day?"

Carruthers' face screwed up as if he was being given a wedgie with a cast-iron pair of briefs that was already two sizes too small.

Turner asked, "Who's the source for the rumor?"

"I got it from my clout down at City Hall. It's all over my area of the city."

Generally, Turner felt at one with cops who were in trouble. Dealing with the public in mostly negative situations was not designed to be a warm and fuzzy experience. Nor was handling criminal perpetrators geared to make you a believer in the milk of human kindness, which, as Fenwick often put it, got curdled pretty quick in their line of work. Or as Turner remembered Fenwick's comments—which included an image he wished was more forgettable—"Curdled more quickly than a carton of milk left between the thighs of a dead whore lying on an asphalt parking lot on a hot July afternoon."

Turner didn't like incompetent fools screwing up police work. Cops had a tough enough image problem without the assholes on the force being showcased on the evening news. He doubted if Devonshire and Smythe would ever be back in Area Ten. The immediate impact on him was that the squad was shorthanded. This had meant more overtime recently. Supposedly two replacement detectives were showing up soon, which in police parlance could be in five minutes, five days, five weeks, five months, or five years.

"We're planning a defense fund benefit for the two of them," Carruthers said. "You guys going to come?" Turner thought it was more than typical for Carruthers to be the one rallying around those who were proving to be even more incompetent than he.

"When is it?" Fenwick asked.

"A week from tomorrow."

"We're taking our kids to a Bulls game that day." Turner and Fenwick had gotten tickets to a game for a family outing. Without a championship in sight, it had been easy to garner reasonably decent seats, but at a still-atrocious price.

"You should try and stop by," Carruthers said.

"Won't be able to," Fenwick said. He picked up some paperwork and returned to pointedly ignoring Carruthers. Turner did the same. Their disinterest finally sank in. Carruthers then did what he did so well: he drifted away to find someone else to talk to.

"You're not going to the benefit?" Turner asked.

Fenwick glanced around. As blusteringly assertive and self-confident as he was, he still didn't want to risk the rumor getting around that he or Turner weren't one hundred percent behind one of their own. He said, "Incompetent assholes of the universe unite. I won't be party to bullshit."

"Got that right," Turner said.

Commander Drew Molton strode into the room. Arriving at their workstation, he perched his butt on the corner of Fenwick's desk. No one else in the entire squad dared be so forward. Fenwick might squirm each second his commander took the liberty, but even Fenwick didn't have the nerve to tell his boss to get his butt off his desk.

Fenwick said, "We've got a hot rumor from a source I would never reveal—Carruthers—to the effect that Devonshire and Smythe are going to be fired. You know anything about it?"

"I know the investigation is on-going. I heard the board isn't scheduled to release their decision for weeks yet. The kid they shot has recovered almost as much mobility as he had before the shooting. Whether or not he fully recovers, they're in huge trouble. I think their case has nothing to do with the rest of us, except as an object lesson to people like Carruthers who wouldn't catch on if great flaming dragons came down from heaven and told him how to do his job better."

"The great flaming dragons thing is way overrated," Turner said. "Just last week they were wrong about several things."

Fenwick said, "They never told me they visited you. You never told me they visited you."

Turner said, "Maybe you're losing your touch."

Molton said, "I hate to interrupt great flaming fantasies and delicious rumors of impending doom for cops in this city, but we've actually got real work to do. The killers in the city have not paused to appreciate the humor, the dragons, or the intricacies of police bureaucracy."

"Good for them," Fenwick said.

Turner mentioned the chocolate and the message on his computer screen.

"Get them checked out," Molton said. "How's the Lenzati case going?" he asked.

"A few computer leads," Turner said. He filled the commander in.

"Not much," Molton said when Turner finished.

Turner handed him the coded gibberish.

"What's this?" Molton asked.

Fenwick said, "Secret plans to conquer the world? A long hidden map showing the way to the lost treasure of the Incas?"

Turner said, "It's a little late for feeble attempts at humor."

"Feeble!?" Fenwick exclaimed.

"Feeble," Molton declared. "Get on with it," he said, and walked away.

In the middle of their paperwork, Micetic showed up.

"Did you find out anything yet on Lenzati's computer?"

"No. I was taking a break and decided to stop over to check on your computer message problem."

Micetic sat at Turner's desk for several minutes and typed at the keys. "You leave this thing logged on?" Micetic asked.

"Usually."

"Don't from now on. Somebody got into your machine. I

think I got rid of all the bugs. You need to turn the machine off when you aren't using it." He left.

On their way out Fenwick marched up to the front desk. Turner followed. Dan Leary, the cop on duty, gave them a wary look. Leary had been a cop for thirty-five years, and had a gut that bespoke of more donuts than you could shake a cliché at.

Fenwick said, "I'd like to get in on the pool."

"What pool?" Leary asked.

"The one about which of the detectives is going to be the next target of the serial killer."

Leary looked confused. "I haven't heard about any pool. Don't you do all of them?"

"You can tell me," Fenwick said. "I'm not offended."

A couple of the other beat cops on duty joined the discussion. One said, "Nobody would organize that kind of pool. It's sick."

Turner said, "Carruthers told us there was one."

"Maybe he made it up," Leary said.

"Why?" Turner asked.

Leary said, "I don't want to intrude on detective business, but maybe he thought it was funny, or maybe he was trying to get back at you. There is no pool."

"Oh," Fenwick said.

Once out the door Fenwick asked, "You really think there isn't a pool?"

"Would they lie to the two most perceptive and well-loved detectives on the force?" Turner asked.

Fenwick said, "We could find out whoever that is and ask them to come over and talk to the desk detail."

Turner responded, "I think the idea that Carruthers pulled the wool over your eyes would bother you more than if they really did have a pool on which of us might die."

"I'll have to find a corpse and have it piss in Carruthers' underwear."

"The guy's working up some nerve, which isn't necessarily all bad."

"I don't want him working up nerve near me," Fenwick said.

"I don't want him working near me, period," Turner answered.

8

Cop hangouts are the best. It's easy to find them if you're methodical. Just be around when the last shift of an evening goes off duty. You might follow a few home to their faithful spouses, but eventually you'll follow one to a cop hangout. You've got to be careful about going into them. There's nothing like cops for being suspicious. You pick times when you know the hangout will be crowded. You sit near a group, but not too close. You never, ever look at any of the potential victims directly. There's a lot of rough camaraderie. I love listening to them, knowing one of them is going to die.

Paul Turner opened his front door a little after eight-thirty. On the couch in the living room sat a scrawny teenager dressed in baggy black pants, a baggy gray sweatshirt, and torn black sneakers. His gelled-back hair was dyed maroon on top and cut razor-short on the sides. His beard stubble was almost longer than the hair between his ears and the mass on the top. He was watching a college basketball game on ESPN, and barely glanced up as Paul nodded in his direction.

His youngest son, Jeff, called a brief hello. He was curled in his wheelchair next to the front window. He was rereading *Harry Potter and the Sorcerer's Stone* for the third time. Like hordes of other kids, Jeff had abandoned his computer for the Potter books. Paul was glad the boy now spent fewer hours immersed in playing games in which the goal was to defeat vast hordes of evildoers as quickly as possible. Paul had picked up the first book in the series one night when he was sitting up with Jeff when the boy was sick. He'd become as enthralled as his son. It wasn't something he was about to tell Fenwick, but he was eager to get the time to read the next book in the series.

Paul found Ben at the kitchen table reading a new issue of *Bludgeoning Computers*. It was an underground satire magazine designed for those frustrated from failed attempts to use their computers—the fastest-growing segment of the population.

They kissed and hugged hello. Paul enjoyed his lover's aftershave and thought of how good it would be to go immediately to bed next to that warmth and good feeling. He was tired and wanted nothing more than to be entangled in those masculine arms.

"I called earlier," Paul said.

"We went out for steak. Brian is now on a high protein diet."

"Which sports star claimed that was the be-all and end-all?"

"Does it make a difference?"

"I suppose not." Paul said, "Thanks for the chocolate."

"What chocolate?"

"I found a package addressed to me on my desk. It didn't have a return address on it. I assumed it was from you, or at least I had hoped it was."

"You opened a package without a return address or name on it?"

"It was a tiny thing, barely big enough for a small piece of buttercream chocolate. I didn't open it. I sent it to the lab for analysis."

"Be careful."

"I'm always careful. It wasn't from you?"

"If I wanted to give you chocolate as a surprise, I wouldn't be shy about admitting it afterwards."

Paul shrugged then asked, "Why is there a surly, uncommunicative teenager, not my own, sitting on my living room couch?"

"Kid's name is Andy Wycliff. He's got a heavier beard than half the daddies in a leather bar. He's another one of Brian's school projects."

"The kid is a 'project'? Would that be science, social studies, literature, calculus, or what?"

"Or what. Brian's in that peer helper group. You know, they help out kids in crisis or who transfer to the high school after the beginning of the year. Brian says this kid has all kinds of problems adjusting, so he came to their group for help. Brian offered to take him to the poetry reading tonight. He has that literary assignment."

"Nuts," Turner said. "I thought about the reading earlier today, but then I forgot all about it, and I promised I'd go."

Brian's assignment was not the reason Paul felt compelled to attend the poetry reading. Several weeks ago Paul had run into an old friend, Trevor Endamire, from his police academy days, who had tried to convince him to come to the gay police officers' meetings. Trevor and Paul had grown up in the same neighborhood. Paul had begged off because he wasn't much of a joiner. The guy had then explained about the poetry reading. It was not a gay group, but a bunch of cops who met once a month in the basement of a shop which sold a mixture of new age, cabalistic, and holistic health food items. The meeting place was half a block from the Eighteenth District police station on Chicago Avenue on the near north side.

Reluctantly, Turner had agreed to go. He'd known Trevor for years. They weren't close friends, but he wanted to be supportive. Although being supportive after a hectic day like this was a bit more of an obligation than he liked feeling.

His older son Brian was going. For his literature class this semester he had to attend at least three cultural events, not to include rock concerts of any kind. If it was going to be music, it had to be a symphony. Getting Brian to a symphony orchestra was like trying to convince anyone that just one more injection from a ten-inch needle would be great fun. Most of his buddies were going to plays. Brian had missed one event with them because of a basketball game, so he had to do something else. Since Brian was going, Jeff, the younger son, wanted to go. Mrs. Talucci, their next door neighbor, had heard that Trevor was performing. As the son of someone from the neighborhood, he earned the sobriquet of "one of us" and therefore worthy of her support. When Paul's reporter friend, Ian Hume, had expressed an interest in attending, the event had begun to take on the proportions of a minor literary stampede.

"Is there any way I can get out of this?" Paul asked.

"Yes. You could have moved to the Yukon yesterday."

"I missed my flight."

"You could call Mrs. Talucci and tell her she'll have to find another ride. You could call Ian, and explain you're not interested in seeing him tonight. I'd be happy to do that part for you." The relationship between his friend and his lover was cool at best. "You could explain to Trevor why you deserted him. You could write a note to your son's literature teacher explaining your shortcomings as a literary parent. You could apologize profusely to your dedicated and loyal lover who agreed to participate in this mad behavior."

"Not a lot of choice to any of that. Double nuts. It's not like Trevor and I were lovers when we were kids."

"He's gay. You said you'd go. Mrs. Talucci is looking forward to it. She says she is dying to go to a truly seedy cop hangout. She claims she hasn't been in one since the late thirties."

Mrs. Talucci was in her nineties and had lived next door to Paul all his life. He lived in the Taylor Street area of Chicago just southwest of the Loop in the house he had grown up in. His parents had retired to Florida some years ago, but Paul loved the old neighborhood and stayed. The greatest annoyance in Mrs. Talucci's life was pressure from her daughters and nieces, who thought she should spend her days in a rocking chair waiting to die. This annoyed her beyond reason. She got out as often as she could, and she had recently taken to international traveling with several of her grandnieces, who were often hard put to keep up with her. She'd found two possible locations for her next trip in *Modern Maturity*. One was horseback riding in the Golden Circle in Iceland. The other whitewater rafting on the Upper Yangtze River in Tibet. Both of these activities were rated by the magazine as "easy tries." Paul hoped that was true.

"I'm going to go, aren't I?" Paul said.

"Yep. We were waiting for you so we could leave."

"I'd offer to go out and come back later, but it probably wouldn't do any good."

"Not the slightest. You've just got time to eat that half of the meatball sandwich left from last night."

Paul wolfed it down with a Miller Lite, and then the two

adults entered the living room. Paul heard his son Brian thump down the stairs. The boy breezed into the room, wearing his black leather jacket, a heavy gray sweatshirt over a white T-shirt, and khaki pants. He said, "Hi, Dad. Did you meet Andy Wycliff?" Brian nodded toward the still recumbent teenager. The kid nodded briefly. "Ben said it was okay for him to come with us."

Paul said, "I can hear the teaser: 'Teenagers slain in wild poetry brawl. Police mystified, parents held accountable. Film at ten.' He called his parents?"

"Yeah. Mrs. Talucci's on her way over. Are you ready to go?"

Everybody piled into Paul's van. Jeff's wheelchair fit into the second seat, and Mrs. Talucci sat next to him. Brian drove. He was still in the recently-acquired-license stage of offering to drive everywhere. Paul sat next to the boy, who was campaigning vigorously to get his own car. So far the you-have-to-pay-your-own-car-insurance gambit had forestalled the purchase. Ben and Andy sat in the back.

Brian fussed with the heat. Before he could blast their ear drums, Paul reached over to the stereo controls and turned them off.

"Dad!" Brian protested.

"Son?" Paul asked.

"We gotta have music," the teen insisted.

"For the less than fifteen minutes it is going to take us to get to the north side, you can live without causing harm to the eardrums of the adults inhabiting this vehicle."

"I won't turn it up loud," Brian promised.

"Loudness is one thing," Paul said. "Stunningly annoying by its very nature is another." For longer trips, he had gotten the boys portable CD players so they could listen to their own music without disturbing the adults.

They parked in a handicapped zone in the alley behind a row of stores and trooped through a door off the alley and into the basement. Paul carried Jeff, and Ben carried the boy's wheelchair. Most of the lights in the basement were out. Someone had placed numerous candles on the unromantic, plastic-topped tables. The floors and walls on the way to the bathrooms looked as if they hadn't been washed or mopped in years. Dim lights from the coffee and health food bar added little illumination to the rest of the room. A podium was set up on a small stage. Paul saw Trevor Endamire and went up to him.

"When do you go on?" Paul asked.

"I'm second from the end."

Paul hid his sigh of resignation as best he could. Endamire didn't seem to notice. "How many people are reading?" Paul asked.

"Seven or eight," Endamire said. "I'm really glad you came. This is really supportive. I think we're going to have a decent crowd."

Mrs. Talucci greeted Trevor with a huge hug and began asking him about obscure relatives. Including those who Paul came with, and the people he assumed were readers, there might have been twenty-five people in the room. At a card table on the side a woman was pouring Coke from a large plastic container into small cups. A hand-lettered sign asked for a donation of two dollars for each drink. Paul bought some for each member of his group. He sat back down in the murk to wait for the show to begin. The performance was supposed to have started at nine—it was now half past. Paul wished they'd hurry and get it over with. He saw that his son Jeff was already yawning.

9

Watching and waiting. Sitting in the dark on the street outside their homes and spying on them through the windows. Sitting next to them in a restaurant or a bar. Being near and getting a feel for your victim. The very best times are killing them—but watching up close, unseen and unknown, that ranks right up there.

Because he had his back to the stairs, Paul was not aware of Dwayne Smythe's entrance until the man stood in front of him.

"I need help," Smythe said, "I've got to talk to you."

"I'm here for the poetry reading with my family."

"This will just take a minute."

Turner would have preferred to say no, but his innate politeness won out.

"Could we talk outside?" Smythe asked.

Paul would rather talk to Smythe with an auditorium full of witnesses present. However, this guy was a fellow cop. He'd faced down gun barrels as had Paul. Smythe had backed him and Fenwick up in tough situations. Paul grabbed his fur-lined, black leather jacket and trudged back up the steps. Outside, the air was crisp and clear. Turner pulled his gloves out of his pockets.

In the street light, brighter than the basement dimness, Turner could see Smythe's handsome face was blotchy with red and creased with worry lines. His hands trembled.

"I need some help," Smythe began.

"Where's your partner?"

"I think she and I are on our own. We're both in deep shit."

"I don't want to be involved in your case," Turner said. "I know nothing about what happened."

"I know. I don't need you for that part. I need somebody from the squad to testify for me."

"About what?" Turner said.

"I need a character witness. You're the first guy I thought of. You've got a reputation for honesty. People respect you. If you talked on my behalf, it might help."

"I don't have any clout. I don't have any influence. Aren't these evidentiary hearings? I have no place there."

"If I need somebody to talk for me, it's got to be you," Smythe insisted. "People listen to what you have to say. I've got to have somebody. You're known in the department for honesty and integrity. Aren't you willing to be supportive?"

"I'm supportive," Turner said.

"You've got to be willing to stand up for me. How will it look if you won't defend one of your own?"

"Is that a threat?" Turner asked. "You want me to help you out and if I don't, you're going to spread it around that I wouldn't back you up? You're not stupid, Dwayne, at least I never thought you were, but you've gone too far." He turned to go back to the basement.

"Wait," Smythe said. "Please, don't go in. I'm sorry."

Turner paused. He realized the man was shivering almost uncontrollably. Smythe was well bundled up in his heavy coat. It wasn't the cold that had brought Smythe to this pitiable state.

Turner said, "You think that was a good way to get me to go out on a limb for you?"

"I'm scared. I've always wanted to be a detective. I didn't break any department regulations. In the Haggerty case they were accused of breaking over thirty of them. I'm not."

Smythe was referring to a case in which three officers were fired by the police board, and another suspended. "I've got a chance. Maybe I won't get fired. I've always wanted to be a detective. I never meant to hurt the kid."

"You screwed up. You don't even know how to ask for help. You never think before you act. You always push too hard. You've made too many mistakes. You should have thought about how to be a good cop before you screwed up the first time."

"I did, you know. I thought about the job constantly. I know I sneered at you and Fenwick a lot, but I watched what you guys did. I tried to do things right, the way you did them. It's probably too late now, but I've got to try everything I can think of to save my job. I know you're reluctant to risk your reputation for me. I shouldn't have made any kind of threat. I'm sorry." He drew a deep breath and rubbed his hands together, then sniffed and wiped the back of his glove against his nose. "Look, Paul, I'm desperate. It's not much of a limb to go out on. You just have to say you've worked with me and that I'm a good cop."

"But Dwayne, I don't think you're a good cop. How can I get up and testify?"

"You really don't think I do a good job?"

"Did you falsify those incident reports?"

"No. I swear to god. I would never do that."

Turner had never falsified a report, had never felt a need to. He'd get his arrests honestly or not at all. He knew Fenwick felt the same way. He said, "This would be a poor time to lie to me."

"I'm not lying. I swear. Please, you've got to help me. You're the only one I can turn to. That fool Carruthers keeps volunteering to testify. I might as well put a noose around my neck as have him speak. They wouldn't stop laughing as they booted my ass out. It's got to be someone who's respected. People said you'd be willing to help."

"Who?"

"Everybody says you're a stand-up guy."

"No one has any business speaking for me." Paul wondered about his reputation and his own conscience if he testified on Smythe's behalf. The cops who knew Smythe would know him for an overly ambitious fool. They'd know Paul was saying as little as possible while trying to keep his integrity intact. Paul was not willing to squander the goodwill of his reputation by speaking dishonestly about Dwayne Smythe. If he lied, people would know Paul had swallowed his real opinion to maintain his solidarity with one of their own. Some of his coworkers would see this as righteous solidarity while others would be delighted to hear that he had compromised himself. Some would see it as him coming down a peg from some unspecified moral high ground. Turner didn't view himself as a paragon of virtue but at the same time he most certainly intended to be able to live with his conscience. If called upon, he intended to tell the truth. Smythe was putting him in a delicate, but probably not career-threatening, position. Nevertheless, he resented even being asked to do something that forced him to confront a moral dilemma not of his own making.

Smythe apologized again. "I'm sorry. I screwed up a few minutes ago. I shouldn't have asked you the way I did."

"No, you shouldn't have."

"Will you?" Smythe pleaded and placed his hand on Turner's arm.

Paul allowed the contact for a moment, then gently pulled away and said, "I'll think about it," and strode carefully back down the stairs.

Turner was furious with Smythe. Despite the apology, the position the young detective had put him in was a nasty one. The blue wall of silence was very real: if you saw something, you kept silent; if forced to speak, you supported your own. Smythe had known exactly what he was doing. Taking back the implied threat was useless. It hung there as soon as Turner was asked, and would be there until Smythe's case was decided. And if Turner made the wrong decision, it could affect the rest of his career in the department. Being a gay cop was one thing. Being thought of as a traitor was another.

As Turner resumed his seat, Mrs. Talucci asked, "Who was that? I thought it might be that Dwayne Smythe that's being investigated." Mrs. Talucci was addicted to television news shows, listening to interviews on NPR, reading three newspapers a day, and indulging in tawdry neighborhood gossip. She would recognize Dwayne from photos in the media. She knew details of current events, whether of revolutions in remotest Moldavia or the birth of a baby in the neighborhood. She knew the names of more foreign leaders than George W. Bush, which wasn't all that difficult a trick.

Paul knew he could avoid her question, and Mrs. Talucci would not pursue it, but he said, "Dwayne wants me to speak on his behalf, to be a character witness."

Mrs. Talucci nodded. "A tough position to put you in. Have you decided what to do?"

"As little as possible," he replied.

Turner saw his reporter friend, Ian Hume, stride down the stairs. As always, Ian wore his slouch fedora. Ian was a reporter for the local gay newspaper, the *Gay Tribune*. He and Paul had attended the police academy together. For a short while after Paul's wife had died, they had been lovers.

Ian had claimed he wanted to go to the reading out of a perverse desire to watch cops attempt to be literary. Paul wasn't sure about his motives, but was glad for the additional company.

Ian pulled up a chair behind him and leaned close. "My sources say you are investigating the Lenzati murder."

"And who would those sources be?" Turner asked. It was a ritual with the two of them, the claiming of an unnamed source and the asking for the name.

"I have information for you," Ian said.

"That's a switch," Paul said.

"You are annoyed tonight."

"I don't want to be here."

"I do. I found out this afternoon that there's a young guy in the gay cop group who's supposed to be really hot. Apparently, he's not a very good poet, but he is reading tonight."

"I figured there was some stud at the bottom of your motivation."

"Isn't there always? And what better motivation could there be to attend a poetry reading? You're probably the only gay cop who isn't a poet."

"For which I am grateful."

"You don't like poetry?" Ian asked.

"It's nice, in its place. I just wish its place wasn't where I was. I feel the same way about opera."

"I know. We're worried about you. Not liking opera may cause us to confiscate your gay ID card."

"Will I have to give back the toaster?"

"Probably. At least you aren't a gay poet."

"What's wrong with being a gay poet?" Turner asked.

"I didn't say anything about right or wrong. It's just there are few people on the planet more pretentious than gay men who write poetry and take it seriously."

Turner said, "I don't think I know any openly gay poets."

"It's a quirk in their gay genetic code. You have to know how to look for it."

"I thought there wasn't a gay genetic code," Turner said.

"There probably isn't," Ian said. "Individually, gay poets are mostly harmless. Put them in a group, and they can be lethal. I wouldn't mess with them."

"What is it you know about Lenzati?" Turner asked.

"Do I get information back?"

"As usual, you will get back in equal measure according to how important your information is."

"The partner, Werberg, is gay," Ian announced.

"Why is that important?"

"Why wouldn't it be?"

"Would it cause him to kill his partner?"

"That I don't know."

"Was Lenzati gay?" Turner asked.

"No, very straight from all I know."

"How do you know Werberg's gay? And don't tell me 'sources.'"

"I had sex with him."

"You did?"

"No, but I thought you'd sit up and take notice." Ian pointed and asked, "What's he doing here?"

Paul looked. Buck Fenwick and his wife Madge entered the room. "He likes poetry?" Turner asked. Buck and Madge took a seat near the stage. When Fenwick looked surreptitiously around, he spotted Paul. Turner left his seat and walked up to them.

"Paul," Madge said. "How nice of you to come and be supportive of Buck. He said you probably wouldn't be here."

"He may have fibbed to you," Paul said. "I had no idea that he was going to be here."

Even in the dim light, Paul could see that Fenwick had turned very red. His bulky partner looked distinctly annoyed.

"You never told him?" Madge said. "You should be proud of what you've done."

"You write poetry?" Turner asked. Turner thought he would be as likely to find a liberal at a Christian Coalition convention as discover that Fenwick wrote poetry.

"I am not to be razzed about this," Fenwick said.

Madge said, "Paul would never do that."

"I can be bribed," Paul said, "but my silence on this will only be bought at a very high price."

Fenwick mumbled, "Whoever thought the most honest cop in the city would resort to extorting bribes from a fellow officer?"

"You know, Madge," Paul said, "there are cops in this town who would pay a great deal to have this knowledge."

"I don't see what the big deal is," Madge said.

"You're being naive," Fenwick snapped.

"I think poetry is great," Madge said. "Anyone in the department could have come here tonight. How would he prevent the news from getting out even if you weren't here?"

Fenwick said, "Everyone in the room knows enough to keep quiet about the others."

Mrs. Talucci joined them. She and Madge hugged briefly. Mrs. Talucci patted Buck's massive shoulder with one of her diminutive hands. She said, "I always figured you'd be the poetry writing type."

"How's that?" Paul asked.

"A hunch," she said. "From the way he loves pasta, from the way he loves to eat, from the way he eyes a woman when he thinks his wife isn't looking. He's a romantic."

"You never told me," Paul said.

Mrs. Talucci said, "I'm not required to reveal all I know to you. The main problem tonight is refreshments. Two dollars for a thimbleful of soda? Outrageous? And why can't they provide an adequate spread at these events?" She headed toward what Paul knew she would regard as a woefully inadequate food table. Mrs. Talucci believed that if you didn't leave an event stuffed, you probably didn't have a good time.

"She deliberately tried to get me to come tonight," Paul said. "It wasn't just for Trevor. She knew you'd be here."

Madge said, "Mrs. Talucci is a smart woman."

"Or at least she has good sources," Paul said. He glanced around the room. It was nearly ten, long past the scheduled starting time and he knew he was stuck staying until Fenwick and Trevor had read. He could always ask Ben or Brian to take Jeff home. Paul returned to their table. He sat between Ben and his younger son. Brian and his buddy Andy were whispering together and giggling. Paul decided he preferred not to know what about. With his fingers, Paul massaged the back of his lover's neck for a few moments. Ben moved his knee to rest against Paul's.

A makeshift spotlight finally went on and outlined a chair on a small raised platform. The next hour and a half was mind numbingly boring. Fenwick read as if the forces of hell were behind him, and he needed to hurry to get done before they caught him.

When Fenwick was finished reading, Mrs. Talucci whispered to Paul, "I think he's nervous because you're here."

"Fenwick nervous?"

"Of course," she said. "He's opening himself up and being vulnerable. It's the same for any performer. You know that."

"I don't voluntarily get up in front of any group," Paul said.

"He did, and it took nerve," Mrs. Talucci said.

Paul admitted this was true. Fifteen minutes after Fenwick finished, Jeff was fast asleep with his head on Paul's shoulder. The two teenagers had asked to be able to walk around outside. Paul had told them not to go far.

Just before eleven, Ian left with the first reader, an attractive young man whose poetry, as far as Paul could tell, consisted solely of an extended and self-absorbed meditation on the shades of light on a falling maple leaf.

Paul knew he had to get up the next morning to work on the Lenzati murder. He hadn't been scheduled to work, but he knew he had no choice. When Trevor finally began to read, Paul almost cheered. In his reading Trevor included dramatic pauses and long stretches of silence, which Paul found as interesting as his verses. Twenty agonizing minutes later he decided he'd had enough. Mrs. Talucci chose to stay and get a ride home with the Fenwicks. Buck would have to be at work in the morning as well, but these were his cronies from a world Paul was not part of. Turner knew Buck would simply drink gallons of coffee and stay awake on caffeine.

Before they left, Paul walked up to Fenwick, leaned down, patted him on the shoulder, and murmured, "Nice job, buddy."

"Thanks," Fenwick said.

.10.

I thought of leaving the cops alone and attacking their families. I've heard it said that leaving someone in misery for the rest of their life is excellent revenge. That may be so, but I want the cops to be the ones who feel pain.

Saturday morning Turner was awakened by someone banging on the front door. He threw on some jeans and padded downstairs. On his front porch was the kid from the night before. He tried to remember his name and couldn't. This morning the kid had shaved his heavy beard and looked much more like a teenager. He was dressed in baggy jeans, a baggy shirt, an oversized jacket, and overpriced tennis shoes. Paul called upstairs for Brian, who trudged downstairs in a pair of gray sweat pants and a T-shirt.

Brian said, "Hi, Andy." Paul remembered then that Andy Wycliff was the kid's name.

The kid said, "We're supposed to stop by the school early today for the science project."

Brian yawned. "I gotta go to school today, Dad. A bunch

of us are going to work on our senior physics projects. They've got to be done."

"Going to school on a Saturday is okay."

"Then a bunch of us are going to the hockey game at UIC this afternoon."

"And Mr. Chores will be done?"

"Got most of them done before you got home last night. I'll finish them between the end of the game and before I go out tonight."

"Tonight is?"

"Hanging out with the guys. Probably a movie."

"Sounds fine. Give the details to Ben. I'll probably be late."

Paul returned upstairs. He found Ben pulling on a pair of black jeans. "I'm too old for these wild late nights and then getting up and going to work," Ben said. "These mad poetry readings take a lot of out of you."

"I could use more sleep," Paul said.

"Me too. I could stay out all hours when I was young, but not anymore." Ben would be working at his car repair shop for at least the next ten hours.

Paul said, "I'd rather not spend another night at a poetry reading."

Ben said, "I'm a little worried about that article in the paper about the attacks on cops."

Paul embraced his lover and kissed him. "I'll be careful. You've got my pager and cell phone numbers. If you feel the need, call." They'd had this discussion before. Ben had become less openly worried about the risks Paul faced in his job. He'd become generally quiet about his fears, but he'd made them clear many times before. Ben said, "I love you."

Paul said, "I love you, too." Paul made sure Jeff was securely ensconced at Mrs. Talucci's, then drove to work.

Turner got to his desk a little before eight. Fenwick

wasn't in yet. On his desk, Turner found another small box like the one from yesterday.

Under the package was a phone message memo which said, "Your fat buddy writes lousy poetry and he reads even worse." Someone not only was sending him stuff but knew of his movements. Turner was able to confirm that note and package did not arrive together. The cop on the desk had simply taken a phone message.

He asked everyone he could find in the station house if they knew anything about the package. No one did. The first one had arrived by mail. He found out this one had been sitting on the front steps of the station when the shift had changed. No one had seen anyone put it there. It had his name on it, so someone had put it on his desk. Again the wrapping paper was from Nutty Chocolates.

Turner sent the package and contents to the police lab for analysis. He also called the lab, which confirmed that the inside of the first box had contained a single piece of chocolate, but they hadn't gotten around to any further analysis than that. He asked them to put a priority on it. Turner had never gotten an unexplained package before, much less two, and he found the experience unsettling. He didn't know if someone he had helped convict for a crime was trying to get even in some perverse way, or someone was trying to be cleverly kind. If the latter, he wished they'd understand it was stupid and disconcerting rather than generous and thoughtful. On the other hand, getting even with chocolate made very little sense either. He knew Ben wasn't the kind of man to string him along. His kids had no reason to. Nobody he knew did. He didn't like it, but for now there was nothing he could do about it.

The note was disturbing and even more baffling. Turner wondered who really cared if Fenwick wrote poetry, and why spend the energy to leave a phone message for him and not his partner. His sense of unease began to grow.

He flipped the switch on his computer monitor. There was another message: ARE YOU WORRIED YET? Turner slammed his fist down on his desk. A knot of detectives gathered around. "Where the *hell* is this coming from?" Turner demanded.

"Our new computers, unlike this building, are state of the art," Judy Wilson said. "They're the only thing new around here. It's connected to a broadband Internet server."

"Which means," Roosevelt said, "that anybody, anywhere, can wreck anything. You better find out what the hell is going on."

"Got that right," Turner said. But he couldn't find anyone who had been near his machine. He had no way of finding out if there was a way for his computer to be turned on from a remote location and a message inserted.

He was still fuming when Fenwick staggered in a little before eight-thirty. Fenwick glared at him through sleep deprived eyes. "Madge set this up with Mrs. Talucci. They got Trevor to talk to you."

"I figured that out last night," Turner said. "I have made the ultimate sacrifice for my cop partner. I showed up and stayed awake." Turner yawned. "It was the best poetry reading I've ever been to."

"It's the only poetry reading you've ever been to."

"Which makes it the best. No offense to you, but I'm hoping, it's also the only."

"Philistine."

"My guess is you're more embarrassed about writing poetry than about my being there."

"Maybe it's kind of both."

"Trevor's your real problem. He talks too much. I'm sure he's blabbed to half the planet. Frankly, I'm not sure why everybody doesn't know already. There's no way everyone in this squad room isn't going to know you were there. And I got a phone message." He handed Fenwick the pink piece of paper.

Dan Bokin from the downstairs desk entered the room carrying a bouquet of red roses, pink carnations, and yellow daffodils. With a bow he handed them to Fenwick, did a smart about-face, and strode out.

Fenwick gaped at the flowers.

Commander Molton sauntered in. "Nice flowers," he said.

Fenwick grabbed the envelope from the bouquet, plunked himself into his chair, and opened the card. "They're from 'an admirer,'" he said.

Turner told Molton about the chocolate, the phone message, and the note on the computer. He finished, "Are the flowers, chocolate, message, and note from the same person?"

"Beats the crap out of me," Fenwick said. "I've got the solution to the messages-on-the-computer problem." He reached over, yanked the plug and cord out of the back of the machine, and tossed them onto Turner's desk. "That takes care of that." He bent down and took a deep whiff of flower scent. "This I like," he announced. "My guess is the flowers are from the guys downstairs and are meant to be sarcastic."

"I'm going to order protection for you for a while, Paul," Molton said. "I don't like this. Whoever's making these threats knows too much and is too clever by half, and could also be a killer. I hope it isn't necessary, but I'd rather be safe."

Turner was about to object, but he thought of his kids and Ben's ability to worry. At the very least Ben would feel better if he knew someone was out there protecting him.

"What's the plan for the day on the Lenzati killing?" Molton asked.

Turner said, "We've got a long list of people to talk to."

Molton said, "If you can drag yourself away from Fenwick's literary career, you should get to it." He turned to Fenwick, "I heard you were quite good last night. Congratulations." He marched off.

Carruthers walked up to them. Turner thought the young detective beamed more brightly than anyone had a right to at work on a Saturday morning. Carruthers clapped Turner on the shoulder and said, "I hear you're going to do what's right."

"What's that?" Turner asked.

Carruthers lowered his voice and leaned down to whisper in his ear, "Be a character witness for Dwayne."

Turner was furious that this news had already hit the cop gossip line. He was even more angry because he assumed Smythe had spread it around. He also realized that Smythe had done it deliberately to push him into a corner. Very carefully he said, "Randy, I don't want you to come near me for the next six months." Carruthers frowned, his shoulders slumped, and he shuffled off.

"What the hell was that all about?" Fenwick asked.

Turner told him about last night's discussion with Smythe. He finished, "I got a plea from an incompetent creep followed by years of listening to poetry, all in one night."

"But it was my poetry, so that should have made it all right."

"Why didn't you ever tell me you wrote poetry?"

For one of the few times in Turner's memory, Fenwick spoke quietly and almost modestly. "I'm not ashamed. It's just a little strange."

"No stranger than a lot of the other stuff you've told me. Are you afraid people will think you're effete, less studly, or maybe gay because you write poetry?"

"I've got a tough guy, masculine image. Admittedly an overweight, tough guy, masculine image, but poetry does

104

not fit in with that. In general we don't like people who are different, and a lot of cops would make of fun anyone who writes poetry. I've got a big ego and can take a lot of razzing, but somehow I felt less secure about the poetry."

"I'm your partner. We're friends."

"I know. I guess I should have said something."

"Then again, if you'd said something sooner, I might have been stuck going to more poetry readings."

"Consider yourself lucky."

Turner said, "I can live with that. I admit, I know nothing about poetry. I think you did a fine reading. Let's leave it at that."

"I guess," Fenwick said. "What are you going to do about Smythe?"

"Shoot him or hire a great flaming dragon to take him away."

"Both excellent suggestions. You know, he's got you by the balls. If you lie, you sell yourself out. If you tell the truth, you sell him out. If there's anything I can do to help, let me know."

"I don't think it's going to come to anything very dramatic."

"It might," Fenwick said. "There's nothing you can say that would be neutral?"

"Neutral is good," Turner said. "but I'd just rather not be involved at all."

"You may not have much choice."

"There's nothing to be done about it now. What time is our appointment with Werberg and our computer guy?"

"We've got fifteen minutes to make it."

Before they left, they procured the pictures of Lenzati and Werberg they'd asked for the night before. They also called Lenzati's accounting firm. Because it was Saturday, it took more than a few calls, but they got through and arranged for a meeting later that day.

Dylan Micetic, the department computer expert, met them at the Lenzati house at 9:00 as scheduled. As they entered, Turner asked, "You have any luck with that code?"

"Code as in computer language?" Micetic asked.

"Don't give me that computer gobbledygook," Fenwick snarled. "We mean code as in secret spy codes written in ciphers. The rest of us know what a secret code is. Just because your over-educated ass wants to—"

"Wait," Turner said.

Fenwick stopped.

Turner said, "I understand the harangue. Let's get on with it."

Micetic said, "I've learned very little. It has at least seven different encryptions. It's the most sophisticated encryption scheme I've ever seen."

"Speaking of sophisticated," Turner said, "I got another one of those strange messages on my computer at my desk." He explained.

"You have one of those new high-powered computers," Micetic said.

"Supposed to be the fastest in the department," Turner said.

"And they're hooked up to everything, which means they're vulnerable to everything," Micetic said. "I'll look at it again later."

At that moment, Werberg showed up. He had his lawyer, Claud Vinkers, with him.

Before they started on the computers, Turner said, "Tell me about the late night parties Mr. Lenzati had."

"I know nothing of such parties," Werberg said.

Fenwick rubbed his hands together. "Excellent. A blatant lie. Our first big one of the case." He clamped a huge paw on Werberg's shoulder. "Ya see, we've got a witness that saw people, individuals and in groups, here late, and you, you poor sap, you were seen and identified as being part of that crowd. Blatant lies whet my appetite. They cheer me up. They make life worth living. They make me think you are a much better suspect than you were even five minutes ago."

Turner was dying to mutter that just about anything whetted Fenwick's appetite. He kept quiet.

Werberg said, "I came to his house late a few times for small get togethers. That isn't a crime."

"Then why lie about it?"

Werberg looked confused but kept silent. Turner and Fenwick waited. Silence was most often the detective's friend. Most people couldn't stand to let silence build. Werberg kept mum. After several drawn out moments, his lawyer asked, "Did you want to get to work on the computer programs?"

"How could Lenzati work after partying all night?" Turner asked.

"Same as you," Werberg said. "Same as anybody. We worked every minute from the time we were both twelve years old until we sold our first company in our twenties. All those years, when we weren't in school, we were working. Neither of us had a life. We were the ultimate computer nerds. We reveled in being different and the possibility of being rich. We had a goal, and we met it beyond our wildest expectations. We've more than earned the right to play and party."

"Who was he partying and playing with Thursday night and Friday morning?" Turner asked.

"I have no idea. I wasn't there. He didn't need to check in

with me. Did you want to go over this computer stuff or not? I've got to get to our offices today. Craig's loss is a tragedy, but I've got to do damage control before the stock market opens Monday."

"Do you know which properties he owned in the city?"

"I have no idea. He invested in real estate. I invested most of my profits in precious metals and long term municipal bonds."

The five of them entered the computer room. "What projects was he working on?" Turner asked.

Werberg said, "We have a bunch of different projects. Probably the most important is trying to create artificial intelligence. That's in these files here." He began inserting CDs in the disk drives of two of the computers. Werberg pointed to several sets of gibberish on the screen. "All these are programs for that."

"What do they mean by artificial intelligence?" Turner asked.

"A machine that works on its own," Werberg said.

Fenwick said, "No matter how sophisticated a machine, won't it all simply be a matter of open and closed, on and off? No matter how fast the thing goes, it will simply be programmed. How can you program a machine to do something for which there would be no program? Why wouldn't it just shut off? How could it go beyond what it is programmed to do?"

Turner asked, "That's what people are really working on?"

"How much of this do you want me to show you?" Werberg asked. "I can show you mathematical formulas and programming language, but I don't see how that would help your case."

"We're not sure what's going to help or not help," Turner said. "If we're going to examine what competitors might be interested in stealing, or be willing to kill for, we need to know what he was doing."

"Another big project at computer companies is coming up with new operating systems. That's always hot. Whoever develops the best and newest and fastest system can always make a ton of money."

"Show us that," Fenwick said. Werberg inserted more disks and called up more unintelligible data.

"Is he faking this?" Fenwick asked Micetic.

"Not that I can tell. I can only follow about half of this. I'm awed. I wish I had time to study it all."

"I would rather not have him study it, period," Werberg said. "These are industrial secrets."

"He's going to study everything," Fenwick said. "You're going to explain it to him. This is a murder investigation. We need to know everything."

"Did you ever have trouble with hackers?" Fenwick asked.

"You mean crackers. Never," Werberg said.

Fenwick chortled. "Another lie."

Vinkers interrupted, "I don't believe such dispargements are helpful. Mr. Werberg is being as cooperative as possible."

Fenwick subsided for the moment. Turner said, "One of your employees told us about Eddie Homan, the computer hacker."

"Oh," Werberg said. "Who told? No one was supposed to."

"Someone did and we know," Turner said. "So tell us about him."

"Some people were against hiring crackers, Rian the most. She's probably the one who told you." The detectives said nothing. He continued, "But even the government is hiring them to develop safeguards. In Homan's case I was wrong, but it wasn't a big deal. We've always had security in place. With broadband becoming more extensively used, everybody is scrambling to improve industrial safeguards."

After more than an hour of poring over mostly incomprehensible data, Turner pulled the encrypted document they'd found yesterday out of his folder.

"What's this?" Turner asked.

Werberg barely glanced at it. "I have no idea. Which file was it in?"

Turner's cop instinct told him the guy was lying. Micetic began moving the pointer to a document file. Turner stopped him. "We want to know what it means. The computer programs are complicated and might be tough to understand, but this is in a secret code."

"I have no idea what that document says."

"We're going to find out," Fenwick said. "When we finish decoding it, I hope it has nothing to do with you, because if it does I will become mightily suspicious."

"I didn't kill my friend."

"We need that list of personal acquaintances."

Werberg rapidly typed at the keyboard. Three names appeared on the screen.

"This is it?" Turner asked.

"Other than those we worked with, this is everybody I know of. Neither of us went out much."

"Except for late night parties," Fenwick said.

"We worked," Werberg said. "That's what we did mostly. We didn't do a lot of socializing."

Turner said, "We were told Mr. Lenzati often appeared in public with attractive women."

"Yes."

"Who were they?" Turner asked.

"I have no idea."

Turner pointed at the list on the screen. "Who are these people?"

"Old friends. People from the old company who decided not to stick with it when we sold it."

"Were they angry about your selling?"

"Not after we explained the deal. Anyone who had worked for us for five years or more was guaranteed a salary for ten years, no matter what they did. Along with that, they received stock options in the new company. They were very rich and very secure."

"Where is his personal address book?" Fenwick asked.

"His Palm Pilot? I have no idea."

"Who is handling the funeral arrangements?"

"I am," the lawyer said.

"Why not some member of his family?"

"His will specifically states that I am to take care of it."

Werberg knew nothing more that was helpful. He and his lawyer left. The detectives turned to Dylan Micetic. "Anything he was telling us that was obviously wrong?" Fenwick said.

Micetic waved at all the computer disks. "They were geniuses. When I say that, I'm not just making a compliment. This stuff is far beyond my experience."

"Who can we get who would understand it?"

"You probably can't. This is the cutting edge of computer technology. If there is something beyond this, I don't know about it. I've never heard of a lot of this stuff. I thought I was pretty smart. I *am* pretty smart about computers." He gave a rueful shrug. "I'm willing to admit my shortcomings in light of what I've seen here. I'd love to work for this guy—it's great stuff."

Fenwick said, "Before we drown in admiration for a possible murderer, can you give us anything on this code?"

Micetic picked up the paper and gazed at it. "This I will be able to figure out. I did my graduate thesis on encryption. But it will take a while."

Turner asked, "Even if they were geniuses, you'll be able to figure it out?"

"If I don't, I can resign."

"We need to make more copies," Turner said. "Maybe we can get other people working on it."

"Sure." Micetic tried to call up the program on the computer. He couldn't retrieve it. "I don't understand it," Micetic said. "It should be here. I didn't erase it. I know I didn't."

"Computers screw up all the time," Fenwick said.

"I know exactly what I did. I didn't screw it up. It should be here." Micetic worked for five minutes, but he couldn't call it up.

"How can it be gone?" Turner asked.

"Somebody came in here and erased it," Micetic said. "Computers don't erase things all by themselves."

"Mine does," Fenwick said.

Micetic said, "It's usually someone who isn't good with computers who screws something up. I'm telling you, someone erased it."

Fenwick said, "Computer age fuckups drive me nuts."

Micetic said, "The impression I have is that any kind of fuckups drive you nuts."

Fenwick muttered, "That's part of my devastating charm."

They asked the local police district to check with the beat cops who had guarded the scene. In a few minutes they learned that no one had been permitted into the mansion.

Turner asked, "Could someone have turned the computer on from another location and worked with it from there?"

"Sure."

Fenwick said, "We need to get a warrant for Werberg's house."

Turner asked, "To find out he has nothing on his computer to match the nothing that's here?"

"There's got to be a record," Fenwick said.

"There isn't one here," Micetic insisted.

Fenwick said, "Let's dispense with the computer age and get back to something simpler I do understand. Go to Area Ten. Make enough copies of this to paper the entire Loop. Make sure a stack of them gets to my desk."

Turner asked, "Have you found a list of the property he owned?"

"Not yet."

"We'll probably have to visit all of them," Turner said.

"I'll be sure to look out for it," Micetic said.

Turner asked, "Have you found any reference to his Palm Pilot in all this data?"

"Nothing I've seen gives a hint about it," Micetic said. He took the copy of the encryption and left.

"That son of a bitch knows a hell of a lot more than he's telling us," Fenwick said.

"Micetic or Werberg?"

"Probably both. I don't trust these computer guys."

.11.

I love the information age. I can find out more about possible victims than they ever imagine. A click here and there and I get all kinds of data, details, and knowledge they don't know I have. Before I kill them I want to feel like I have power over them.

The entryway of Area Ten headquarters was a mob scene. Reporters clustered in the foyer, down the hallways, and on the stairs. Fenwick bulled through the maelstrom. Turner followed in his wake.

"What the hell was that all about?" Fenwick asked when they arrived on the second floor.

Bokin, the beat cop who was normally on the front desk, said, "Two things. The Lenzati case, and somebody tried to kill Dwayne Smythe early this morning."

"How bad is he?" Turner asked.

"All I know is Dwayne was cut up real bad, and he's still in the hospital."

"Knifed?" Fenwick and Turner echoed.

"Yep."

Turner asked, "Has Smythe been able to give any information about what happened?"

Bokin said, "All I know is that I was told to tell you guys to get your butts over to Northwestern Hospital."

As they rushed to their car, Turner said, "Our guy was knifed."

"All these cases can't be connected," Fenwick said.

"We've had odder connections. And be wary of absolutes. Often enough as soon as we use one, the opposite turns out to be true."

"Cops around the country were knifed," Fenwick said. "That's going to be the connection everybody makes."

Turner said, "We've got to find out if it's a real one or not."

They hurried to the hospital. Even with the milling groups of cops abounding, the hospital corridors were quiet. Their badges got them up to the fourth floor, where a uniformed officer was on duty. Commander Molton and the deputy superintendent of the department, Calvin Sturm, were in the hallway. Sturm had iron gray hair, cut within a quarter inch of his skull. He was short and fat.

"Is Smythe all right?" Turner asked.

"He's in and out of consciousness," Molton said. "He lost a lot of blood. Some of the wounds were to some vital spots. They aren't sure he's going to make it."

"The victim in the Lenzati murder was stabbed numerous times," Sturm said. "Are the two cases connected?"

"No idea," Turner said, "but none of us believes in coincidences."

"Be certain of everything," Sturm ordered. "We can't take chances on any mistakes. We've got several detectives in Area One working on this attack. Work with them. Don't talk to the press. We'll handle all contact with reporters."

Turner wondered about the universal ability of moronic

administrators to speak in commands and imperative sentences as if all underlings were stupid beyond belief. That manner of speaking and that presumption of stupidity were two of the things he hated most in administrators.

Molton said, "It is possible that the attack on Dwayne is connected to the cop murders east of here. We're going to have a million reporters around trying to horn in."

"Be extra careful with this case," Sturm added.

"Where did all this happen?" Turner asked.

Molton said, "A beat cop coming out of the Fraternal Order of Police offices on Washington Avenue found him in a nearby parking lot. He didn't see the actual attack. There could be other possible suspects. Dwayne's marriage was in trouble—all this scandal was taking a toll domestically. His wife is unstable and has physically assaulted him several times."

Turner didn't ask Molton how he knew this. The police department was a notorious haven for rumors and gossip. Or perhaps Molton had been Dwayne's' personal confidant.

"Anybody know where his wife was?" Fenwick asked.

Molton said, "Her alibi's being checked. Another real possibility is that it was a relative or friend of the boy he's accused of shooting."

Fenwick said, "All kinds of people hated Smythe, not just us. I feel better knowing that."

"Lose the gallows humor, asshole," Sturm decreed. "He was one of ours."

Everyone shifted uneasily for a moment. Even Fenwick wasn't about to directly challenge the deputy superintendent.

Finally, Molton spoke. "He's been asking for you, Paul. That's why we sent for you."

"Why?"

"He wouldn't say. He didn't ask for his wife or kids."

"I'm jealous," Fenwick said.

Molton said, "We've got two active cases that we aren't sure are connected."

"Check to see if they are," Sturm interjected.

Molton said, "That reporter who broke the serial killer story has been hounding half the detectives in the city for interviews. Go ahead and speak with him. He hasn't given us any more details. You need to have everything he's got."

Sturm blustered, "It's all bullshit speculation. I'd like to string that little bastard up by the balls."

Turner said, "Maybe he's really onto something. If he is, we'd catch hell if somebody in this town died and we did nothing to prevent it."

Sturm thought for a moment. "Talk to him. Only him. Nobody else from the press. Make sure he knows it is not an interview."

"We definitely don't want to see him at the paper," Turner said, "and not at the station. Someplace neutral would be good."

Molton agreed to work it out.

"Talk to Smythe," Sturm ordered. "And you need to stop harassing Vinnie Girote."

Fenwick said, "He's a suspect. Are you saying if he did it, we should cover it up?"

"I'm saying do your job," Sturm said.

"Are you sure it's okay to talk to Smythe?" Turner asked.

Molton said, "He asked for you. The doctor said that if he was awake and willing, we could try but no one should stay very long. One of the most serious wounds was to his throat but he can whisper." They found a doctor who reiterated permission for a brief visit.

Turner and Fenwick walked into the hospital room. As

they entered, Smythe was trying to get out of the bed. He wore only a pair of white boxer shorts and white socks. A hospital gown was around his feet. He desperately clutched one corner of the nightstand. The other was holding onto a bandage on his stomach. Large swatches of cotton covered wide patches of his body. His neck was almost completely encased. His IV cord trailed behind him.

"You supposed to be out of bed?" Turner asked.

"No." Smythe's voice was more of a ghastly rattle than a modulated whisper. It didn't sound even remotely healthy to Turner.

Smythe pointed at the nightstand next to the bed. "Open . . . drawer . . . please . . . what's in?" He gasped between nearly every syllable. His butt thumped back onto the bed.

Turner hurried over and propped him up. He wondered if they shouldn't just call the doctor and then turn around and leave.

Dwayne stretched his arm toward the drawer and began to slide off the bed. Turner held him while Fenwick opened the drawer.

Fenwick said, "It's got your clothes, wallet, keys, some change."

Almost slipping out of Turner's grasp, Smythe reached over, slammed the drawer, and fell back on the bed sheets. He closed his eyes. For a few seconds Turner thought he might have passed out. He was about to ring for the nurse when Smythe opened his eyes. Smythe's efforts in attempting to close the drawer had caused his shorts to ride down nearly to his pubic hair. Even with all the stitches and bandages, Turner noted that it was obvious Smythe must work out often. There wasn't an ounce of fat on his abdomen.

Smythe breathed evenly and deeply for several minutes.

His skin was a ghastly pale, his lips dry and cracked. Turner gave him a boost back into the bed. When Dwayne finally spoke, he paused after every phrase, but no longer gasped after every syllable. Turner leaned close to catch the words. The wounded cop said, "I think I'd be better off dead."

Turner raised an eyebrow.

Smythe pointed at Turner. "I want to talk to just you."

Fenwick shrugged, spun one hundred eighty degrees, and walked out.

Turner pulled up a chair beside the bed. "Why just me?" he asked.

Smythe spoke haltingly and with much labored breathing. "I talked to you last night. You were honest with me. I need somebody I can trust. Everybody else is out to get me. Fenwick would as soon shoot me as look at me."

"I don't think he cares enough about you either way," Turner said.

"You could try being a little less honest."

"What is it you wanted to tell me?"

"The attacker got my gun and star."

"You haven't told anyone?"

"That's what I just had you look for. I don't remember anything until I woke up here. I've been woozy for a while. I didn't know if it was missing."

"You should concentrate on getting better. You can worry about the gun and your ID later." The loss of either one of these items alone would be a major hassle in the department, but the loss of both at the same time constituted a minor crisis.

"Everything I do is wrong. Every twist of fate works against me."

Turner asked, "What happened?"

"This morning I'd just been to see my Fraternal Order of

Police rep and the lawyer. I was walking back to my car. I'd parked in a lot a block away. It's a Saturday morning, so there wasn't much traffic. I was putting some stuff in my trunk when I felt this searing pain in my left side."

"You didn't hear anything?"

"Nothing. I had no warning at all. The fucker just stuck me. I fell half into the trunk, and banged my head pretty hard. I tried to reach for my gun and fight off the guy at the same time. A lot was instinct. The big problem was that I was off guard, off balance, and half in the trunk. Before I could do much of anything, he'd stabbed me a few more times. I couldn't reach my gun. I had my car keys in my hand, so I pressed the panic button on the key chain. The car alarm must have startled him. I began to pass out. I knew I was losing blood, and still he was stabbing me."

"Why aren't you dead?" Turner asked.

"Huh?"

"He could have easily killed you. He kept stabbing you. You were passing out. Why not finish the job?"

"Maybe I was just lucky. Maybe someone was coming. While I was passing out, it felt like he was trying to yank my coat off. I had my winter coat on: a heavy down vest, flannel shirt, and two T-shirts. That's a lot of material to go through even with a very sharp knife. The doctor said that's why I'm probably alive."

Turner said, "I'll have to check and see if the detectives in Area One have any witnesses. I'm sure they're working extra hard on this with you being one of us."

"Am I?" His breathing became more labored than ever. Turner knew he needed to draw the interview to a close.

"Dwayne, you may be a supercilious snot with a huge ego, and you are in deep trouble, but, yeah, you're still one of us." To himself he thought, *and you're badly injured and pos-*

sibly dying, and I'm wondering how much of a idiot I am for still being here talking to you. I'm also wondering how sad it is that of all the people you know, you asked for me and not someone closer. Or, if I'm the one you feel is closest to you, how dismal your life must be, because I certainly do not feel close to you.

Smythe clutched Turner's hand, "I'm glad you're here." He breathed deeply and evenly for several moments. "I think I was attacked because of the kid I shot. The two older brothers and an uncle threatened to get even."

"I'm sure somebody's interviewing them. Were you able to give any kind of description? Did the attacker say anything?"

"He breathed heavy. I thought near the end he said something like, 'Now you know how it feels.'"

"A male voice?"

"I sure thought it was a guy. From the voice and because the attacker seemed strong. I guess it could have been a strong woman with a deep voice. I can't even tell you if the guy was white or black. I'm worse than the stupidest witness I've ever talked to. I've fucked up as a witness. I fuck everything up, and things are only going to get worse."

Turner didn't do much wallowing in self-pity. Dwayne and his partner Ashley had turned self-serving angst and self-analysis into a lifestyle. Since Dwayne was possibly dying, Turner was willing to listen to whatever Smythe chose to say at the moment. But the young detective was quiet, eyes shut, breathing more evenly.

After a few moments Turner said softly, "If you think of anything more, let me know."

Smythe opened his eyes and asked, "Are you going to testify on my behalf?"

Turner said, "I'd worry more about getting well. If they call on me, which I doubt, I will do my best."

This seemed to satisfy Smythe. He shut his eyes again and murmured, "Thanks." Turner squeezed the man's hand gently and left.

Out in the hallway Sturm and Molton were not in sight. Fenwick asked, "So what was the big secret that he couldn't tell me?"

"He's been in love with you from the first day he met you, and he didn't want to reveal his crush."

"I didn't know the guy had taste. I may have to reevaluate my poor opinion of him." Fenwick paused for several seconds. "I've reevaluated. He's still an asshole. Why did he want to talk to you?"

Turner shrugged, "Maybe he just needed to connect with someone who he thought didn't actively dislike him."

"A very small list on this planet," Fenwick said.

"And he might be dying," Turner said.

"I do feel sorry for him," Fenwick said, "and I am going to do everything I can to avenge the creep. I'm just saying that no matter what condition he's in, he's still a creep. Did he remember anything about his attacker? White, black?"

"Nothing. He got him from behind."

"We've got two stabbings," Fenwick said. "There were probably ten or fifteen more in the city last night. We could try and connect them all. I have no notion that these two were related in the slightest."

"Which is always the best time to be suspicious that they are related."

"Nuts," Fenwick said. "I love it when you do circular logic. I'm starting to think you've been taking lessons from Carruthers."

Turner said, "We need to stop using that man as a crutch for all of our failures."

"I didn't think we ever failed," Fenwick said.

"Not this week, yet," Turner said.

Molton rejoined them. He said, "The meeting with the reporter is all set."

"We're questioning him, right?" Fenwick said. "He understands that we are not being interviewed?"

"I leave that delicate task in your competent hands," Molton said. He gave them the address of the Caribou Coffee shop on the northwest corner of Aldine and Broadway.

Once there, it took only a few inquisitive glances to establish who was looking for whom. The young reporter sat at one of the tables just inside the room on the right. Noah Morgensen was in his late twenties. He had short red hair, more freckles than someone who had spent a childhood out in the sun, and didn't look big enough to stand up against a strong wind in a blizzard. He seemed to bounce in his seat. One foot was crossed over his left knee; the foot was constantly in motion. A laptop computer sat with its lid up in front of him. Turner saw lines of type on the monitor. The young reporter constantly fiddled with a pencil he held in his right hand. He had a smile filled with perfect teeth.

They sat at a table next to a floor-to-ceiling window. They had a perfect view of the passersby on Broadway.

"I'm glad you guys came to talk," Morgensen said.

"We need to get some information from you," Fenwick said.

"I'm not revealing my sources." Morgensen moved his computer closer to himself and hit the sleep command. The screen winked out.

Turner said, "We aren't interested in violating or even attempting to violate your First Amendment rights."

"I'm not sure I should trust you guys."

"Why? What do you think we're going to do to you?" Fenwick asked.

Morgensen pointed at Fenwick. "I've heard about you specifically."

"All bad, I hope."

"Pretty much. Did you really dangle a reporter outside of a window from the tenth floor of a high-rise off Division Street?"

"That's a lie," Fenwick said. "It was not the tenth floor, and it was most definitely *not* Division Street."

Morgensen touched a button on the computer and the screen flicked back to life.

"This is not an interview," Fenwick said. "You want police brutality and corruption, you're going to have to come back another day."

"You were kidding, right?" Morgensen asked, his fingers poised above the keyboard.

"Look," Turner said, "we're interested in details about what you discovered connected to the cop killings. We want to put it together with what we know and see if we can find a pattern."

"What you know about what?"

"Any connections with crimes here in Chicago."

"I want to be in on any news story. I'm not giving out information for free."

Fenwick said, "You'll be in on everything the moment we know anything."

"I don't believe you," Morgensen said.

Turner said, "We're not going to cheat you out of a scoop. If what you know helps us, we can reciprocate in kind."

Morgensen's blue eyes searched his. His foot rattled a bit faster for a few seconds, then he nodded. "Okay," he agreed. "That's fair enough." Turner knew that reporters could be helpful, although the relationship between them and the Chicago police was not what it once was.

In Chicago the old boy network of cynical, hardened reporters and tough, brutal cops working together in a conspiratorial haze of silence to deal with the dregs of human life had changed since the Democratic convention in 1968. That symbiosis had been missing since those long ago days. It wasn't that individual cops didn't remember details of those days, although there were some still working from that time. It was a change in institutional memories and behaviors. Over thirty years may have passed, but the atmosphere between cops and reporters had never returned to what it had been. Many said this was not necessarily a bad thing. Turner didn't think it was bad or good. He just knew it was generally better to keep on an even keel with the press. At times they could be useful to you in your job and there was no reason not to reciprocate whenever possible.

"How did you get the insight that a serial killer was on the loose?" Turner asked. He didn't rule out the notion that Morgensen himself could be the killer. It would not be the first time that a murderer had deliberately drawn attention to himself. He had no notion if it was logistically possible for Morgensen to have committed the crimes, but it was too early to close off any line of speculation.

Morgensen leaned forward. "It was serendipitous. It was so cool. When they hired me at the *Tribune*, they assigned me to the police beat. It's pretty much one of the entry level positions and I knew nothing about city cops. I grew up in a wealthy enclave near Green Bay, Wisconsin. But my dad had connections at the paper here and that's how I got my job at the *Trib* right out of college. The boss they forced me on didn't like it, so I got assigned a lousy beat. He thought I'd get fed up and quit. I decided I'd be the best damn cop reporter on the planet. Every day for years I cut out every cop article from the *New York Times, USA Today*, the *Washington Post*, and the *Los Angeles Times*. In fact, I still do. I filed all of them under specific headings: police corruption, killings of police, killings by police, police heart-warming, all kinds of things."

Turner said, "Sounds very thorough."

"Yeah. So, I had all these articles. Most of the cop shootings were part of random gang things, or part of domestic squabbles, or explainable in some simple non-mysterious way, until three years ago. The unexplained murders started in Boston. After the third one, I began making special references about each death listing every detail I could find. I made a big chart. Everything I could find out, I put down."

"I'd like to see it," Turner said.

"I guess, maybe. I got most of the information from the newspaper articles themselves. Some of the stuff I got from interviews I did with reporters and officials in the different cities. The killings started in the northeast and moved west. At first no one here would listen to me, so I just kept records. Finally, even my dim-witted boss realized there was a story in all this. Although without the final connection, I don't think they would have printed the story."

Fenwick asked the inevitable, "So what was the final connection?"

"It was hard to find. It wasn't reported in any of the newspaper stories. I interviewed hundreds of people, no matter how peripherally connected they were to the crimes. A reporter in New York who had talked to an assistant ME just happened to mention this one little detail. Then I went back and dug for it in all of them." He gazed from one to the other of them. They waited for the revelation.

Morgensen announced, "The killer had pissed on all of them."

Turner and Fenwick did not gasp with recognition. Big light bulbs did not flash over their heads, but they knew a connection when they heard one.

"Are you sure?" Turner asked. "You didn't put it in your story here."

"After I talked to police in all the cities, and after consulting with my boss, and the paper's lawyers, we decided not to print it. It is one of those things that only the killer would know. We want to keep it quiet."

"It's a solid connection," Turner said. "Is there anything else?"

"I put everything that was verifiable in the article. For instance, the killings were all done with those large hunting knives, the kind with a nasty serrated edge. Since the article appeared yesterday, I've been getting calls from all over the country about cop stabbings, some going back over thirty years. We're trying to put it all together. It's going to take some time."

Morgensen picked up his pencil and opened his laptop. "What can you tell me about the cop who was knifed here this morning?" He began tapping his pencil against the table top. "An attack on him could easily be connected to what he's been accused of. I know the uncle of the victim has made all kinds of threats in very public places."

"Or it could be a random nut," Fenwick said.

Morgensen said, "Or our serial killer."

Turner felt no obligation to mention Lenzati's murder and the possible connection there. He said, "I think assuming Smythe is part of the pattern would be premature."

Morgensen nodded then said, "I don't have any reports of failed attempts, although unsuccessful attacks on cops probably wouldn't make the national papers."

"Probably not," Turner said.

"Did the guy try to piss on him?" Morgensen asked.

"I don't know. Dwayne put up a fight. He managed to fend off the attacker, or at least last long enough for someone to stop the assault. The area was too open, too public. He might not have had time."

"Where was he attacked?"

Fenwick replied, "In a parking lot near the Fraternal Order of Police headquarters. Not as public as the street, and not very busy at that time of day."

"What other patterns were there to the killings?" Turner asked. "Even if you put them in the paper and we can read them, sometimes it just helps to talk about them. I'd also like to hear what you think might be connections, but weren't sure enough of to print. Or what you couldn't verify."

"I can speculate a lot if you want. Some details vary greatly. There were lots of little connections, but lots of differences as well. The locations aren't the same. Sometimes it's near their home. Once it was inside. All the cops had kids living at home. The time of day is different from city to city."

Fenwick asked, "Were there a lot of these variables that didn't fit any pattern?"

"Yeah, bunches of differences: age, race, ethnic background, religion, left-handed, right-handed. Lots."

Turner said, "I wonder how much of that variety and consistency are deliberately planned or pure happenstance. A smart killer could really screw up an investigation."

Fenwick said, "Half the time, I think the serial killer profilers are full of shit."

Morgensen said, "I don't think they claim to be infallible, but lazy reporters take those guys' professional opinions or best guesses and state them as facts and set them in concrete. To make it worse, the press tends to characterize the possible or probable as fact to get people to read their paper or watch their newscast."

"What other sure connections were there?"

"They were all plain-clothes cops. All were male. They all had among the best conviction records in the departments they worked for—they were good cops. All had more than five years on the job."

"The killer must do his homework."

"I think he or she is very organized," Morgensen said. "Frighteningly so. If I were a cop, I'd be worried."

Turner asked, "Is there any specific forensic evidence that links all the crimes?"

"My article just came out. The cops in some of the cities are dismissing it but most are scrambling to begin cross-referencing data. I'm not sure who's got DNA of what. It would be absolute proof if we could get a DNA match in every city. Of course, even after we establish a forensic connection, the DNA won't be much help until someone is caught to whom we can compare it."

Turner nodded. DNA worked the same as fingerprints. You might have a national registry with which to compare prints, but if the prints you found weren't on file, then they did little good until you found a suspect.

Fenwick asked, "When can we see the flow charts with the information you've gathered on these cases?"

"I'll talk to my editor and get back to you."

The detectives left.

*　*　*

In the car Fenwick said, "We can set up our own goddamn flow charts. He'd save us time, but we don't have to rely on him. Or we could just arrest him."

Turner said, "To the ME's office post haste."

"Already got it covered," Fenwick said. "We need more details."

, 12 ,

I'd like to go to an autopsy. I'd like to see my victims opened up. I'd like to see them more defenseless, more helpless, and more dead than they probably ever imagined. I'd like to see mostly indifferent medical examiners handling the most vulnerable and inviolate parts of those who thought they were so high and mighty just a few hours before.

They met with the ME at the Cook County morgue. In the autopsy room, Lenzati's body was on the slab. Various internal parts were visible. Bits of him lay in sterile containers. The stainless steel throughout the room gleamed, as it always did, as if it had been burnished five minutes before. The blood on the floor and the table, the hanging meat scales, and the chalkboard with dripping blood became all the more vivid against the stark metallic background.

The ME said, "My best guess is your killer got in a lucky blow early on, or maybe your killer knew exactly where to strike. After that Lenzati would have been mostly helpless. The shock itself would have immobilized him somewhat, but he didn't die right away. I think your guy had him pretty help-less and then began stabbing randomly. Perhaps trying to see how many wounds he could inflict without actually killing him. Brings a meaning to the word disgusting that even around here, we don't often see. The actual death wound was most likely one in the middle of his upper back."

"What about the murder weapon?" Turner asked.

"Big damn thing. One of those knives with a serrated edge. Lots of damage inside from twisting from one of those things."

Here was another connection with the cop killings around the country.

"Be sure to check the state of his bladder," Turner said, "as well as the DNA for the piss. We think it could be impor-tant. It could be his or maybe the killer's."

"DNA in urine might not give you what you need. You don't always get cells that are helpful."

"Try anyway," Fenwick said.

"Speaking of the male reproductive system," the ME said, "your boy had an orgasm within an hour of his death."

"He fucked his killer?" Fenwick asked.

"I can tell you we've got residue of semen. He might have beat off. He might have had wild sex beyond your imagina-tion with fifty chorus girls."

"I can imagine some pretty wild sex," Fenwick said.

"What precisely he did, I have no idea. That he did come is a certainty."

"Sex and grit," Fenwick said. "I'm in heaven."

The ME said, "You've got a stabbing, torturing killer who pisses on his victims? We're beginning to move beyond really nuts."

"And if it be true, it would be a wonderful clue," Tur-ner said.

"I thought Fenwick was the poet," the ME said.

"I could never write a rhyme that sublime," Fenwick said.

The ME said, "Go away."

Turner said, "The piss might be part of a pattern connected with the cop killings that reporter wrote about in the *Trib*." He explained what they'd learned.

"You've got possibilities," the ME said. "What you've got here is a healthy male in his mid-thirties. He has all his own teeth. He must see a dentist regularly. No scars, no broken bones, barely a scrape or a scratch, prior to this."

They returned to Area Ten headquarters.

Turner found a box with the Nutty Chocolates logo on his desk. "What the fuck is this?" he demanded of the room at large.

"You sound like me," Fenwick said.

"This could piss me off," Turner said.

"Not in a case like this."

Once again Turner sent the box to the crime lab. This time, the box had been left on the admitting desk downstairs. With the usual crowds in the station, no one could pinpoint who had left it there.

They talked to the evidence tech on a conference call.

Turner asked, "Have you found anybody's blood besides the victim's?"

The evidence technician said, "We're still going over a lot of it. So far it's only his. We'll have to wait for DNA samples from the bedrooms to see what they indicate about other partners. Of course, the downstairs bedroom might simply have been for guests, and we'd only get DNA from people who were non-sexual visitors. Also, anything we find could have come from days or weeks before, depending on how often he washes his sheets. If he's rich, maybe somebody else puts them on for him. We're likely to find traces of a maid. After we examine for human tissues, we'll have to go over all the fibers and every speck of dust. This is gonna take a while."

Fenwick said, "We don't have 'a while.' The rich die and people want answers. For this case, the department is willing to pay for lots of expensive tests."

"When the remnants of the dead show up here, it doesn't matter how rich they were."

"If you could get on it, we'd appreciate it," Turner said.

"I'll do my best like I always do."

"Was the piss his?" Turner asked

"We haven't examined it. You have reason to believe it isn't?" the evidence tech asked.

"We need to be sure."

They spent an hour going over the tapes from Lenzati's security cameras. They saw mostly nothing. No solicitors showed up at the front gate trying to sell encyclopedias. No possible identifiable suspects appeared on camera.

"I don't see any late night visitors," Turner said. All the tapes had time codes on them. "We don't have any for the last week. A good guess would be that the killer took them. Presumably, there is something incriminating on them."

Fenwick said, "There weren't many tapes. I bet they simply recorded over them numerous times. Maybe there weren't a lot of visitors or parties. It wouldn't take the killer long to grab the ones that might be incriminating."

They indulged in a mountain of paperwork. Dylan Micetic showed up an hour later. He wore a black peacoat, faded jeans, a white, bulky-knit fisherman's sweater, and grubby sneakers. The sweater almost made him look less than scrawny. His hair was flattened in several places, as if he'd slept on it, or had his hand pressed against it for a long time, or he had worn a knit stocking cap for too long.

Micetic swung over a chair on rollers and plunked himself next to Turner's desk. "I've got something for you." His scrawny wrist stuck out of the sweater and coat as he handed sheaves of paper to Turner. All of the pages had the same six-column structure, but with different contents. The first column was a list of names. The second a date or dates. The third was still gibberish, which often continued for four or five lines. Columns four, five, and six repeated the same pattern: names, dates, gibberish. Turner glanced at every page and saw they were similar. The first few pieces of paper were only about a third to half filled. The later pages were filled nearly to the bottom. Next to a few of the names in the first and third columns were small red dots. Turner tossed them over to Fenwick.

"What is it?" Turner asked.

Micetic said, "I'm not sure what it is, but I finally cracked the code, or most of it, anyway. I still haven't got the third column. The problem is that each word in each column has its own code."

"You're kidding," Fenwick said.

"Nope. My encryption program was barely able to figure out some basics. I even got hold of one of my teachers, and he helped me with some of it. I knew there were lots of codes, but it dawned on me an hour ago that there was a separate code for each word. This guy was a computer genius. He could make up codes the way Fenwick makes up poetry."

"Make another crack like that," Fenwick warned, "and I'll write another poem and read it to you."

"A truly notable threat," Turner said.

To Micetic, Fenwick said, "I thought we were the ones not supposed to be razzing people?"

"I figured I'd give it a try," Micetic said. "Maybe you'd beat me up or throw me against a wall."

"You'd enjoy it too much."

"Probably not enough. Anyway, once I had the first insight, things began to fall into place. After a while the codes for each word in the first two columns weren't all that different, as if maybe he got overconfident, or lazy, or didn't care as much. Once I figured out there were columns and the first one was names, it became much simpler."

"Why are there six columns?"

"That's how it broke down on the master file. I tried to replicate the original exactly. None of the names are duplicates."

Turner picked the papers from off Fenwick's desk. "Who are these people?"

Micetic shrugged. "I cross-referenced it with the Chicago phone directory. There are a lot of names that match. I highlighted them with a red dot. They are most likely coincidental. You could try universal searches on the Internet, but not knowing what city a person lives in makes that a pretty useless activity. Even knowing the city doesn't help much if they're really common names."

Turner asked, "Why are most of the ones in the first column men and most of the ones in the fourth column women? Although a few of the names in both are nongender specific."

"Nothing in what I found explained that."

Turner inspected the dates in the second and fifth columns and said, "Some years there are more men than women. Some it's the opposite. There's only eleven for the first year and . . ." he counted, "a total of thirty-eight, nineteen each, for the last year. The last entry is in the column with male names. It was for the night Lenzati was killed."

"The dates go back twelve years," Fenwick said.

"Yeah, I made a separate page for each year. The code

put them chronologically. It's going to take me a while longer to uncover the meaning in columns three and six."

"I think we need to talk to Mr. Werberg about these in general," Turner said, "and to find out how this disappeared from Lenzati's computer."

"It was downloaded from a remote computer. I traced it."

"You've been busy," Turner said.

"And successful. The computer in the house is connected to Lenzati's office at work and to Mr. Werberg's home computer. I got into the computer's memory and traced where connections had been made to. It was turned on by a computer at Mr. Werberg's address. I'll keep working on columns three and six. How's your computer been working?"

Turner said, "I haven't plugged it back in."

"You want to try it while I'm here?"

Turner got the nasty little message that his computer had been turned off incorrectly or that if he was experiencing frequent crashes he should call a special number. He pressed the return key.

After it booted up, no message appeared on the screen. "This is good," Micetic said. He had Turner log in and check his e-mail. The department had gotten them all e-mail accounts at some fantastic discount. They had hoped to improve departmental efficiency with faster communications. So far that was still a fantasy. There was one message. The sender was unidentified. It said, "Don't turn this thing off again."

"Can you trace it?" Turner asked.

"Give me a couple minutes," Micetic said, "I'll see what I can do."

Turner and Fenwick used the time to make multiple

duplicates of each page of the half broken code. The copy machine jammed three times while they were working.

"This place must be cursed," Fenwick said. "And if it isn't, it should be. Doesn't anything in this building work for more than five minutes?"

Turner said, "Remember when we chipped in for the new coffee maker? It worked for two days before it broke."

"There must be an arson guy in this city who could burn down this place so no one would ever notice."

Micetic shook his head when they returned. "No luck. I got frozen out completely when I tried to follow where it came from. Sorry. This thing is pretty screwed up inside. My guess is you're going to have to get a whole new computer."

"It's brand new. How could it be destroyed?"

"It's hard to tell," Micetic said. "Have you gotten any e-mails recently?"

"A few memos from police headquarters."

"I didn't get any e-mails from police headquarters," Fenwick said.

Micetic nodded. "I think I found your problem. It's a simple one. Everyone knows not to open e-mail from somebody or someplace they don't know. If you got an e-mail, supposedly from headquarters, you went and opened it. Perfectly natural. All the person who wants to ruin your computer has to do is include an attachment to that e-mail. You wouldn't know it was there. Whoever did this got in through the back door. I can do a few things that might help for a while."

"But can't you trace where the e-mail comes from?" Turner asked.

"I doubt it. If whoever's doing this is good they'll know lots of ways to hide who they are. Remember, most of the computer crackers who get caught brag about what they've done. They want to be noticed and get praise. They're stupid. You could hide yourself simply by sending each one from a different public library. If you were rich enough, you could have multiple DSL lines in different parts of the city or multiple IP addresses with fake ID's."

"Lenzati and Werberg would have been rich enough," Turner said.

"All you have to do is figure out how Lenzati would send you e-mail after he was dead." He paused a moment. "Of course, he could have some kind of timing device."

"Let's not get too nuts here," Fenwick said. "Is this like when they broke into those commercial sites?"

"No, that was denial of service. For that a hacker runs a program that scans for computers vulnerable to a break-in program."

"They have break-in programs?" Fenwick asked.

"Sure. Then they find a vulnerable host. Sometimes they break into complete strangers' computers and launch the attacks from those machines. Once they get in, they install a distributed DOS program on the hacked computer. Maybe they toss in corrupted packets trying to crash a computer."

"Is that still English?" Fenwick asked.

Micetic smiled. He worked on Turner's computer for a few minutes then left after warning him not to use the machine for anything remotely important.

When they had reassembled the newly decoded papers, and were sitting back at their desks, Turner said, "I think I'd like to contact a few of these people before we talk to Werberg."

Fenwick asked, "How can we be sure if we're talking to the actual person on the list or a random name that happens to be the same?"

"Dull, boring, police work. We go to everyone. We start

with the more unusual names. Then if we have to, everybody with the same last name in the city and in the metropolitan area. We can try and get a couple of detectives and beat cops to help us out. Everybody's screaming about how important this case is. Perhaps that will cause them to unbend a little in our direction."

Turner's phone rang. It was the reporter Morgensen. "I talked to my editor. He said I should give all this stuff to you." They agreed to try and pick it up later that day.

They walked into Commander Molton's office and showed him the printouts.

"This has got to mean something," Molton said. He agreed to give them whatever personnel they needed. "I'm getting flooded with calls on this one. If we're ever going to make an arrest, I'd like to do it soon."

"Me too," said Fenwick.

◣ 13 ◢

I feel serenity and peace for at least a little while after I've killed them. The pain goes away for at least a few brief moments. It just hurts too much not to do something about it.

Dan Bokin walked up from downstairs. He stuck his head in Molton's office and announced, "I just got a call that Brooks Werberg is dead. We've got beat cops at his house on the north side."

Turner and Fenwick rushed out. It took them extra minutes to navigate the crush of Saturday afternoon traffic on the near north side. Finally, Fenwick took Wacker Drive out to Lake Shore Drive and came back in on LaSalle Street from the north.

Manny Merlow, a beat cop from the Eighteenth District, met them at the east entrance to Werberg's considerable mansion.

"What happened?" Turner asked.

"We got a call about twenty minutes ago that there was something suspicious going on here."

"From whom?"

"Some guy who said he found a strange message on the Internet. He was surfing the web and got into a chatroom. The guy he was talking to claimed he was being attacked."

Fenwick asked, "Werberg was being attacked, and all he did to defend himself was type on his computer?"

"Maybe he was trapped," Turner said. "Why don't we wait until we see what happened? Did you see any security system?"

Merlow said, "All we saw was a closed circuit television next to the front gate. We tried knocking and ringing the bell, but that didn't get any response." He pointed at the closed circuit monitor. "That was off. We tried the door and it opened. If it was a distress call, we figured we'd better check it out. He's in there dead all right."

"Lots of city officials, police brass, and the press are going to show up in minutes," Turner said. "We had better establish a perimeter."

Merlow said, "I called for backup as soon as we found the body."

"Call Dylan Micetic, the department's computer expert," Fenwick said, "get him over here. Then, no matter who shows up, do not let them into this house. I don't care if the mayor and the cardinal show up. They are not to be catered to. You can let in the ME and the evidence technicians. Your stay in hell will be expanded by extra eternities for each wrong person that appears inside this house."

"How can you expand eternities?" Merlow asked.

"Watch me," Fenwick said.

Turner and Fenwick stepped inside. The large foyer was silent, the smell antiseptic, as if the occupant had a powerful and unpleasantly aromatic odor-eater running full blast.

As Merlow had said, they found Werberg in an office on

144

the second floor. Someone had shoved his head through the screen of a twenty-nine-inch monitor on his desk.

"Maybe the computer finally got its revenge," Fenwick said.

They approached the body carefully. Turner felt for the carotid artery. The skin was cold. There was no pulse.

Werberg wore gray boxer shorts, a gray T-shirt, and white athletic socks. All were tattered and flecked with blood.

Fenwick pointed at the wet stains on the boxers. "Smells like piss."

Turner nodded agreement. "He's been stabbed, but not nearly as much as Lenzati."

The room looked like a category five hurricane had lingered for several hours before moving on and then decided to make a return trip just in case it left anything even remotely close to upright. The paper strewn about would eliminate the need for anyone to make confetti anywhere in the country for several New Year's Eves to come. Every page had been ripped from every book. The paper shredder was jammed to overflowing. Someone had taken the fax machine and broken it over the printer. Hundreds of CDs and their cases had been smashed and flung about. Two impressively large stereo speakers were now little more than kindling. They found a baseball bat broken in half. By the date and signatures, Turner realized it had been signed by each member of the 1969 Chicago Cubs. Presumably the bat had been used to cleave through the receiver, CD, and tape player, plus anything else that the killer felt like destroying. The guts of a cordless phone were scattered across the rug.

Turner and Fenwick could see nothing that was once whole still intact.

"Anger," Fenwick said. "Anger like I've never seen before.

More pissed off than I get at the Cubs during an entire season, which is a very great deal."

"They always lose," Turner said, "why don't you give up on them?"

"One of the great philosophical truths of the universe," Fenwick said, "is that being a Cubs fans teaches a person the true meaning of life. Most of us are not champions, the good guys lose as many as they win, and all we can really do is go out and endure day after day, no matter how hopeless things look."

Turner said, "You're dangerously close to being a philosopher as well as a poet."

Turner heard his name on the police radio. It was Merlow. "I've got paramedics out here. Do they get in?"

"Yes," Turner said.

The paramedics were quick to assess the situation. They were trained enough to know to be careful at a murder scene. They did not try to revive Brooks Werberg. He was very obviously dead.

After they left, the ME and the evidence technicians arrived. While waiting for them to finish, Turner and Fenwick spent the time inspecting the mansion. They began with the bedroom next to the office. Compared to the mess next door, it was startlingly neat. Along with a Palm Pilot they found an address book and other personal data in neat piles that made sense.

Fenwick asked, "If the rest of the place isn't a mess, I presume the killer was just angry and not looking for anything?"

"We can't be sure yet," Turner said.

Dylan Micetic arrived and joined the inspection tour. The downstairs was cleaning-service neat with nothing out of place. They found a large room without any windows. It was luxuriously furnished with a king size bed, overstuffed chairs, and pillows in warm bright colors. They found a room with a bank of television screens filling an entire wall, each tuned to a different station. Turner thought many of them looked like they originated in international locations. The opposite wall was floor-to-ceiling monitors with numerous computers and controls sitting on a low, twenty-foot-long table in front of them. All of the monitors showed different images. Some were filled with vibrantly colored graphics the likes of which Turner had never seen on a computer monitor. He thought some looked like Web sites. Others were filled with complex equations or dense with single-spaced ten point prose.

Fenwick pointed at the wall of monitors. "He didn't use screen savers?"

"No need in this day and age," Micetic said.

"Why doesn't anybody ever tell me these things?" Fenwick asked.

"In the computer industry if you blink, you're behind the times," Micetic said.

Fenwick said, "Or maybe if you blink, you miss the point that all the hype about out-datedness is because lots of slick sales people are trying to get you to buy useless junk."

Micetic smiled, "Perhaps that does happen."

They found an ashtray shaped like a profile of Bill Gates's head, with a picture of the Microsoft CEO laminated in the middle. Someone had mashed a cigarette butt into Bill's left nostril then glued it in place.

"Why have all this electronic stuff in here, and all the other junk in the room we found him in?" Fenwick asked.

Micetic said, "My guess is that this was more for display rather than actual work. Kind of a bragging rights thing, I suppose. He's got the top of the line model from most, if not all, of the computer manufacturers in the world in here."

After checking the machines to make sure Micetic's guess was plausible, they met with the medical examiner. He said, "Werberg was restrained before he was killed, probably by a piece of rope, although there is no longer any at the scene. Both his wrists and his ankles were tied."

Fenwick said, "He was alive while someone was destroying this room? Someone wanted him to see everything wrecked?"

"Very possibly," the ME said.

"What killed him?" Fenwick asked.

"He was alive when his head was thrust into the computer screen. I think his head was rammed into the thing several times before the blow that actually killed him. Your murderer kept banging away until he was dead. The stab wounds strike me as an afterthought. I don't see a lot of bleeding from them. I can't be totally sure just yet how much the stab wounds contributed to his death."

Turner said, "I didn't see anything under his fingernails that would have indicated that he fought back. No scratches on his arms or bruising that would indicate there was a fight."

The ME said, "He's been dead a couple of hours."

Turner said, "I wonder if he went to work like he told us, or came back here first."

"That I can't tell you." The ME left. The detectives watched them remove the body.

Fenwick asked Micetic, "How about the computer itself? We were told that someone who was with him in a chatroom on the Internet called the police."

Micetic said, "The monitor is wrecked but the computer itself might be okay. I'll try and follow his logs, or he might have the kind of computer that keeps track of where he's been on the Internet."

"Precisely where he was probably isn't going to be a big

deal," Turner said. "My question is why he used a chatroom and didn't simply call the police?"

"If Werberg was surprised by whoever it was," Fenwick said, "then how could he have time to keep typing, or why did the person let him keep typing? If he was trapped in here, why not use a cell phone? He's the kind of guy who always has one on him."

"He was in his underwear," Turner pointed out. "Or maybe he knew the killer and let him in. Maybe he realized he was in danger and couldn't risk making a call or get to his phone. You can type quietly. The bedroom's right next door. If you're having sex with your killer, and you get suspicious, you dash to the nearest thing you have to send a message from. You don't want to risk making noise, so you use your computer."

"Why don't you dash out the front door?" Fenwick asked.

Turner said, "We'll have to ask the killer when we find him. For some reason he came in here."

Turner called the number for Lenzati and Werberg's company. He spoke with Terry Waldron, the CEO. Turner said, "Mr. Werberg told us he was going into work after our interview this morning."

Waldron said, "We had a meeting scheduled for noon. He never showed up. I called his house and e-mailed him. I got no answer. With things so chaotic, I didn't know what to do."

Turner spoke softly, "I'm sorry to tell you this. Mr. Werberg is dead."

There was a slight gasp and a choked, "No," then silence.

"Mr. Waldron?" Turner inquired after several moments.

"This is unbelievable. Are you sure?" Waldron asked.

Turner didn't comment on the absurdity of this last question. Anyone hearing such news was not required to be intelligent, witty, or sensible. He gave him a few, bare details.

Waldron said, "I have to call some people," and hung up.

Turner reported the conversation to Fenwick.

Micetic informed them, "The computer is still working." They moved one of the monitors from the display room to the office. Micetic hooked it up. After a few moments, he said, "The computer is still connected to a chatroom. I can download a list of all the things he's done recently on the computer. He didn't need to actually type. The word processing program is voice activated, probably keyed to his own vocalizations."

"A computer can do that?" Fenwick asked.

"His could probably design programs to take rocket ships to the stars and cook his breakfast in the morning—maybe simultaneously. Lenzati's could do more than any machine I ever saw. I bet this one is the same. I can't wait to get further into it. I doubt if there are many computers like theirs in the whole world. Mine at home can't come remotely close."

"So his could be recording everything," Fenwick said. "We better watch what we say around it."

"I'll save everything on his hard drive to several high-capacity Zip disks. I can get you copies. I imagine his software disks are going to take a long time to analyze and decipher. My guess is at least as long as Lenzati's did."

"Maybe we've got the killer's words on there," Turner suggested.

Micetic said, "I didn't see anything, but if Werberg's machine is voice activated, it could be. He wouldn't have to be typing to send a message."

Turner said, "But if he was in the chatroom and it was recording because it was voice activated, wouldn't it take down whatever was said in the room, and wouldn't then the people in the chatroom have been privy to the whole conversation?"

Fenwick said, "Or maybe the killer was typing in the chatroom to announce he was here or was trying to send a message. Macho bravado crap."

"We'll have to talk to the guy who called it in and find out exactly what was being said," Fenwick said.

"If I can find him," Micetic said.

"Be sure to check for secret codes," Turner said.

"Absolutely," Micetic said.

To the evidence tech Turner said, "I want you to cross-match every fingerprint and DNA sample here with what we found at Lenzati's house. If nothing else, that could help us rule suspects out."

The evidence tech nodded.

Fenwick said, "Two guys in the same company meet violent ends within less than forty-eight hours of each other. If they aren't connected, I'll become a hula dancer."

"I do not want to think about you in drag," Turner said.

"I'd pay to see it," the evidence tech said.

"How he'd get him restrained in the first place?" Fenwick asked. "No other room shows any sign of being disturbed. I think it began and ended in here."

Turner said, "If it began in this room, how did Werberg get free to type in a call for help?"

"How about if Werberg was trapped?" Fenwick suggested.

"Possible," Turner said. "If he was free to type and the message went out, the killer was taking a big risk. It took time to do all this destruction."

Fenwick said, "Maybe all this stuff was wrecked in the fight, and the killer didn't need to go on a rampage."

Turner said, "The timing of all this isn't working for me yet. Even a fight in here with all the men currently on NFL rosters couldn't cause this much damage. I think it had to be deliberate."

Fenwick said, "I still want to know why the security system wasn't working."

Micetic said, "The security system is over there." He pointed at a console covered in twisted plastic and smashed glass. In the maelstrom of destruction, this was possibly the most pulverized part. The killer had left the plastic tape holders on the scene, but the actual tapes were missing from all of them.

"So much for security," Turner said.

"Doing that took more than a couple of minutes," Fenwick said.

"Wrecking the console might have, but not grabbing the tapes themselves," Micetic said. "You just rip 'em all out." He went back to his work.

Turner said, "We're going to have to push for quick DNA results on both of these deaths. If each of these guys had sex with their killers, then it is possible to assume we've got two killers. Lenzati is presumably straight and would have had sex with a woman. Werberg, from our information, is gay. Assumedly he'd have had sex with a guy. Unless the sexual residue on Lenzati was simply from beating off."

"Maybe we've got an anti-masturbation killer," Fenwick said.

Turner replied, "He'd wear himself out trying to murder everybody on the planet. At any rate, we don't have proof that Werberg was having sex with his killer. Although I doubt that he entertained visitors in his underwear."

Fenwick said. "We might as well go over some of this computer stuff right now. It could be the key to this whole thing."

"Unless it's sex," Turner said.

"Give me some time here," Micetic said. "I can begin getting information for you in fifteen minutes or so."

While Micetic worked, they examined the rest of the

upstairs and downstairs thoroughly. They had the sheets and pillows from the master bedroom and the cushions from the living room furniture taken to be examined for possible traces of DNA.

Next to the master bedroom suite they found a room with leather-lined walls and lit by electric lights with nineteenth century wall fixtures spaced evenly around the sides. Against each of the four walls were large antique mahogany dressers. The one on the east wall contained different styles and sizes of men's boxers and briefs. Most of these were in their original packages or were pristinely clean as if they'd never been worn, perhaps leftovers from packages that had been opened and partially used. A wide variety of types and styles and sizes of jeans filled the one on the west wall. The dresser to the north had only leather accouterments: pants, chaps, vests, belts, wrist bands, bicep bands, hoods, and head bands. The south dresser contained swimming suits and rubber gear, again, as in the other three, in various sizes.

Fenwick asked, "Why does he have all these sizes? His pants in his closet are all size thirty waist. The shirts might vary a little—sixteen and a half or seventeen and a half—but not like this."

Turner said, "My guess is, he liked the men he brought home to dress up for him."

In one of the large rooms they found state-of-the-art exercise machines and a small running track. Halfway through the inspection, a beat cop brought in a woman who he introduced as Werberg's sister, Brenda Darium.

Brenda Darium was nearly six feet tall. She wore dark blue jeans, a heavy beige sweater, and a down winter coat.

She said, "There was a news flash on the radio that something had happened to my brother."

Turner and Fenwick found a quiet corner and sat down with her. Turner said, "I'm sorry, Ms. Darium, your brother is dead."

She wept. "This is so hard," she whispered after gaining some modicum of control. She dabbed at her tears with tissue she took from her purse. "How did?" She gasped and drew a deep breath. "What happened?"

"I'm afraid he was murdered," Turner said.

"My god! Just like Craig Lenzati. What is happening?"

"We're not sure, Ms. Darium," Turner said. "If you could answer a few questions, you might be able to help us find the killer."

She continued speaking as if she had not heard him. "My mother is quite ill, but she is still lucid. This is going to be toughest on her. She doted on him. I told him he needed to be more careful."

"More careful about what?" Turner asked.

"That stupid, silly sex game he played with Craig Lenzati. I told him it would lead to trouble. He wouldn't listen to me."

"What was the game?" Fenwick asked.

She heaved a deep sigh. "The two of them had an extremely hard time growing up. They were picked on unmercifully for being such nerds." She gulped. "Well, they *were* nerds. Brooks was three years older than I was, but I still found him embarrassing. I never brought friends home. Craig Lenzati was pure evil from the time I met him as a child."

"How was he pure evil?" Turner asked.

"He didn't hurt little puppies or anything. He just wasn't right. You just knew something was awfully odd about him. I didn't like him."

"How much did you know about this game?"

"My brother and I weren't very close growing up, but

after he went away to college he started to open up. I was the first one he told he was gay, even before he told that slime bucket Lenzati. I loved him and our bond grew over time. As for that stupid game, I'm not sure what it was all about. He bragged to me about it in this kind of obscure way, but he never gave me details. I knew it was about sex, I knew it was about money, and I knew it sounded dangerous and stupid. I warned him and warned him. Paying strangers for sex was a wide-open invitation to violence. One time I asked him if he was ever going to settle down. In his whole life he never actually dated anyone seriously. His longest relationship lasted less than three months, which was probably longer than any Craig Lenzati ever had."

Turner said, "Among the items we found on Mr. Lenzati's computer was a coded list." Turner showed her the printout Dylan Micetic had given them. Brenda Darium barely glanced at it. Turner said, "It's in a code that our computer people have managed to break some of. Do you know what it is?"

Darium said, "I told my brother over and over again it was stupid, stupid, stupid. He told me several times they had this encrypted method of keeping track." She pointed at the paper. "That might be it. I don't know."

"What were they doing exactly?" Turner asked.

Darium said, "I think they were just so desperate, so lonely. I think that's why Brooks confided in me and I think that's why I listened. He had to have somebody real to talk to. I was appalled by what he hinted at, but I was willing to listen. I felt so sorry for my brother, hanging around with that creep Lenzati and not having any other friends."

Turner said, "The records we found go back twelve years."

"I suppose they might. I really don't know when they actually started." She sniffed a few times and wiped her nose.

Turner held out the list to her. "There are a lot of names here. We're going to have to interview all of them. Do you recognize any of them?"

It took several minutes for her to scan the entire document. She shook her head and handed back the list. "I don't recognize anyone. You aren't going to try and ruin my brother's reputation?"

"We have no reason to leak this information to the press," Turner said, "but if we can find it out, my guess is there are reporters who would be able to do so as well."

Darium said, "I warned him and I warned him. If this gets out, it will break Mother's heart."

Turner said, "We were told Lenzati had late night parties. Do you know anything about them?"

"No. He was such a jerk. He was creepy to be around. He leered at you in a very repressed, absolute nerd kind of way. It took them both years of intense workouts to change their body shape. What they really needed was intense psychotherapy. They never could or would do anything to improve their social skills for attracting an intimate partner. When they got rich, they figured cash was the best aphrodisiac. Maybe they weren't all that wrong."

"Did Lenzati ever make advances to you or your friends?" Fenwick asked.

"Never. Back then, he might look at a woman for a few seconds, but then he'd run for his computer."

"We were told they were the toast of the town here in Chicago," Fenwick said.

"Money attracts friends, doesn't it?" she said. "No, my brother and Craig Lenzati never had many real friends. Except each other. Even the rest of my family didn't have much to do with Brooks. I was the one who maintained the connection between Brooks and our relatives. He didn't care for them, and to be honest, they didn't care much for him. They didn't hate each other or anything. He just never gave them much time. When he made a lot of money, a few of them expected jobs and fabulous gifts and presents. Nobody but my mother got anything. That was fine with me. Mom has private nursing care at home. She has a live-in nurse and every possible part-time caregiver, all hired by my brother to satisfy her every whim. My mother has a lot of whims. He is very generous to her."

"We found all different sizes and kinds of men's clothes in your brother's bedroom," Turner said. "Do you know what they were for?"

"No. He's been the same size for years. When he started working out, he lost one pants size, but he was never heavy."

They asked her to look at the names of people in Werberg's address book. She was able to confirm only a handful of people who the police might be able to talk to about his private life. A few minutes after she left, the detectives finished inspecting the house. Micetic said he'd stay and go through as much as he could on the computers. They agreed to meet late the next morning.

They did a canvass of the near neighbors. No one had seen anything. They got several beat cops to do the rest of the neighborhood.

14

I think sex is dirty. I think public displays of affection are ghastly. Why people can't leave each other alone is beyond me.

As they drove back to headquarters, Turner gazed at the score sheet. "We need to talk to these folks. How the hell are we supposed to find them? While a plurality are probably from Chicago, we can't be sure of that. For all we know, they were from all around the country and the world. We don't even have full names for all of them. For many we have only first names." He peered closely at the print out. "We've got to get those third and sixth columns translated."

Fenwick said, "Let's stop at the paper and see if Morgensen's got all his data ready for us." They called and caught the reporter just as he was ready to leave. They met at the newspaper's offices in a small conference room with a computer terminal.

"Have you found any more connections?" Morgensen asked.

"Nothing we're even close to sure on," Turner said. "We'd like to see all of yours."

"My editor said it was okay for me to show you this stuff because I got a lot of the initial information from newspaper stories and other public records. The rest was from interviews I did. Telling you who I got it from isn't possible, but giving you the results is. Watch." He tapped a few buttons on the computer and the screen filled with a spreadsheet with wide columns.

"Someday I'm going to be able to do one of those," Fenwick said.

Morgensen made the comment that has driven computer students nearly mad for years: "It's easy." To his credit, contrary to his many vows in the past to shoot the next person who made such a crack, Fenwick restrained himself.

Morgensen pointed at the screen. "Here's all the victims, and everything I could find out about them personally, and then everything I could find out connected with their deaths. I cross-referenced each bit of data in as many ways as I could. I've got one page for each crime, with an index at the end."

They got their copies and left.

Back at Area Ten another tiny parcel had arrived for Turner. This one had been sent by Federal Express. It had been posted at a drop box in the middle of the Loop.

"What is this shit?" he demanded. A small crowd of detectives gathered around his desk. He flipped the box in the air and caught it.

"Do you think you should do that?" Judy Wilson asked. "Maybe it's somebody's idea of a joke that's gone sour, or maybe it's really explosives."

"I'm not sure why it has to mean something sinister," her partner Roosevelt said. The other detectives glared at him.

160

He added quickly, "Although, it certainly opens itself up to that interpretation."

Turner held the box out to all of them and said, "Boo!"

Wilson drew back slightly. "I expect that kind of flippant braggadocio from Fenwick, but not you."

"I've been taking lessons," Turner said.

"What about the cities where cops were killed?" Fenwick asked. "Is there any pattern of gifts there?"

They tacked the spreadsheets from Morgensen to the corkboard that covered the entire north wall of the room. They used space opposite pictures of a partially dismembered corpse, a case that Roosevelt and Wilson had solved that morning.

All of them pored over the documents, trying to find patterns that had not revealed themselves before. Nowhere was there mention of gifts to the cops who had been killed.

After fifteen minutes Fenwick announced, "There's nothing here."

When they were done looking, Turner called to get results of the analysis of the previous boxes. He hung up and announced, "None of them have had prints on them. This one won't either." Turner tossed the box up and down several times.

Wilson said, "Maybe there'd be prints on that one. If there are, you're destroying any that exist."

Turner took the box and flung it as hard as he could against the nearest wall. There was a small pop and a smoky foof.

"This one was a bomb?" Wilson asked.

They rushed to the remnants to find that it had been filled with white powder.

Fenwick said, "At least the others had chocolate in them."

Commander Molton strode over to where they were all

gazing at the box and its contents. When they finished explaining, he said, "The heat has been turned up on the Lenzati case. I've had my job threatened if we don't get results. I've gotten complaints that Fenwick has been abusive to witnesses."

"They wanted more or less abuse?" Fenwick asked.

Wilson said, "You always get those kinds of complaints, especially from anyone who's heard any of his jokes."

"At least I didn't shoot any crippled kids," Fenwick said.

"One of the complaints comes directly from the superintendent's office, which means it is most likely coming directly from the mayor's office."

"The mayor himself?"

"I don't know. Sturm delivered it in person. If I don't make you toe the line, they will find someone who will."

"What did you tell him?" Wilson asked.

"We traded bureaucratic barbs."

"Huh?" Roosevelt asked.

"We obfuscated. We danced around the issue. We were exceedingly polite."

"And got nowhere," Wilson said.

"We got threatened," Molton said. "I may be used to this kind of threatening bullshit, but the pressure is real. For all the brass's bluster, as you know, your jobs aren't really at risk. But this high profile crap gives a case a sense of urgency all out of proportion to real detective work."

"Is Girote involved in the murder?" Roosevelt asked.

"Did Werberg say he specifically called Girote?" Molton asked.

"No," Fenwick said.

"Pressure Girote if you have to," Molton said. "Find out for sure what he knows. The son of a bitch has been a pain in

162

the ass to me over this and other things in the past. He hasn't told you everything. If he does know something about the murder, or more likely an attempted cover-up, I want to know about it."

Wilson said, "It's their jobs you're putting on the line if they pressure him."

"I'll call," Fenwick said. "It's not a problem."

"Shall we gather at the computer for the checking of messages?" Turner asked. "I'd hate for any of you to miss out on this."

Turner flicked on his computer. He called up his e-mail. There was only one new posting. The name listed was "from one who hates you the most." The message was a simple, "Ha!"

"And that means?" Fenwick asked.

Turner said, "It could be anything. Maybe it's from the killer, crowing about Werberg's murder."

They sent Turner's box and its powder out for analysis. No one had offered to do the television and movie trick of putting a finger into the unknown substance and tasting it. Tough cops they might be, but none of them took stupid pills either.

The phone rang on Turner's desk. He picked up the receiver. The voice on the other end said, "I think you're going to be next." He heard a click and then a dial tone. Turner began punching in numbers.

"What?" Fenwick asked.

Turner told them what the caller said.

Molton said, "Get onto the computer hookups at headquarters. Find out where that call came from."

"Already on it," Turner said. The operator identified the call as coming from a phone inside the fast-food restaurant at the corner of Dearborn and Congress Parkway. They nearest beat car was dispatched immediately. Turner and Fenwick rushed over as well. When they got there, the restaurant was crowded. With the beat cops, they talked to all the employees and patrons. No one admitted to having seen anyone near the phone.

Turner said, "I've got three separate types of communications with unknown origins. I've got the phone calls, the chocolate, and the e-mail. Are they all connected to each other? Are they all separate? Two out of three? Is it the serial killer? A random nut? A computer hacker who desperately needs a life?"

"That last could apply to all of them," Fenwick said.

"I think this is serious," Molton said when they got back upstairs.

"Me too," Turner said.

Fenwick said, "My guess is that it's our killer from Interstate Ninety."

"Or a copycat," Turner said. "High profile cases bring out the loonies. Morgensen doesn't report any prior warnings or messages or chocolate."

"Check with him on that," Molton said, "and with the cops in the other jurisdictions. I think we need to begin working on the assumption that the call and the message represent real danger. I'm not sure about the boxes, but I don't like it. The police protection I've ordered will be in place whenever you go home. I want to alert the department, get it mentioned at all roll calls."

Turner said, "After that article yesterday morning, every cop in the city is on high alert."

"Danger to a specific officer needs official attention. We can be organized. We can get out information in a coordinated fashion. If nothing else, we can find out if there have been other threats."

"This isn't the first threat I've gotten over the years," Turner said. "It won't be the last."

"You want to move Ben and the kids out to my house?" Fenwick asked.

"I'm not sure yet."

Molton said, "You'll have all the protection you need. I'm not losing any personnel to some nut."

Turner thanked him. Molton left.

Turner called Morgensen's pager number from the card he'd given them when they met. He asked about warnings or messages. Morgensen said, "Why, is somebody getting messages there?"

Turner had to decide quickly whether to trust him or not. He said, "Cops get threats all the time. There's been some here. We need to know if there's a possible connection."

"I don't have anything so far. I'll check."

A few phone calls got them Girote's home number. Fenwick called.

Girote said, "You have some nerve calling me on a Saturday night at home."

"I'm working on a murder case," Fenwick said. "I thought that's what you wanted—results. I hear you've been making all kinds of calls trying to pressure us and our boss about this case. I don't like you. I don't like pressure. Maybe you're trying to orchestrate a cover-up. Or maybe you're the killer."

Girote hung up on him.

Fenwick finished announcing the results of his call by saying, "It's going to get ugly."

"It already is," Turner said.

Turner and Fenwick did paperwork for an hour. Finally, Turner said, "It's nine o'clock on a Saturday night. My family is waiting for me at home and I'm going. I don't care how dead Werberg is."

Fenwick agreed. Molton had ordered the surveillance he'd promised for Turner. His protection, a blue and white Chicago cop car, followed him home and parked halfway down the block.

⌐ 15 ⌐

Domestic bliss! Ha! Domestic death is how I see it.

At home Paul changed into jeans and a heavy sweatshirt and walked next door to Mrs. Talucci's house. Ben, Jeff, Mrs. Talucci, and three of her great-grandnieces had recently been spending Saturday evenings taking turns reading chapters of the Harry Potter books out loud. They were halfway through *Harry Potter and the Chamber of Secrets*. Paul especially enjoyed reading them out loud. Jeff confided that he liked his dad's deep, sonorous voice best.

Paul hated being late. He sat down close to Ben and ate an Italian sausage sandwich provided by Mrs. Talucci as he listened to Lucinda Talucci finish reading chapter ten. Paul took a turn on the next chapter.

Half an hour later they gathered in the kitchen for ice cream and fresh-baked scones.

Mrs. Talucci said, "Paul, you look exhausted."

"I didn't get enough sleep last night. Yesterday morning I didn't know I'd have another one of these big cases."

"It seems all of them lately have been big," Jeff said.

Paul said, "I had plans this weekend. There's things I need to do around the house. I wanted to spend time with the boys and Ben. I haven't had time to talk to you, Rose. You haven't told me about your latest trip."

She said, "We'll inflict slides and videos on anyone who can't run fast enough at some point, but not tonight."

"What's going on with that computer guy case?" Jeff asked. "I read about him all the time in the computer magazines. It was on the news that Mr. Werberg is dead, too. The two cases are connected, right, Dad? The mayor's press secretary was on the news before we left. He said they were."

Mrs. Talucci snorted. "Vinnie Girote is mortally stupid. I remember him growing up. He tried dating several of my daughters. If I was a putting-a-stop to it kind of person, I would have put a stop to it. I'm afraid I played a very mean trick."

"You're never mean," Jeff said.

Mrs. Talucci laughed. "What I did is invite him over. Constantly, for dinner, for family gatherings, for picnics. That way my daughters would get to know him. I think he's just as obnoxious and overbearing at sixty as he was when he was sixteen. For most sensible people, his presence made the heart run as fast as it could in the other direction. For several of my daughters, it took more time than I wished, but fortunately, he never became part of this family."

"You're pretty smart," Jeff said.

She laughed and patted his arm.

Ben said, "He's really applying all kinds of pressure about the case? What good does that actually do?"

"None," Paul said.

"That is so typical of him," Mrs. Talucci said. "He's the kind who can't do things himself, but he thinks he can make others jump at his whim. That's because he jumps at everybody else's whim. He's a fool." Paul saw her lips set and her jaw clench. He suspected she'd come to a decision. "I know his mother," Mrs. Talucci said. "A fine woman, as long as you weren't married to her. She buried three husbands, drove them all to an early grave. We'd all be better off if she drove her son there too."

Ben said, "That's a harsher judgment than I've ever heard you give."

"He's is *not* a nice person," she said.

Paul, Ben, and Jeff left. It was nearly eleven. The night was cold and fine with no wind as they wheeled Jeff home. It would have been easier to carry him, but he'd gotten more insistent lately about not being carried. Paul figured this had something to do with Jeff's needing to feel less like a little kid. The short trip home took only a few minutes more time to accomplish this way, and if it made the boy feel better, Paul was willing to accommodate his son. Time was one thing he was determined to never begrudge his family.

As they neared the front steps, the blue and white squad car containing Paul's protection lurched forward. The Mars lights began to spin, the headlights began to flash on and off, and its siren began to *whoop*. The voice on the loud speaker said, "You in the van, stay where you are."

A van load of teenagers was parked in front of the house across the street from Paul's. The two uniformed officers exited their car. One of them had one hand on his gun and a flashlight in the other. He shone it into the van's interior. His partner stood at the open squad car door. Less than five seconds later, two more squad cars pulled into their street. Mrs. Talucci joined Paul, Ben, Jeff, and other neighbors as people began to converge on the scene. Paul strode forward.

"Everybody out of the van," the cop ordered.

Paul saw his son, Brian, Andy Wycliff, Brian's project kid, Jose, Brian's best friend, and another teenager he knew from Brian's football team hop out of a van.

"What's up?" Paul asked.

"These kids have been sitting here for fifteen minutes watching the houses."

"Dad?" Brian said.

"One of these yours?" the uniformed cop asked.

"Yeah. I know all of them," Paul said.

"I thought I saw light glinting off metal. I didn't know what they were doing. It's getting a little late to be sitting in a van."

"I'll vouch for them," Turner said. "I appreciate you being vigilant."

"What's going on?" Brian asked.

"Yeah, Dad," Jeff said, "what would happen if Brian got arrested?"

Paul said, "You'd have more chores to do."

"Oh."

Mrs. Talucci said, "That's an awful lot of cop cars for a group of slightly suspicious teenagers."

Paul said, "Because of that newspaper article, everyone in the department is being more careful, and I got a crank call at work. For a day or two, there's going to be someone outside the house."

"Good idea," Ben said.

Mrs. Talucci nodded, "I'll make sure everyone in the neighborhood stays on the alert." In this old Italian neighborhood, people tended to watch out for one another.

When they finally got settled in the house, Brian said, "That was a little more excitement than I expected."

"Why were you guys sitting out there?" Paul asked.

Brian said, "Sketching out plans for international drug

deals and finalizing details on selling our sisters into white slavery."

Ever the practical one, Jeff said, "We don't have a sister, and you don't do drugs."

Brian said, "I guess that wasn't as funny as I thought it would be."

Paul didn't really want to talk about the threats he'd been receiving, but he spent some time reassuring them about how careful he was, and how statistics were on his side in returning home safely each night. Paul thought Jeff still had a romanticized notion of what a detective did and the dangers involved. Television and movies exaggerated the dangers and the heroism. Brian never said much, but Paul noticed that at those times when there was possible danger to his dad or headlines about cops being killed, the boy stayed home more, as if his simple presence would be enough to deter any attacker. Paul wished it was that simple.

Paul said to Brian, "For now, maybe you and your buddies better not sit outside."

"You think there really is a danger?" Brian asked.

"I don't know. And since I don't know, I don't want to take any chances. As much as you may want to live the life of an action adventure hero, I don't, and I don't want you to."

"That's boring," Jeff said.

"I prefer boring," Paul said.

"What action adventure film did you see tonight?" Jeff asked Brian.

Brian said, *"Dead Witches Eating Machine Gun–Shooting Spies Who Know What Everyone Did Last Summer."*

Ben said, "I thought those kinds of movies were the rage last year."

"Can there ever be enough 'dead teenager' movies?" Brian asked.

"But you're a teenager," Jeff said as he spun his wheelchair in a circle. "Aren't they supposed to be scary?"

"They're supposed to be," Brian said, "but my friends and I rarely stop laughing through most of them. The best part of this one was the helicopter showing up at the end for no logical reason. Except maybe because the script writer was desperate to come up with a spectacular ending."

"Did it blow up?" Jeff asked.

"It was a helicopter in a movie," Brian said. "Of course it blew up."

An hour later, the house was quiet. In T-shirt, briefs, and white athletic socks, Paul was downstairs getting a drink of water from the bottle in the refrigerator. The house was quiet. He heard steps on the stairs, and seconds later Brian padded into the room. His son wore only flaming red boxer shorts on his well-muscled frame. He sat down at the table.

"Dad, I think Mrs. Talucci was right. Wasn't that kind of a lot of protection simply because of one crank call?"

Paul sat down. "You're right. I didn't want to say too much in front of Jeff."

"You always talk about being honest with us."

"I know."

"I can handle whatever you tell me. If there's a big problem, I want to know. I can imagine a lot of horrible things, which are probably worse than the truth."

Paul told him the whole story.

When he finished, Brian said, "Sometimes I wish you weren't a cop." The refrigerator compressor clicked off, leaving the house very still.

Paul said, "I'm always glad you're my son. I'm glad you worry about me."

"How could I not?"

172

"I won't say don't worry. I will say what I always do. No one on the force is more careful than I. I always want to walk through that door and see you guys."

"I know, Dad." They got up. Brian hugged him in a fierce embrace for several seconds. He mumbled into his dad's shoulder. "I love you, Dad."

"I love you, son."

Upstairs in their bedroom, Paul tossed his T-shirt and socks into a pile and got in bed next to Ben.

"You were gone a while," Ben mumbled.

"I talked to Brian." Paul told him what they'd discussed, and included the full story about the threats.

When he was done, Ben said, "We all worry. We don't need to discuss it anymore tonight. Discussing it won't increase or decrease the danger you're in, or the amount of worrying we do. I love you. I never want harm to come to you. I know it's your job. I don't like it sometimes, but I love you." Ben pulled him close.

They made passionate love.

◣ 16 ◢

Kids. I hate little kids. I don't want them near me. It's always a big test among those infested with children to inflict them on the childless, to see how we handle their little monsters. All kids need to suffer the way I was made to suffer. And they will. Lots of them will.

Early the next morning the temperature was in the mid-twenties. They walked the few blocks to church. Afterward, Ben made a large breakfast. The other three took turns cooking on weekday mornings. Since Ben had moved in, he'd taken to making a feast for the four of them every Sunday. He tried new recipes and unique variations. Today was eggs Florentine with more garlic in the spinach than any of them had imagined possible. They loved it.

Jeff's plans for the day included a meeting of a new computer club he had joined. He was learning advanced website design. Brian was continuing his peer helpers project with over twenty mentors and helpers. They were all going on a tour of the city's lakefront museums.

Paul kissed Ben and left for work around ten. Fenwick was at his desk. The obligatory box of chocolates and threatening phone message were already on his desk. A quick e-mail check showed another unpleasant note.

Fenwick pointed at the box and message, "Kind of like your morning coffee."

"It gives a hell of a kick to a morning. I don't have time for this crap now." The box went to the lab for analysis, the messages to their files.

Turner examined the encrypted list. After several minutes, he said, "We're going to have to talk to as many of these people as we can. If it was just recreational sex, fine, but it could also be part of the murder."

Micetic showed up a minute or two later. He beamed at the two detectives. "I found a ton of encryption work on Werberg's computer. It helped break the whole thing wide open. Once I found the key, I couldn't stop. I haven't been to bed yet. About six this morning I even found a bunch of anecdotal comments Werberg left behind."

Micetic spread numerous pages of printout on top of their desks. Turner and Fenwick leaned close as Micetic explained. "The encrypted stuff is a record of the private contest between Werberg and Lenzati. I found a bit of history. The night they sold their company, they took a jet purchased for the occasion and zoomed off on a trip around the world. In his anecdotal record—I guess it was a sort of diary, but not very consistent—Werberg said that they were filthy rich now and could have sex with anybody they wanted. They decided to have a contest to see who could get the most desirable and unattainable people into bed. As kids, no one was interested in them. Girls didn't look twice at Lenzati. Werberg himself says he didn't have sex until he was in his twenties."

Fenwick said, "This is beginning to sound like the movie *Indecent Proposal*."

"Werberg refers to that. He claims they never lied to people. They didn't string people along like the Robert Redford character did to Demi Moore, you know, finally dumping her later. These two were clear up front that it was an exchange of money for sex and nothing else. Werberg claimed the movie did give them some ideas. Werberg wrote that they actually had sex with a few married couples."

"Why not just pick up a prostitute?" Fenwick asked. "Why go through all the extra hassle?"

"I think it was the thrill of the chase," Turner opined. "For two guys who never had sex growing up. Picture frat boys being given a billion dollars. This sex game was their chance to play, to make up for slights they got as teenagers, their chance to have fun."

"That sounds accurate," Micetic said. "They were in fact unsuccessful the majority of the time. According to Werberg, people turned down surprising amounts of money. However, enough were more than willing to go along, usually women more than men. Over time the game got pretty complicated. It started in Sydney, Australia. They met a couple who were on their honeymoon."

"How on earth did they convince all these people?" Fenwick asked.

"Werberg said it took a lot less than a million. Some you couldn't buy for any money. Some would go for stunningly little. That couple in Australia was from a small town in the Outback and never had much of anything to begin with. They'd blown their meager life savings on the marriage and honeymoon."

"Why didn't anybody ever turn them in for solicitation?" Fenwick asked.

"Werberg comments on that once or twice," Micetic said. He picked up one of the unencrypted pieces of paper and showed it to them. "They had to get out of Singapore very quickly one time. Werberg makes a few jokes about it. He said they got even by putting glitches in every program sold in that country that they could get their hands on."

"Could they really do that?" Turner asked.

"They were rich and stupid and geniuses at the same time. Who knows how much they could really do."

Turner asked, "Weren't they ever afraid of getting the crap beat out of them?"

"When you're rich you can get away with a great deal, and they were careful," Micetic explained. "Werberg talks constantly about how much care they took. They never asked a roomful of college hockey players to participate."

Fenwick asked, "Why did they keep a record?"

"It developed into a contest to see which of them could get the prettiest, or most handsome, or most famous, or richest, or most difficult to get person. They created an elaborate scoring system. Whoever had the most points at the end of the year had to give that much of a percent of the point differential of the company to the other person. Like, say if you won by three points, you gave three percent of the company to the other guy. Nobody ever won by more than six percent. The records show that it was pretty even over the years. It seems more like a friendly rivalry, a running tally."

Turner asked, "How did the scoring system work? How could they prove you had been to bed with someone?"

"The more proof you had, the more points you got. Look at one of Werberg's longer entries." He held out a piece of paper to the detectives.

They read:

178

One time I was at a gas station in Arizona, and I thought the guy who waited on me was totally gorgeous. It was a lonely town, and I got lucky. More often we got to know the person, found out what they wanted or needed. That's all you really need to do. Find out what people really want and offer to give it to them. With a computer you can find out a lot about people. With a little patience you can find out enough to get a lot of people to do what you want. Most of the time you don't have to find out much. When you're rich you can provide what they want.

"There aren't that many explanations of that length. Most have only a few sentences. It's the third and sixth columns that give details about each sexual encounter. They tell what their partners were willing to do at the outset. Locations, both the city and where in the city they made it, time of day, level of trustworthiness of the reporting. What the men and/or women were convinced to do during. What they wound up doing. Duration, orgasm, or lack of same."

"The entries weren't that long," Turner said.

"It was a code. Very simple. The first number is one to fifty on the states, matching them alphabetically."

"With a code that simple, why couldn't you figure it out sooner?"

"Omniscience is not my strong suit. In addition, they changed it with each page. Like sometimes they numbered backwards on the states and since neither of them had every state, it could vary wildly from year to year. As of last week, Werberg had gotten forty-four out of fifty states, Lenzati thirty-nine. They did countries of the world the same. Then they had numbers for specific sexual acts. The last letter is for how much they paid. On some pages 'z' was lowest, 'a' the highest."

"What was the price range?" Fenwick asked.

"Actual cash, ten bucks to a hundred thousand. I've found references to paying off people's bills. At least once they paid off somebody's home mortgage. I haven't been able to find how much these last two categories added up to."

Turner asked, "Did they take pictures? How did they prove their conquests?"

"The whole proof thing is discussed in Werberg's computer," Micetic said. "Sometimes they couldn't, so they simply took a lower score. Once in a while they were in a bar together, and the one could overhear the other make a connection. A few times they stayed in the room and watched. Another time one of them hid in the other's house while it was going on."

"Why weren't they being blackmailed?" Turner asked. "Nobody ever got angry? No loving husband or wife got mad at what they'd done? Nobody made threats or demanded payoffs?"

"Werberg says nothing about that. As far as I can tell, some of their partners knew their names, most didn't. They didn't go out of their way to tell who they were. I doubt if identities were important. The money was. Proof was always a problem. Werberg was obsessed with it. He writes about the frustration of getting exactly what they needed. Having absolute certainty with a famous person would be the best."

"How often did that happen?" Fenwick asked.

"If it was someone famous enough for me to know, I haven't seen it in the records."

"Did you find any pictures?" Turner asked.

"I found references to some pictures and records, but nothing concrete. It certainly wasn't on that computer."

"Maybe they were blackmailing people," Fenwick suggested.

"Not as far as I could tell. Every document I found referred to it as a game."

"Which one cost a hundred thousand?" Turner asked.

"Brooks swore that he had sex with the entire starting infield of a minor league baseball team in Iowa."

"All?" Turner asked.

"That's what he said. First, second, third, and short."

"What was his proof?"

"Four used jockstraps, and a baseball bat signed by all of them."

"We didn't find any jockstraps," Turner said. "The baseball bat we found had the signatures from the 'sixty-nine Cubs, not four obscure players."

Micetic said, "In the game you got more points for full names and addresses. If they got taken to their partner's homes, it was all for the better. If they got a souvenir from their homes, it was excellent. They got extra points for a genuine piece of underwear."

"How would you prove you got the real underwear?" Fenwick asked.

"DNA. They had a lab they paid to examine it. Like a couple times, they'd get a glass the intended conquest was observed drinking while they were in the bar, and the DNA from it would match flecks of skin left on a pair of underwear left behind, or even better match their bodily fluids. Aside from the minor league players, Werberg claimed one of his greatest triumphs was making it with a professional hockey player. He got a jockstrap and a mouthpiece as souvenirs."

"How?" Fenwick asked.

"He took them when the guy wasn't looking. This all sounds a bit sordid, but knowing all this, I don't see how you're any closer to finding out who killed either of them."

"Where are all their souvenirs?" Fenwick asked.

"I don't know," Micetic said.

"Do we know anything about Lenzati's conquests?" Turner asked.

"As far as I've been able to find, he kept no anecdotal records. He won seven years and Werberg won five."

"How often was the list updated?"

"Hard to tell. There is is that entry from the night Lenzati was killed, but it's in Werberg's tally."

Turner said, "That's why his clothes were all rumpled when we saw him when he got to Lenzati's house. I bet Werberg came to meet Lenzati straight from his latest conquest. After he found his friend dead, he was probably too upset to think about changing."

"Very possible," Fenwick said.

Micetic continued, "There were no entries for Lenzati's for about a month."

"Which means what?" Fenwick asked. "He didn't get around to it? That he didn't always keep track?"

"That I can't tell you." Micetic added, "There are also mentions of a new playhouse."

"What does that mean?" Fenwick asked.

"I don't know."

"A hiding place for souvenirs," Turner said. "I'd bet on it. We need to find it."

"All this stuff was in the security portion of their software. They were working on computer security for hundreds of companies. It doesn't seem to be complete, and there are references to materials that I can't find. I'll keep looking. The oddest thing I've found in that section so far is constant references to a guy named Eddie Homan. Who's he?"

"A hacker who walked out on their business," Turner said. "We need to find and talk to him."

"I still have a lot of files to go through in the security section," Micetic said. "I'll get a little sleep and then get back to it." He left.

"We need to talk to Werberg's lawyer and accountant," Fenwick said. "They must have records of what they owned and where it was. They must have had to pay taxes on any property. We'll visit every site if we have to. If there really is a secret location, we've got to find it."

"For now let's concentrate on the sex list," Turner suggested. "We need to talk to as many of these people as we can."

"How are we going to find them?"

"Simple," Turner said. "We start with the ones Micetic put a red dot next to. They're the most likely ones."

Fenwick asked, "Because their names are listed as having sex in Chicago, does that mean they lived in the area, or simply that the sexual act was successfully completed in Chicago?"

"For now let's assume if it says Chicago, they lived somewhere in the metropolitan area."

Fenwick checked Micetic's materials. "We don't have full names for a lot of these."

"Be grateful for that. We go to all of them in Chicago, and then we start in the suburbs. If this case is such a priority, we should be able to squeeze some help out of the commander."

They strode to Molton's office and explained their plan. He readily agreed. After they left his office, Fenwick said, "That was easy. Not like a gang shooting, is it?"

"Would you like it to be?"

"No pressure, no hype, and a dead body for an inane reason," Fenwick said. "Sounds like a winner to me."

Turner and Fenwick went over the printout and matched it to local directories. They came up with a list of ten leads to follow up. They decided the most common names would probably be the least productive. There would be too many possible duplicates in the six county area. Starting with the odd names would be more likely to get them a match to the correct sexual partner. They knew that if they didn't find out what they needed from those, they'd have to try the common names. They could at least start the beat cops on those.

Turner did not relish talking to all the Smiths in a fifty-mile radius.

They organized a detail and gave them instructions. Before they left, they set up a meeting with the accountant and the lawyer for later in the day and checked the phone company and driver's license records for Eddie Homan. They found nothing. Further searching for him would have to wait until their interviews were done.

▲ 17 ▼

Finding unique gifts in each city is a nuisance. Figuring out dif-ferent delivery methods can be tricky. If they aren't frightened before they get the gifts, they are soon afterwards.

Turner and Fenwick started with the As. Malcolm Ashburton lived in Presidential Towers on the near west side. Late on a Sunday morning they found him watching NFL pre-game coverage on television. He was in his mid-twenties. He wore unadorned gray sweatpants and a baggy sweatshirt with an East Chapel High School logo on it.

They introduced themselves and asked to come in.

"No. My place is too messy."

They conducted the interview in the hallway. "Mr. Ashburton, your name appeared on a list in Craig Lenzati's computer."

"The rich guy who's dead?"

"Yeah."

They waited. He waited.

Ashburton finally said, "Is that all you wanted to tell me?"

"Did you know Mr. Lenzati?" Fenwick asked.

"Nope. I saw him on the news once in a while. He was filthy rich. Why was I in his computer?"

"We don't know."

"You sure it was me?"

"No."

"Oh."

They showed him the picture of Lenzati. He shook his head. "I never met the guy. I kind of recognize him from television." They showed him Werberg's picture. "Nope, not him either."

Fenwick asked, "Do you know what you were doing August twenty-ninth five years ago?"

"I beg your pardon?"

"That date was next to your name."

"Five years ago? You gotta be kidding."

"Try to remember."

"What day of the week was it?"

"Does it matter?"

"I'm probably not going to remember anyway. That's a hell of a long time ago." When he couldn't remember what he was doing, they left.

As Fenwick drove, Turner asked, "What were you doing five years ago August twenty-ninth?"

"Beats the shit out of me," Fenwick said.

"We should find out what day of the week these were."

"They're never going to remember what they were doing. It would be nice if they were doing something memorably criminal and were willing to confess it to their kindly and wise neighborhood police detective."

Turner said, "We could get you a smiley face badge. Unfortunately, you keep using them for target practice on the pistol range. We should try talking to the names next to the most recent dates. That's the last page and there are more of them."

They consumed an hour in fruitless pursuit around the city. Of the next five people, one was out. The four who were in responded as Ashburton had.

As they drove to their next interview, Fenwick said, "The people on that list could be from anywhere on the planet."

"We've got to try as many as we can. Maybe other people on the team are having better luck."

The sixth person was Blaine Dworkin. His wife directed them to the garage behind the Dworkins' bungalow just south of Archer Avenue on Kolin Street. The January sunshine wasn't warm, but there was no wind so the cold was less piercing than the twenty-five degree temperature might indicate. Dworkin had the garage door open but a space heater was on. He was maybe five feet six inches tall, and was lucky if he weighed one hundred twenty pounds. He wore a gray sweatshirt over a black T-shirt, which covered a white, long sleeved thermal shirt. His black jeans clung to his narrow hips. He might have been in his early twenties.

Dworkin's fingers were grimy, and Turner saw he'd been working on an electric snowblower. Turner also noted that Dworkin's eyes lingered ever so briefly on his crotch. Turner didn't really believe in "Gaydar"—the supposed ability of gay men to identify one of their own—but he noted the look.

They identified themselves and explained why they were asking questions.

Dworkin said, "The rich computer guy who died? I didn't know him."

"Do you have any idea of why your name might be in his computer?"

"Are you sure it was me?"

"You're the only Blaine Dworkin we could find in the metropolitan area."

"Yeah, can't be a lot of me around. Does it have to be connected to someone in this metropolitan area?"

"We're not sure," Turner said. "You from here? Got family around here?"

"No, I'm from South Dakota. I worked in my dad's gas station there while I was growing up. I'm supporting my wife and kid here by working in a garage on the north side fixing cars while I attend the Art Institute. I've got a scholarship, but it doesn't cover everything." He shook his head. "Maybe your guy just collected odd names."

Turner asked, "You ever met a Brooks Werberg?"

Dworkin hesitated briefly before saying, "Wasn't he the guy's partner in the computer business? Wasn't it on the radio that he died yesterday?"

"Yeah." All Turner knew that would cause even a hint of suspicion to grow in his mind was the briefest of hesitations in this answer and the earlier glance that had lingered on his crotch.

Turner checked the printout. "Next to your name, we found the date October first last year. Do you remember what you were doing on that day?"

"I'd have to look at an old calendar."

"Would you?"

"I guess."

They trooped into the house. Dworkin's wife asked, "What's going on?"

"Some crazy computer guy had me on a list in his computer."

"Why?" she asked.

"I don't know," Dworkin said.

188

In the living room, Dworkin produced a calendar from the bottom drawer of a desk. "I saved this because I wrote some phone numbers and directions on it. I was going to copy them over." He flipped several pages. "It was a weekday. I must have been at work."

"You remember anything significant about that day?"

"No."

Later, in the car Turner said, "Something odd there."

"I caught the hesitation in his answer."

"He looked at my crotch a bit longer than is usual in a supposedly straight man."

"And that means?"

"I don't know."

The seventh person on the list lived in an apartment house in Evergreen Park just south of Ninety-ninth Street. Larry Switzel was five feet four inches tall and, like Dworkin, very thin. He had heavy, unshaven Sunday afternoon beard stubble. He wore work boots, tight faded blue jeans, and a blue and white checked flannel shirt. A toddler played with a dump truck on the floor in the living room as he talked to them. Switzel sat with his legs spread wide, his elbows on his knees, and his hands hanging loosely between his legs.

"How old is your child?" Turner asked.

"Fourteen months. I've got custody."

"Looks like a nice kid," Turner said.

"Thanks. What is it you guys needed?"

"We found your name on Craig Lenzati's computer."

"Who?"

"The computer genius who died Friday morning."

"I never heard of him."

"You've heard of Bill Gates."

"I guess. He's so rich and all. He's always on television. Is this Lenzati guy famous?"

They showed him the photo of Lenzati. Switzel frowned. "I don't know this guy. I'm sure I've never met him. Are you sure it was me on his computer? Did it have a description?"

"We found your name. Did you know him?"

"No. I don't know why I'd be on his computer. What kind of list was it?"

"A list of names and dates. Your name was listed next to February tenth last year."

"That's my soon-to-be-ex-wife's and my anniversary. I worked that night. I've got a part time job busing tables at the Pit."

"Maybe he was a customer," Turner suggested.

Switzel shrugged. "When the rich come in to the restaurant, they're made a fuss over in an understated way. The owner is very careful to make the well-off feel comfortable."

"Where's the restaurant?" Fenwick asked.

"On Dearborn, just north of Chicago Avenue. The Pit is a restaurant and bar, very hot and trendy."

Turner pulled out Werberg's picture.

Switzel blanched. "Him!" was all he said.

"There are two other names listed next to February tenth," Turner said. "Alex Jones and Dave Jackson." They had found too many A. Joneses and D. Jacksons in the metropolitan area to begin contacting them, yet. If they had to, they probably would see all of them. February tenth was one of the few multiple date listings.

"I work with Al and Dave. That was the night . . ." He muttered, "Holy shit," and then turned red.

"What do you remember?" Turner asked.

"I can't tell you guys. It's too embarrassing."

Fenwick said, "This is a murder investigation, Mr. Switzel. You don't want to withhold information that could lead us to a killer, no matter how embarrassing it might be."

"What happened can't be connected to any murder. It was as far away from that as possible."

"How can you be sure?"

Switzel ran his hand over his beard stubble. He leaned over more closely to the detectives and began speaking in a low voice. His child continued to play contentedly, only ten feet away. Turner assumed the precaution was to ensure that the child did not hear them. Turner figured the kid was too young to understand what was being said, but there was no accounting for paranoia.

"My divorce isn't final. She could use it against me, but this can't be connected to Lenzati." He stood up. "This is goofy." He ran his fingers through his blue-black, slicked back hair.

The detectives let him pace for a few moments. Finally, Turner said, "You and the other busboys must have done something."

"Got that right."

"Unless it was blatantly illegal, we don't care," Turner said. "We're only concerned about finding a killer."

"It wasn't illegal—at least, I don't think it was. Maybe it was a little."

"How little?" Fenwick asked.

Switzel grimaced. "I wish I knew."

"We'll talk to the other two," Turner warned. "You don't want this to get messy, being dragged down to the station. Someone's going to open up eventually. You might as well get it over with now."

Switzel sat back down. "You guys can't tell my wife."

Turner said, "There's no point, no benefit to us in doing that."

Switzel dithered for a few more minutes then finally heaved an enormous sigh. He said, "That night, this rich guy showed up alone at the restaurant. He got the royal treatment. He ordered the most expensive items on the menu, including a bottle of wine that cost more than three thousand dollars. The whole tab must have been over five thousand."

Turner thought that was a hell of a lot to pay to be hot and trendy for an evening. Then again, a night out at a fast-food restaurant with his sons and Ben was as trendy as he got these days.

"Why was that so memorable?" Turner asked.

"We've got plenty of other guests who spend more," Switzel said. "It's what happened when I was cleaning up after dessert, while they were preparing him some exotic coffee. Supposedly it's grown on only one patch of ground in a secret grove in Columbia, and sold only in our restaurant. In truth, it's probably leftover Starbucks blend. Anyway, this guy beckons me over, and puts his hand on my arm. Then he says, very calmly and quietly, 'I'll give you ten thousand dollars, and each of the other busboys the same, if you come with me to have sex. It has to be all three or none of you.'"

This time Switzel's hand rubbing through his hair left it in disarray.

"All three?" Fenwick asked.

"Yeah."

"What did you say?"

"I said, 'You've got to be kidding.' But the guy didn't smile or laugh. He just said he was very serious. He asked me if I was interested, and that if I was, could I talk to the other busboys? I'd been solicited before. What busboy hasn't been at the Pit? We wear these tight black pants and white muscle T-shirts. We're *supposed* to be alluring."

Turner thought, all the unattractive ones don't get solicited. He didn't think Switzel looked particularly hot—he wasn't Turner's type. Looking at him objectively, he thought the guy might appeal to some men, in an undersized-athlete kind of way.

"Did you ask the other busboys?"

"No. I told him I was straight, and that I didn't go in for that kind of thing. Then I shook my head and walked away. A few minutes later I saw him talking to Alex, who is a goof. He's this tall, lanky blond who always claims he's ready for anything. You know, hinting like he's this big sexual adventurer. He talks about being a free spirit, but I think all that he does is ingest recreational drugs and screw women every chance he gets."

"What did Alex do?" Fenwick asked.

"I saw Alex talking to Dave. They looked from me to the guy. I guessed the guy must have propositioned Alex. Now, Dave is real quiet, never says much. Just does a decent job and goes home. He's trying to finish his undergrad degree and work at the same time. I've seen Dave with several women he dated. I didn't think he was interested in men."

"What happened?"

"Alex and Dave came over to me and said the guy had offered fifty thousand for the three of us to spend the night with him."

"The price had gone up."

"Yeah."

"They were interested?"

"Alex was, for sure. He kept repeating he was straight, but for a one third portion of fifty thousand, he'd be ready to do it with a camel. He also kept saying that just because he did sex for money, didn't mean he was gay. Dave said his third would pay for a lot of his bills at the University of Chicago." Switzel took another deep breath. "This was all pretty illegal, huh?"

"Pretty much," Turner said.

"Are you going to arrest me?"

"No," Fenwick said. "We're after a murderer."

"I still don't see how this is connected to any killing," Switzel said.

Fenwick said, "Three names on a dead man's computer. Three guys who happened to know each other and worked together, and on a night listed in his computer were doing something out of character and illegal."

"Did anybody ever try to blackmail you because of what you did?" Turner asked.

"No."

"You said you were getting divorced," Turner said.

"That's because my wife refuses to stay home. She goes out with her friends to party every weekend and most week-nights now. She never stayed home to take care of the baby. I have to work. I've got to get sitters, day care, or my mother to watch little Charlene."

"So you had sex with him," Turner stated.

"Look, I think I better be careful here. This guy made an offer. After what he had paid for that meal, he certainly seemed like he could deliver. The other two guys were certainly willing. Alex was convincing. It was only money. What did I care if some fag groped himself while he stared at me naked?"

"What actually happened that night?" Fenwick asked.

"He left. We worked the rest of our shift. I assumed it was a joke. Who would pay that much money for sex? He said there'd be a cab waiting for us outside the entrance when we got off. Alex insisted we walk out together. There

194

was a cab with the door open, just like the guy said there would be, and we got in. The driver spoke no English. He drove us to this address on the north side. The cab was already paid for."

Fenwick said, "You didn't know who the guy was, yet you went along with it? He could have been a killer."

"He seemed pretty harmless. There were three of us. What was one queer going to be able to do to us?"

Turner said, "The word queer is off limits for the rest of this conversation."

"Huh?" Switzel said.

"Just tell the story," Turner ordered.

Switzel continued, "We were at this mansion, all clustered around a gate. We could see ourselves on a security monitor set into the wall. Alex rang the bell, and a few seconds later the gate swung open."

"You guys still weren't worried?" Turner asked.

"I was a little. The front door swung open, and we entered this hallway. A door opened at the far end while the one behind us closed with a soft click. The guy was there. He led us to a room that didn't have any windows. It was huge and luxuriously furnished, maybe half the size of my whole house. Lots of overstuffed chairs and pillows. Warm and bright colors. Beds and mirrors. A high ceiling, but not as high as a gymnasium."

"Then what happened?" Turner asked.

Switzel did some nervous hand wringing. "It got even more strange. He had stacks of money on a desk. He said each one contained sixteen thousand, six hundred sixty-six dollars. Then he said, 'You're guaranteed that. You can earn a great deal more.' Alex asked, 'How?' The guy said something like, 'It depends on what you're willing to do and how far you will go.' Alex agreed right off to everything he asked us to do. Dave turned out to be real passive. He didn't make any objections. For some of the stuff, I had to be convinced."

"Like what?" Turner asked.

"He wanted us to rim each other, each of us had to screw the other. The more often we came, the more money we would get. It was weird, a bunch of straight guys doing all this fa—gay stuff."

"Gay for pay," Turner said.

"I guess."

"Did you ever see anybody else?"

"No."

Fenwick asked, "He wasn't afraid the three of you would gang up on him and rob him? Even kill him? That's a lot of money."

"One of the first things he said was. 'You may try to rob me. Harming me would be pointless. You have been recorded by the security cameras which are hooked to a recording device miles from here.' I believed him, but it didn't make a lot of difference. He was willing to pay so much, why get greedy? Every time we performed another act, he added more money to the piles."

"Did he go out of the room to get the money?"

"No. He had like an automatic teller machine attached to a computer right in the wall of his mansion. He'd type in a code, and money would come out."

"What did the guy do while the three of you were having sex?"

"He watched."

"That's it?" Fenwick asked.

"Just about. He never even took his clothes off. Halfway through, he spent nearly a half hour caressing Alex's waist, hips, stomach, and abs with his finger tips. I got pretty bored. Alex is really skinny—I guess the guy liked that. After that, the guy didn't do a thing. He played straight porn videos all the time we were there. That helped me do stuff sometimes. I could shut out the guys and picture being in the scene on the television."

"You spent the night?" Fenwick asked.

"We were there until about five. We stopped when I finally balked and refused to be talked into something. It was pretty disgusting. Doing sex stuff with guys," he shrugged, "most of it wasn't real bad. I mean a lot of the time I had to beat off to stay hard, but there weren't any whips or chains or anything. What ended it all was when he asked us to piss on each other. I was too tired to listen to the guys anymore. It was all too much. He offered us an extra five thousand to piss. Those two guys did it on each other and got the money, but that was the end."

"Did he tell you his name?"

"No."

"This all seemed normal to you?" Fenwick asked.

"There was an awful lot of money on that table. That's mostly what I thought about."

"What did he look like?"

"He wasn't an ugly guy, kind of young. You get used to being offered money by older, out-of-shape guys. He looked like he worked out a lot. He had these big enormous shoulders, a thick neck, and short hair."

In the car Fenwick said, "We got piss from here to the east coast."

"A vivid description if I ever heard one," Turner commented.

Fenwick continued, "We got Lenzati. We got Werberg. We've got connections. We've got kinky sex."

197

"If we add drugs and rock and roll, do we get a prize?"

"If there's chocolate involved, I want to win."

Turner said, "We did find that one room that matches what Switzel described, but we didn't find a teller machine or a money outlet at the house."

Fenwick said. "I wonder if maybe they did have a secret location, or maybe they moved their operation."

"That's real possible."

"And Werberg claimed they were being secretly recorded and the records were miles away. We've got to find that place."

Turner said, "Unless he was bluffing. Did you notice a lot of the guys we've talked to have been thin to the point of emaciation? Maybe that's the kind of guy who turned Werberg on. Even that Terry Waldron was really skinny. Was he a conquest? Or did he have to let himself be conquered before he got the job?"

"We'll have to ask," Fenwick said. "What I still want to know is if Werberg wanted to hire a whore or whores, why risk asking guys who might very easily turn him in for solicitation? Or might be inclined to beat him up? Why engage in risky behavior?"

"Why are *we* in jobs that could put us at risk?"

"It's not the same thing," Fenwick said.

"I'm not sure sometimes." Turner shrugged. "Why would he? The thrill of the asking? The thrill of the chance of making it with, or in this case watching straight guys do it?"

"You get turned on by watching straight guys?"

Turner said, "I can imagine a famous sports star naked, like Chipper Jones, who plays third base for the Atlanta Braves. He's got a kid. I can assume he's straight. I can picture him doing it with a woman. There's an attraction to fantasizing about hot, straight guys doing sexual things, but I think that's more of a kid fantasy. I prefer willing partners. However, I don't think seeking risky sexual partners is an exclusively gay phenomenon."

"I love it every time you say phenomenon."

"Whatever turns you on, so to speak."

18

Before they kill me, I'd like to be able to touch one. Not one that I've killed. It's no good touching them when they're a corpse. I want to touch a live one. I'd like him to touch me back.

The next two they wanted to speak with were Nancy Korleski and her husband. They lived on Webster Street in Lincoln Park several blocks from the DePaul University campus. When she answered the door she was wearing a Harvard University sweatshirt and faded jeans. She had a damp cloth in her hand and a babushka tied backwards around her hair. She was blond with a statuesque body. They introduced themselves and asked if they could come in.

"What's this about?" she asked.

"We want to ask you about Craig Lenzati."

"It's a little late now to do anything about my complaint. I called every official I could think of about that son of a bitch. He had more protection than the pope."

"Would you tell us about it?"

"You bet. Come on in."

She led them into the living room, which was a mixture of chrome and comfort. Pillows and overstuffed chairs surrounded gleaming steel beams.

"What happened?" Turner asked.

"I went to Lenzati and Werberg for a job when I finished all of my training. I have three advanced degrees in computer operations, computer science, and engineering, plus undergrad degrees in physics and math. In college they told me I could write my own ticket. I tried to start a business with my husband, several businesses in fact. They all failed. We just don't have any business sense.

"I promised myself I'd never work for someone else, but we were so far in debt, I had to get a job with a company. Theirs is the best, no doubt about it. I had fantastic credentials, so they interviewed me themselves. I could have gotten a job anyplace. Their offer was the best, with the highest salary and a huge bonus. Lenzati took my husband and me out to dinner. He said the job was mine if we agreed to have sex with them."

"He out and out asked for sex?" Fenwick asked.

"He was actually pretty subtle. He kept hinting around about what he could do for Charley and me and what we should be able to do for them. Finally, when my husband was in the washroom, he said he had the power to make all our debts from our businesses go away. We wouldn't have to wait years."

"How far in debt were you?" Turner asked.

"A couple hundred thousand. And we had no income at all."

"He knew this?"

"He seemed to know everything. Afterward, I realized he must have gotten into our financial and credit records. My husband had been laid off, with no severance package at all.

I can't prove it, but I think Lenzati may have had something to do with my husband losing his job at his company."

"What was that?" Turner asked.

"He was a programmer at Silicon Techno Laser in Oak Brook. One day he was just let go. I bet that creep put them up to that."

"Do you have any proof of that?"

"No, but you can add things up, and they make sense. At the time he asked for sex, we were about to lose our house and everything, but I said no. I didn't wait for my husband to get back. I got up and left. I met Charley as he was coming back. I told him what happened. We left."

"So you never had sex with him?" Fenwick asked.

"I called the sex discrimination offices at the city, state, and federal levels to report the son of a bitch. A guy named Girote showed up from the mayor's office."

"Vincent Girote?" Turner asked.

"Yes. Lenzati was creepy, but Girote was disgusting. I hated him on sight, and what he had to say was worse. I asked him how come the mayor's office was interested in our case. He answered me with threats."

"What kind of threats?" Turner asked.

"He told me that if I didn't drop our sexual harassment complaint, he could make our lives miserable. We hired a lawyer, who we could not afford. That jerk told me I couldn't prove anything. It would be my word against Lenzati's. Later, I realized we should have lied and said my husband did hear the offer. We should have said that from the beginning. It was too late then. He advised us to give it up. We didn't have the money to pursue the issue.

"After I called the police to complain, things started to happen. Inspectors showed up at the house: electric, water, sewer. They stopped picking up our garbage. I spent hours on the phone, which began to work intermittently. Our lawyer refused to pursue the case, and stopped returning our calls. We couldn't find another lawyer in town who would touch the case. That first cut-rate guy we hired screwed everything up. No one showed up at the press conference he called. He tried visiting the newspapers. He got nowhere. I don't know why not."

"Why didn't you just leave town?" Fenwick asked.

"On top of the business losses, the house was an albatross. Our car was repossessed. Our savings were gone. We both had huge college loans to pay back. Then Lenzati showed up one night. We'd figured he was behind what was happening. He apologized profusely for everything that had gone wrong. He assured us over and over again that he knew nothing about it. He told us that it would all stop, *if.*"

"If what?" Fenwick asked.

"If we both agreed to have sex, my husband with Werberg and me with Lenzati. We said 'no' and showed him the door. We realized our situation was hopeless. There was nothing we could do. The next day we made plans to sell the house and move. Real estate agents wouldn't return our calls. We visited one, who was very kind and helpful, but we never heard from her again. We thought our house was being watched. The neighbors were complaining about the garbage. We told them the problem, and they began letting us use their trash cans. Then they began having problems.

"We grew up in California. We'd never seen political power used like this; we were beaten. I called Lenzati and told him we'd give in. The day after we performed our rituals with those two creeps, everything stopped. All our bills were paid, and ten thousand dollars appeared in our bank account. We immediately put the house up for sale. We tried hiring a lawyer again, but it was useless. I wish I'd taken pictures or had some proof, but I didn't. Nobody would listen to us, and I was afraid that if we started making more official complaints, things would go wrong again."

"Did you take a job with his company?"

"No. They offered, but I wasn't willing. It was enough that the harassment stopped. My goal for the rest of my life centered around working for their rivals and bringing them down. I'm glad they're dead, but I'll keep working until that company is in bankruptcy."

"Even after all that money?" Fenwick asked.

"How much made no difference. I hated him."

"Was there anyone else present when you had sex with him?" Fenwick asked.

"No, but I heard Lenzati did have orgies."

"From whom?" Turner asked.

"I found that information on the Internet. I began hunting for anyone who had something bad to say about him. In secret little chatrooms we would talk. You look up sleaze in the dictionary, and you'll find a picture of those two."

"Did he use threats and coercion to get all the others into bed?" Turner asked.

"With all the ones I chatted with."

"Can you give us their names or addresses?"

"I never met any of them."

"How can you be sure they were telling you the truth?" Turner asked.

"I believe anything nasty about that man."

"What did he make you do that night?"

"He began the night with a simple statement. He told me I could lie on the bed like a cold fish, or I could get into it. He wasn't very aggressive. I didn't get into it: I think he got kind of bored or disgusted. He stared at me naked for a long time and then performed. I made him wear a condom—he didn't like that."

"What did Werberg make your husband do?" Fenwick asked.

"He never told me. I didn't want to know. I still don't."

"You haven't seen either of them since that night?"

"No."

"Where were you and your husband Thursday night into Friday morning, and yesterday afternoon?"

For the first time, her flow of words stopped. She gazed at them carefully. "What are you trying to say?"

"We aren't trying to say anything," Turner said. "The question is a simple one."

"Oh, no," she said. "I tried to get a good job and the world went to hell. I am not going to let myself be taken down for life by being accused of doing something to that man. I didn't kill him. We were here with each other that night and yesterday afternoon."

"We'll need to talk to your husband."

"He's out shopping."

"Why not take your complaint to the press?" Fenwick asked.

"After the press conference fiasco, we tried individual reporters. Nothing worked. The man was rich enough to insulate himself completely. If I had a cum-stained dress or a tape of something, that would be great, but I don't. I guess they get people trying to trash celebrities all the time. One even came to the house and took some notes, but I think they all dismissed me as a disgruntled job hunter. I think somebody got to them before we did."

"Why didn't you leave town afterwards?"

"My husband landed a dream job with a financial firm in

the Loop. In spite of that, I swore I'd leave town if I ever saw either Lenzati or Werberg again."

"Do you know anything about computer hackers or sabotage against Lenzati and Werberg's company? Especially a guy named Eddie Homan?"

Her eyes shifted in the classic suspect-lying-mode. "I have nothing to do with that."

"Why didn't you try those investigative shows?" Fenwick asked. "*Sixty Minutes*, or *Twenty-Twenty*?"

"We did. Nothing ever came of it. They didn't return our calls."

Turner and Fenwick left, promising to return to talk to her husband.

Turner asked, "Why did Lenzati pursue her with such fervor?"

"She's hot. She's smart. She was tough to catch. Part of some games is the thrill of the chase. The harder the fight, the greater the glory."

Turner said, "I'd give a great deal to find this Eddie Homan guy. I want to ask him a few questions."

⏴ 19 ⏴

It isn't always necessary to follow someone around. Sometimes you can anticipate their moves. Sometimes you simply miss out. Sometimes you just get lucky, and sometimes you have to take whatever you can get. Sometimes you screw up and miss somebody completely. No matter how awry your planning may go, it really doesn't make any difference, because you know somebody's going to die eventually.

They headed for the LaSalle Street office of Lenzati and Werberg's accountant. Early Sunday afternoon was quiet in the financial heart of Chicago.

Claud Vinkers they had met. The accountant, Evelyn Jasper, was a woman in her fifties who seemed to be brisk and efficient. The lawyer wore a dark business suit obviously expensively tailored. The accountant was dressed in a beige suit that was cut perfectly for her model-slender figure.

They met in a fifty-fourth floor conference room.

"How can we help you gentlemen?" Jasper asked.

Turner said, "We're wondering what financial shape Mr. Lenzati and Mr. Werberg and their company were in."

"All were in excellent shape. Their current business had shown a profit every year since it began, something unusual in a dot-com business. Of course, they were wealthy from the sale of the first company. They never had to touch the principal from that sale. That money was wisely invested and continued to grow. Craig in real estate and Brooks in precious metals and municipal bonds."

"Who inherits all this?"

"Craig's and Brooks' wills were very similar. Their current company gets a half of everything. It doesn't need it. If you're thinking anyone needed their deaths to provide an infusion of money into the business, you would be wrong. There is no motive for murder there."

Turner asked, "Who inherits the rest?"

Vinkers said, "Just like Craig's. A variety of charities are going to be very happy. None of them knew they were getting the bequests. There is no motive there. Sorry."

"The relatives get nothing?" Turner asked.

"They'd both provided for any living parents some time ago. All the other relatives of either one got the same thing: a thousand dollars. Counting distant cousins of both of them, there would be about thirty thousand. Not much to kill for, if they even knew they were going to get it, which I doubt."

Turner asked Vinkers, "We spoke with a woman about her sexual harassment complaint against Mr. Lenzati."

The lawyer said, "You're talking about the rumors on the Internet. I can find you rumors on the Internet that would make even the toughest cops in this city quail, and those are about sweet little grandmothers who love their grandchildren."

"Mrs. Korleski says she couldn't get anybody to listen to her."

"I know the whole story there. She was a disappointed job seeker. She wanted to work for the best and most cutting edge computer company in the world, but she didn't get the job. She was unstable, and she kept harassing him. After a while, we had her investigated. She was a wacko."

"She seemed pretty sane to me," Fenwick said.

"You're an expert?" Vinkers asked.

"Enough to know that I need to be suspicious about anything a lawyer tells me," Fenwick responded.

"Nancy Korleski had an ax to grind," Vinkers said. "We were suspicious that she put a lot of the rumors on the Internet herself. We could never prove it. Whoever was doing it was very clever. We also had trouble with attempted hacking and sabotage—she was suspected."

"Are either of you aware of late night sex parties at Lenzati's house?"

"I find that hard to believe," Vinkers said.

"Why?" Fenwick asked.

"He was the consummate nerd. Every once in a while he'd squire around a very beautiful and very stupid woman for a short while, but he always was far more interested in his work, not sex."

Turner asked, "Do you know anything about a sexual conquest game the two of them played?"

"This is getting beyond absurd," Vinkers said. "Although I've never heard that bit of ridiculousness before."

"Unfortunately," Fenwick said, "that little bitty-bit of ridiculousness happens to be annoyingly true."

"I beg your pardon," Vinkers said.

"We discovered a coded scoring record on Lenzati's computer," Turner said. "We made a copy before Mr. Werberg could erase it—he tried to. Our computer expert has broken the code, and we've talked with a number of people they used for their game."

The accountant said, "Unbelievable."

The lawyer asked, "They really kept score?"

Fenwick said, "Yep."

Vinkers said, "They must have been out of their minds."

"Neither of you knew a thing about it?" Fenwick asked.

Both insisted they hadn't.

Fenwick asked, "Do you have a list of properties that Mr. Lenzati owned?"

"Yes, for here and around the world. Mostly here. Their two main residences you already know about."

"Can we get the addresses for all of those in the metropolitan area? We'll want to check them out."

"You think a real estate deal might have gone bad?" Vinkers asked.

"No," Turner said, "but we have reason to believe they had a separate site for their love nest."

"I can make copies of the addresses for you," Jasper said. "They'll be the places they had to pay taxes on."

After she did, Turner and Fenwick left.

On the way down in the elevator Fenwick said, "He wasn't killed by a grasping relative waiting for an inheritance."

"I could have told you that," Turner said. "That would have made this too easy, but this whole concept of sexual need is making this almost as gritty as you like it."

Fenwick said, "I can hear the crowds in the background chanting, 'more grit, more grit, more grit.' I want it for the mantra on my tombstone."

"That's 'epitaph,' and ain't nobody chanting in this neighborhood."

"That's because it isn't gritty enough."

"Not very ethnically diverse, either."

"Worse luck. And," Fenwick added, flourishing the list of property addresses as they approached the car, "they did *not* own half the Loop. Not anywhere near it. Ha!"

"I'm glad to see you feel triumphant about their lack of real estate holdings. They were still millions of dollars ahead of you or me in this city, and that ain't bad in this day and age."

20

What I'm really doing is what all the rest of you want to do, get-
ting even. The rest of you are too frightened or too complacent.
You've got to get beyond the fear. It's a beautiful, pure country
beyond fear.

It was the middle of the afternoon when they returned to the
station. Turner found another box on his desk, small, com-
pact, and tightly wrapped. On the outside were the words
Nutty Chocolate with the dancing cocoa bean logo.

"What *is* this shit?" he demanded.

Fenwick said, "How the hell does this keep happening?"

Bokin from the front desk said, "It came through regular
channels, departmental mail."

"Somebody in the department is sending this to me?"

"Hell," Bokin said, "somebody could walk in off the
street and dump it in the interoffice mail, but they'd probably be seen."

"Was anybody?"

"No."

"Who the hell?" Turner asked. "If this is a joke, somebody's going to be very sorry."

Bokin said, "You could try and check the places where these are sold."

Fenwick said, "This stuff is sold in every grocery store and convenience store in the entire metropolitan area. Do you have any concept of how many that is?" To Bokin's silence, he said, "A lot."

As with the others, Turner sent the package to the crime lab for analysis.

"Better check the e-mail," Fenwick said.

The message this time was simple, "Eat shit and die." Turner swiveled the computer around so Fenwick could see.

Turner said, "I think I prefer the chocolate."

"We gotta get Micetic down here again," Fenwick said.

They called in the beat cops and detectives who had been working on the other interviews. While waiting, Turner phoned the police in the other cities where cops had been killed. In each city it took a while to connect with someone official who had worked on the investigation. It was also Sunday afternoon, and many of the cops were off duty.

First, Fenwick and Turner confirmed the data they had. Like good cops, they were determined to verify every fact. They weren't about to let lack of attention to detail screw up a case. Each conversation took time. All the cops who'd been killed had children under twenty living at home. Turner added the detail that they'd all had more than one child. There were no fingerprints that were unidentified at any of the scenes. He was able to confirm that all had been pissed on.

In each city cops were scrambling to assemble details and cross-reference data based on Morgensen's story. The reporter was cooperating with all of them.

216

"Had any of the cops been getting threats or unsolicited gifts prior to the killing?" Turner asked his contact in Albany.

"The reporter who broke the story called and asked the same thing. We're checking it out. We all get threats once in a while. We'll let you know."

After the calls, the detectives finished some paperwork. Fenwick broke the silence saying, "I don't know if there's much we can do to prevent an attack by an anonymous serial killer."

Turner leaned back in his chair. "I know. I thought of that."

A murder by someone not known to the victim was the toughest to solve. Discounting gang shootings, most murders are committed by someone who knows the victim, and are therefore relatively easy to solve.

Fenwick said, "Locking up the usual suspects isn't going to cut it?"

"No."

"Does the attack on Dwayne fit into this? I asked about attacks on cops in those other cities before the ones that succeeded. I got two yeses and one no."

Turner said, "I got two noes and one yes. It could have been just some random violence against a cop. The stabbings are still out of the ordinary. Violence against cops occurs almost daily. Being a cop doesn't prevent violence from happening to you."

Fenwick said, "All these stabbings combined with all this piss? These can't be just coincidences."

"What's the last crime coincidence you believed in?" Turner asked.

"Goldilocks and the three bears," Fenwick said. "And the bitch was guilty."

"But that wasn't a coincidence," Turner pointed out.

"Close enough for me," Fenwick replied.

"We still have no proof that our cop stabbing and Lenzati's and Werberg's deaths are connected to each other, or to the other murders around the country."

"We need facts," Fenwick said.

Turner and Fenwick met with the cops who'd been interviewing other possible sexual partners. The beat cops had questioned seven women and eight men. They had found no one who admitted knowing Lenzati or Werberg. They'd been working on the more common names on the list. Turner figured this was all they'd get.

Turner said, "I want to concentrate on the crossovers we've got. Two couples in the area made it with each of them. We talked to Korleski. The other was that couple that wasn't home earlier. We need to try them again."

"Questioning people about kinky sexual practices is what I've dreamed of being able to do," Fenwick said.

"Let's get on with it," Turner said.

Before they left, they asked Commander Molton to permit two clerks to research every murder along Interstate 90 east of Chicago during the month prior to the deaths of the detectives in the listed cities, and to examine every injury to every cop in any city along Interstate 90.

"Why?" Molton asked. "That's an awful lot of possible murders and injuries."

"Looking for patterns," Turner said. "There probably aren't any, and there's always the possibility of random chance intruding, but I want to check as much as we can."

Fenwick added, "Get Micetic to help. He's got a computer. Let him use it for something besides surfing porn sites."

"Is that what he does?" Molton asked.

"Isn't that what they all do?" Turner asked.

"And you never do?" Fenwick asked.

"I've got a block on the computer so the kids can't. It's too much of a hassle to figure out how to undo it."

They grabbed fast food at Beef on the Hoof and ate it as they drove.

The couple they wanted to interview lived in Berwyn, a near western suburb of Chicago. They took the Harlem Avenue exit from the Eisenhower Expressway and turned south. They turned left on Cermak Road and drove several blocks east, parking in front of a solid home of refurbished red brick. Alberto Zengre and his wife Conchetta were listed as having had sex with Lenzati and Werberg over five years ago.

Steam billowed out the door when it opened. A man holding a squirming, nearly naked three-year-old glared at them. After IDs and introductions, the man said he was Alberto. Turner thought he had the most soulful puppy dog eyes he had ever seen. He was five foot six, and looked like he was in his mid-twenties. He had a dark mustache and hair cut close to the scalp on the sides, with a longer dark covering on top. His skintight black T-shirt and the left leg of his faded skintight jeans were almost completely soaked. The jeans hung low on narrow hips. He wore white socks and no shoes.

Zengre had a mellow tenor voice. "If you want to talk, we'll have to do it while I give the kids a bath. My wife's mother is coming to get them soon to baby-sit. If I don't have them cleaned up, I'm dead." He scooped up a one-year-old from a playpen in the living room and led them to a bathroom on the first floor. All the furniture looked to be about five years old. At the time of purchase it must have been of the highest quality. Now it looked as if it had years of heavy use. The wall hangings were religious icons: a Jesus on a crucifix with a loincloth so low on his hips as to be nearly obscene, holy cards blown up and framed, pictures of the Virgin Mary in various poses, and one framed picture of a pietà. The floors were polished oak and looked as if they'd been restored.

As Zengre ran some water, he asked, "What's this about?"

Turner said, "We're investigating the deaths of Craig Lenzati and Brooks Werberg." He showed him pictures of the two men. Zengre's eyes flicked from one to the other of the cops. He tested the water, finished undressing the three-year-old, and placed him in the two inches of water in the tub. Chatting soothingly, he handed the child a brightly-colored ball, a pink plastic cube, and a bar of soap. The latter immediately skittered away. The child happily splashed about with the other two items. Zengre sat on the edge of the tub. He placed the one-year-old in a small basin inside the tub into which Zengre gently poured a stream of luke-warm water from a plastic container.

"Did you know either of these two men?" Turner asked.

"You wouldn't be here if you didn't think I did."

"Which one did you know?" Turner asked.

"Both, actually."

Turner asked, "When was the last time you saw either of them?"

"Five, maybe six years ago."

"Not yesterday afternoon, or Friday morning, or the night before that?"

"No."

"Where were you two nights ago?" Fenwick asked.

"Home with my wife and children."

"And yesterday morning?"

"I got up early to get in the unemployment line. It took until nearly noon."

"How did you meet them?"

"I met Werberg when I was part of a crew delivering some furniture to his house."

"How'd you wind up in bed with him?"

"Is nothing private anymore?" The younger child gazed placidly at the adults. The three-year-old ignored them.

"They were murdered," Fenwick said. "We need to know all the connections in their lives if we're going to piece together what happened to them."

"I don't have to tell you anything."

"Look," Fenwick said. "We know they paid you and your wife to have sex with them. We don't want to arrest you unless you killed them, but we need information. Let's skip to the details that are going to help us catch the murderer and forget this macho posturing crap."

Zengre sighed. "This is crazy." The cops waited. The kids were quiet. Finally, Zengre began, "I was dating my wife at the time. I needed some money. It's not like I'd never . . ."

While Zengre was lifting the three-year-old out of the tub, the child began to splash and stomp. The man reached for a towel with one hand, and steadied the kid with the other. The one-year-old put out his hands toward the action, and the basin he sat in began to tip. Turner squatted down and held the child upright while the father finished with his brother.

"If we're going to get into this, I need to finish with the kids first." He proceeded to change, dress, and set the little ones on the floor back in the living room.

With the children playing quietly on the floor, Zengre sat on a hassock and explained, "Here's what happened. I was working for a furniture delivery company. We were at this big mansion. At one point, my buddies left to get more furniture. I stayed to begin setting up the frame for a specially-designed bed, a heart-shaped thing. Werberg watched for a few seconds then said, "I'm gay. I think you're hot. I'll pay you a lot of money to spend the night with me."

"He was that bold?" Fenwick asked.

"Yeah. I said no way, I said I had a girlfriend, and we were getting married. He said I could bring her along, then the guys came back with more furniture. We had to put more things together, which took a while. The guy was rich, and it seemed like he was refurnishing half his house. The next time I was alone in a room, he reappeared. He asked if I wanted to know how much he was willing to pay. Okay, I hadn't lived a sheltered life. I fooled around once or twice with guys. I let one blow me once when I was sixteen and horny. He wasn't very good. Werberg offered me a thousand dollars if I would agree to spend the night, ten thousand if it included my girlfriend.

"We were young, planning to get married in a couple of weeks. We each had minimum wage jobs, and we had wedding bills, a house to buy or rent. We had no furniture. Nothing. He said, you don't have to do anything, just lay there, although the more you do, the more you'll make. I told him I'd ask my girlfriend. I only said that to shut him up. He said it didn't have to be a package deal. I never mentioned it to Conchetta. Nothing happened for a couple of days, then one night I get home from work and Werberg is sitting in my living room."

"How'd he find you?" Turner asked.

"I'm not sure. I guess it wouldn't be hard for him to find out who was on the delivery crew. When he first propositioned me, I asked the head of the crew who he was. The name didn't mean anything to me. As far as I knew, he was another rich guy who wanted to get his rocks off. That night he seemed to know an awful lot of stuff about us: credit card numbers, the name of our caterer for the wedding, how much money we made, how much was in our bank accounts—which wasn't much."

"Was it blackmail?" Turner asked.

"He'd already convinced my girlfriend. She wasn't upset or anything. With my fiancée in his corner, I didn't feel like I had much of a choice."

"Why not?"

"Conchetta was no virgin when we met. She was a party girl."

"She a prostitute?" Fenwick asked.

"Hey, don't get personal," Zengre said. "She wanted nice things. She wanted money. For one night she said she didn't care. She'd got him up to twenty thousand dollars. That's a lot of money for two people with minimum wage jobs. Conchetta said yes, so I didn't give a big shit. I was kind of dazed that night. It wasn't like a big moral dilemma. Werberg insisted it had to happen that night. He had a limousine outside, and we picked up this Lenzati guy. The four of us had dinner at some fancy restaurant. Then Conchetta went to Lenzati's, and I went to Werberg's.

"At his house he had some clothes for me to wear. He gave me a pair of size twenty-eight pre-faded jeans and white jockey shorts a size too small. He had several sizes of clean white T-shirts and clean white socks. The only thing I wore of my own was my running shoes. At his place he had me shower and change. The whole night was strange."

"How so?" Fenwick asked.

"We watched television for a couple of hours, like we were just a couple spending the night at home. Once in a while he would ask me if I wanted a little snack or a soft drink. During that time he only wanted to snuggle together but not continuously, just once in a while. Finally, he had me lay on the couch with my clothes on. He spent over an hour touching me and caressing me all over with only his fingertips. He barely got near me after that."

"Over an hour?" Fenwick asked.

"Closer to two hours," Zengre averred. "The craziest thing came when we were getting ready for bed."

"You spent the night?"

"It was part of the deal. The craziest thing was when he wanted to watch me take a piss. I had to be fully dressed with my dick hanging out of my fly. Before I left, he paid me to piss on everything I'd worn. When we got to bed, he had me take all my clothes off except my shorts, then had me turn around a few times before I got into bed. I think he stayed awake all night. I slept off and on. Whenever I woke up, there was a little night light on. He was either reading or watching me."

The door opened and a startlingly beautiful woman walked in. Turner and Fenwick rose. Zengre introduced them.

"We're here," Turner began, "to talk about your involvement with Craig Lenzati and Brooks Werberg."

Conchetta Zengre glared at her husband. "We don't know any such people."

"I told them—" Zengre began.

"You did *what?*" The three words rose in volume, ending in a shriek. The one-year-old began to cry. Zengre looked stunned and helpless. Conchetta thrust her purse onto a chair and picked up the wailing child. When the baby was finally cooing quietly, she whispered savagely, "How could you be so stupid?"

Turner intervened. "We already knew. How else would we have known to be here?"

"How did you find out?"

224

"They kept track of their conquests." Turner briefly explained the computer printout, and breaking the code.

"We did nothing illegal," she insisted. The whisper was still harsh.

"Actually, you did," Fenwick said. "A bunch of stuff. With your husband's admission and with the computer files, we've got plenty of broken laws."

"But we're not interested in arresting you for prostitution," Turner said. She visibly relaxed. "We just need information about Mr. Lenzati. You know he died?"

"I saw it on television."

Turner asked, "Where were you Thursday night and early Friday morning?"

"Here. Asleep next to my husband."

"You have any other witnesses?" Fenwick asked.

"No."

"And yesterday afternoon?"

"I was working. Al was looking for work."

Turner asked, "Did you ever try to contact Werberg and Lenzati after that evening?"

"What for?" Zengre asked.

"Blackmail," Fenwick said.

"Is that what this is about?" Conchetta asked. "You think we tried to threaten them and get money from them?"

"Did you?" Fenwick asked.

"No."

"What did Mr. Lenzati want you to do that night?" Fenwick asked.

"He wanted to fuck me and party. He had two other women there that night."

"Did you know their names?"

"I think one was Bambi, the other might have been Jennifer or Candi. I don't remember."

"Were they prostitutes?"

"Weren't we all?"

"You've got some nice things here," Fenwick said. "Twenty thousand can buy a lot, but everything looks about five years old."

"So we got some good stuff," she said. "Then we saved a little."

"Having sex with strangers didn't put a strain on your relationship?" Fenwick asked.

"Some," Alberto Zengre admitted. "The more I thought about it afterward, the more I didn't like it."

Conchetta said, "We haven't gone into couples prostitution, if that's what you mean. We don't hire out at sicko parties. We did this one thing this one time for a lot of money. What's the big deal?"

"Lenzati didn't try to get you to do anything kinky or illegal?" Fenwick asked. "Maybe passing out a few drugs to lubricate the evening?"

"The only lubrication was KY jelly. He mostly wanted ordinary guy on top, woman on the bottom sex. It was five or six hours that were mostly boring, standing or laying around watching him with them, or putting up with him being with me."

After going through everything again, they got no further insights into the murder from the Zengres.

In the car Fenwick asked, "No blackmail? It's a perfect setup for it."

"How would they prove it?" Turner asked. "Who would believe them?"

"Every sleazy reporter on the planet. Somebody *had* to have been blackmailing these guys."

Turner said, "Even if I agreed with that, the wrong people

are dead. It's more traditional to kill the one who is black-mailing, rather than the other way around."

"I hate it when you're logical. I still think blackmail has got to be part of this, but I'm still back on our earlier question."

"What's that?" Turner asked.

"Why did these guys pay for sex? They weren't bad look-ing. Why not expend the little extra effort and save them-selves some cash? There's got to be plenty of women and men who would be willing to be their friends, simply be-cause they're rich."

"I'm not sure it's ever going to make sense," Turner responded. "Maybe it was just easier, or they were lazy. I'm okay with the concept that they did it for the thrill. Before they die, we'll have to ask."

"Like we do all our victims. Who's next?"

"We've got some guy in Rogers Park."

Their next person was Shawn Groshmeister. He lived on Albion, east of Sheridan Road in the last apartment house before the beach. They had to wait quite a while for their buzz at the downstairs door to be answered.

When Groshmeister opened his apartment door, he was wearing only a pair of navy blue boxer shorts. He held a towel in his left hand and his hair was damp. He smiled at them. Groshmeister had a flat stomach, broad shoulders, and well-defined muscles. The brush-cut hair on top of his head was dyed blond, and the sandy brown sides were cut short. His ears were pierced with earrings the size of nickels. Looking at the outsized jewelry, Turner thanked himself that his oldest son had yet to propose ear-piercing to this extent.

"You guys really cops?" he asked. He toweled his hair as they talked.

They showed their IDs.

"Gosh, real cops. What's up? I don't play the stereo loud since Mrs. Reilly complained. She's really kind of nice, and I hate to bug her. I didn't think she'd call the cops on me."

"She didn't."

"Oh."

He tossed the towel on the top of a dark blue horsehair sofa. "You guys want to sit down? You want something to drink?"

They declined. It was a studio apartment, and besides the couch and a recliner there were only two plastic chairs and a tiny kitchen table. There were no dirty dishes in the sink, and the floors looked like they were vacuumed regularly. Paul figured the bed was a hide-a-way. On the walls were posters from two rock groups Paul had heard of only in passing from his son Brian.

"What can I do for you guys?" Groshmeister asked. He pulled on a pair of faded jeans.

"We're wondering if you knew Craig Lenzati or Brooks Werberg," Turner said.

"Who?"

Turner held out the pictures.

Groshmeister gazed at them for a second. "Oh, yeah. I knew him." He pointed to Werberg.

"How did you know him?" Turner asked.

"We had a one-night stand about six months ago."

"Did he pay you?"

"Well—"

"You're on a printout," Turner said. "He kept records of who he messed around with."

"That's kind of creepy."

Turner said, "The records says he paid you a hundred bucks."

"Yeah, I didn't give a shit. I'd have done it for free, but he

228

mentioned money. I didn't care. What difference did it make? I spent time with the guy, and it made him happy. He wasn't real ugly or nothin', so I figured what the hell?"

"Did you know who Werberg was?"

"Some guy with money?"

"He was a billionaire. You could have made lots of money."

"Yeah?"

"How'd you happen to spend the night with him?"

"I was in a bar last summer, the Pleasure Palace, over on Sheridan Road just north of the Loyola El station. He came in and stared at me. I figured he was gay. Lots of gay guys stare at me." He grinned. "I'm used to being hit on by guys and girls. It doesn't bother me. I go with whoever I want. He propositioned me while I was away from my friends. I had nothing else to do that night, so I figured, why not?"

"Maybe he had some dreadful social disease," Fenwick said.

"Yeah, ya gotta be careful, but he didn't want to do much, really. He was kinda boring, although he did ask me if he could take a few pictures. I didn't care. He wanted to know if I had a girlfriend, and if he could watch the two of us have sex, but I don't know any girls who are into that."

"But he took the pictures?"

"Sure."

"You weren't worried about blackmail?"

"Why should I be? I'm not some politician. I'm never going to be. I'm not too bright, but I'm kind of good looking. I wouldn't mind posing nude for some magazine, but I've never connected with anybody. I guess I haven't tried real hard either."

"Where did you go with him?"

"I'm not sure. We got driven in a limo. I never saw the driver. We drove into a garage with a couple other cars in it. Then we went straight to a room that didn't have any windows."

"What happened?"

"He was into this cuddly thing. He turned the lights down low and turned the television on. I figured he was playing out some domestic bliss scene. That was okay with me. I didn't have to do anything much. He didn't even want me to take my clothes off. Pretty soon, he began to touch me all over and that was kind of it. He spent a lot of time on my ears. I guess my earrings fascinated him.

"The oddest thing was that he wanted to watch me piss. When I kind of hesitated, he offered me more money. I guess I could have held out for a lot more." He shrugged. "I didn't. Later he asked me if I'd piss in my pants and let him keep them. I told him I didn't have an extra pair. He told me he'd give me some he kept on hand. He showed me this dresser. He had more clothes than a department store, in all kinds of sizes. He even had underwear, briefs and boxers, in sizes from twenty-six to thirty-two. Different colors, styles. He offered to let me have my pick if I pissed in mine." He shrugged. "So I did."

"And he never took his clothes off?"

"Nope."

"Never mentioned Craig Lenzati?"

"Nope."

The cops left.

In the car Fenwick said, "That has got to be the most amiable man on the planet."

"He's just a friendly goof without a lot of cares."

"I guess."

⌐21⌐

I like to fantasize that all those slasher movies are documentaries. That all the irresponsible, thoughtless, and promiscuous good-looking people are punished for their behavior. They shouldn't be allowed to break the rules.

"Let's go visit Vinnie Girote," Turner said.

They called Molton and got him to find Girote's home address.

"Why didn't reporters pick up on this sexual harassment?" Fenwick asked.

"Hard to tell. It all does sound a little far-fetched. We want to believe it, and we've got the hard copy of their sexual history to prove it. Now, if we released that to reporters, think how popular we would be—popular and fired."

Fenwick said, "I don't care enough about any of these people to lose my job over them, but I do care enough to use their sexual history to find the murderer. Lenzati must have clout beyond imagining to make life such a hell for the Korleskis."

"This is Chicago. Hard to tell what wouldn't be possible."

Fenwick asked, "You think the mayor was behind it?"

"Let's start with Girote. I'm not ready to take on the mayor yet."

Vinnie Girote lived in Lake Point Towers which stood at the entrance to the renovated Navy Pier. They parked in the garage and entered. Girote's apartment had a view south and west toward the distant Adler Planetarium and the Loop. His wife answered the door; Girote wasn't home. She informed them that he was at a political dinner at the British Consulate.

Turner and Fenwick looked out of place on the periphery of the party. Everyone who passed them in the entryway was in elegant evening dress. The white-gloved gentleman at the door asked if they wouldn't mind waiting in a room off the lobby while he brought Mr. Girote to them.

Fenwick said, "Yes, I mind. We're in the middle of a murder investigation. We need to talk to this guy. We don't want him walking out a back door while we're waiting out front."

"We have diplomatic immunity," the gentleman said.

"We aren't after one of the diplomatic staff," Turner said. "He's an American. We need to talk to him."

Another white-gloved figure was summoned, and a compromise was reached. One detective would accompany one white-gloved figure to the room where the reception was being held.

Girote proved equal to the occasion. He smiled pleasantly at the discreetly elegant usher, nodded to the companions he was talking to, and strode cheerfully toward where Turner waited unobtrusively next to a potted palm. Girote walked up to him, smiled, and held out his hand. Turner felt a bit of a fool shaking the smiling man's hand. The two of them joined Fenwick in an office on the third floor. From the windows Turner could look down on a Burger King on the west side of Michigan Avenue.

As soon as the door closed, every ounce of affability and geniality disappeared from Girote's countenance. "What the hell do you two think you are doing? Who the hell do you think you are, coming here? Do you know who these people are?"

Neither Turner nor Fenwick was inclined to interrupt his flow. An angry suspect was more likely to make a mistake than a calm one. The tirade lasted all of three minutes. At the end Girote was breathing hard and the parts of his face that weren't red were tending to purple. Turner wondered if perhaps the man didn't have problems with high blood pressure. Abruptly Girote plopped himself into a purple leather armchair.

Fenwick stood over him and said, "We understand you were behind the cover-up of a sexual scandal involving Craig Lenzati."

Girote gasped, "Never. Nothing. No."

Fenwick said, "You weren't part of it, or there was no scandal, or you're stuck on negatives and can't get out?"

Girote concentrated on breathing for several minutes. His normally loud tone was still in evidence when he finally said, "By the time I'm done with the two of you, you'll be giving out parking tickets in Hegewisch for the rest of your careers."

Fenwick said, "The standard psycholegal analysis of someone who resorts to threats instead of rational discussion is that he or she is a lying sack of shit and guilty as all hell."

Turner said, "We've spoken with Nancy Korleski. We've broken the code that Werberg and Lenzati used to keep score in their sexual exploits. We can prove their activity with names and dates. We have Nancy Korleski and her husband who are angry enough to come forward as witnesses. I bet there will be others."

"Korleski is a crazy bitch."

"She struck me as completely sane," Fenwick said. "She doesn't have big, blousy hair like some recent accusers of famous people nor does she strike me as trailer trash. When she's in front of the cameras, I bet she will strike lots of people as very believable. We'll follow the trail of her complaints from subordinate to subordinate. We'll subpoena phone records. Or perhaps we'll have to start with higher-ups and work our way down to whoever was doing their dirty work. I nominate you for that position. We know you visited her. Why would you, if you weren't part of a cover-up or an attempt to halt an investigation?"

"What we need to know," Turner said, "is what did you know, and when did you know it?" Turner had been looking forward to using that line on a politician for years.

"You guys are nuts," Girote said. But the struggle had gone out of his tone. Even his volume had diminished. "Why bother to smear innocent men? They're dead. Why drag their private peccadilloes into the open?"

"We aren't nuts," Fenwick said. "We don't care if they tried to make love to a charging rhinoceros, unless it has something to do with the murders. If it does, we'll want to talk to everyone connected to them, including the rhino if we have to. This is a murder investigation. They indulged in explicitly criminal and very possibly dangerous activities."

Girote said, "Maybe Korleski murdered him out of spite and revenge."

"Quite possible," Turner said, "but we're going to be thorough. We're not going to take anybody's word for anything. We want hard data, and we need as much information as we can get. We're going to know everything about their lives that we can. I'd think you'd be eager to help us catch their killers. Unless you're still protecting a prominent person."

"I'm protecting no one."

"What's so sacred about these guys' reputations?" Fenwick asked. "They're dead. Trust me, they won't care. It strikes me, you're the one worried now, and only about yourself."

Girote harumphed, but said nothing.

Turner said, "Tell us about the complaints you got about Lenzati."

"There was only the one."

Turner and Fenwick waited patiently.

"Korleski had a lawyer. She was dangerous."

"Bull pizzle," Fenwick said. "Some big deal rich guy screws a woman he shouldn't. A few moral crusaders talk a lot, several of the unwashed titter a bit, but most everybody else doesn't give a shit."

Girote flew into a rage. "What planet are you from? This is America, land of the morally superior and home of the indignantly self-righteous. A taint on someone's reputation can have all kinds of consequences. Why can't you even begin to understand? Public outrage does make a difference. Dealing with wealthy business people is vitally important. Keeping them from being harassed by ignorant fools is paramount."

Fenwick asked, "If he was a sex-crazed maniac using his powerful position to force women to have sex with him, then doesn't he deserve to take a fall?"

"He wasn't a sex-crazed maniac. He was a good man. All kinds of people have it in for the rich and famous. They have a right to be protected from people like Korleski, who are nothing more than opportunistic whores, trying to inflict guilt on mostly innocent people or to milk them for money or personal gain."

"Why not just settle out of court?" Turner asked. "So she makes an accusation. Why not just find out how much she intends to sue for and pay her? He's got enough money. There's got to be a lot more to this. What you've explained so far doesn't add up to a need to go to such great lengths to cover up—and certainly does not lead to murder."

"Don't you see? Don't you understand?"

"I guess I don't," Fenwick said. "Try again."

"It's all public perception. The competition is greater than ever in the computer industry. If it got out about what he did, people might not run from him, but they might trickle away in a steady stream until he had nothing left."

Turner said, "And the city of Chicago cares that much? That's just one major crock."

"Perhaps there's a more personal reason," Fenwick said.

"What!?"

Fenwick said, "Maybe you yourself had something to gain. You've been covering up, and maybe the whole scheme was beginning to unravel because of Korleski, or some other woman who wasn't willing to play his games. You were going to be caught in the middle and you had to get rid of him."

"If that were true," Girote said, "why get rid of Lenzati? Wouldn't it be a lot easier to get rid of the woman involved?"

"I thought I was on a roll," Fenwick said.

"Not if there were a lot of women," Turner said.

"There was only one. After Korleski, he got smarter. He got his dick out of his business. Lenzati may have been a sexual moron, but he wasn't stupid. He got talked to. He understood what he could not do, no matter how rich he was."

Turner asked, "Why didn't the national news magazines or gutter television shows follow up?"

236

"A fortuitous concurrence of life, fast work on my part, and back then these guys weren't all that famous. In Chicago, sure. Give them another couple years, and it might become a huge problem. My ability to stonewall and obfuscate is second to none, and Nancy Korleski and her husband came across as true dopes. The Internet is a great place for stupid rumors. And maybe the Korleskis were big into hacking. Maybe they had some criminal problems in their past."

"She didn't tell us about that," Fenwick said.

"Are you surprised?" Girote asked.

"Maybe Lenzati had something on you personally," Turner said. "They were computer geniuses. They could find anything."

"There's nothing to find." But his tone by now was more defeated than defiant.

"Did you kill them?" Turner asked.

Girote said, "This is ridiculous. I didn't kill either of them. Yeah, I helped cover up some sexual shenanigans. So fucking what?"

Fenwick said, "So one of the people involved in his orgies may have fucking killed him."

Girote said, "To quote a wise sage of short acquaintance, 'bull pizzle.'"

"Werberg called you that morning, didn't he?" Turner asked.

"Yes."

"Why the big secret about it?" Fenwick asked.

"Cover up. Cover up. Cover up. The modern politician's mantra." He stood up. "I'm not finished with you two yet." He marched out.

In the car Turner used his cell phone to call Ben and tell him he would not be home for dinner.

⟂ 22 ⟂

I don't want them to know anything about me. I'm not stupid like some killers. I don't write manifestos. I just want these people dead, and I want to enjoy doing it.

In the winter gloom of the late afternoon, they began touring the city in search of all the properties on the list they'd gotten from Lenzati's accountant. They found four businesses closed for the day, three apartment houses, several fast-food franchises, and a convenience store.

Fenwick said, "Any of those apartments could have vast warrens of hidden cells designed for concealing the secret headquarters of a computer genius."

"I picture something bigger," Turner said.

Their next stop was west of the Goose Island redevelopment section of the city, just north and west of downtown. There were a lot of micro breweries and trendy upscale developments mixed with the crumbling older structures. The one Lenzati owned was an apartment house with all the windows gone and the roof missing.

"He was a slum lord?" Fenwick said.

Turner said, "Or he was on the cutting edge of where the next real estate boom was going to take place."

They walked around the perimeter of the building. There was no doubt it was vacant. Broken windows let in sufficient light for them to see a barren interior. There was no need for a key. They easily forced a door and walked in. The place had been abandoned, even by the rats.

The next building was a monolithic yellow box half a city block long at the corner of Grand and Damen Avenues. Swirls of stucco surrounded solar collector cells, which were flush to the building. None was the same geometric shape as another.

"What the hell is this place?" Fenwick asked.

Turner said, "It's listed as a business address. Drive around to the alley." There was a small cube-shaped garage which repeated the color scheme and solar panel look of the larger structure.

Turner and Fenwick got out of the car and approached the only entrance they could see. Hanging next to the portal was a square box with a slot on the right side for inserting a personal identification card.

"Those are not smears of blood," Fenwick said pointing to what for all the world looked like smears of blood on the ground and parts of the door.

Turner shone his flashlight on them. "If I was a smear of blood, that's what I'd look like." The two of them stooped down to look.

"Someone was attacked here?" Fenwick asked. "Or is this random blood?"

"Nobody has random blood in a murder investigation," Turner said. "We need to get inside here."

The door was built flush with the back of the building.

There was no handle. Fenwick took out a Swiss army knife and smashed the little slot box. The door opened.

They entered darkness. The light from outside showed a carpeted floor. Turner felt on the wall on the right and found a light switch. The new brightness revealed a reception room out of a Victorian whorehouse. The ceiling was completely mirrored. The furnishings were red and maroon plush. The coverlets on the seven-foot couches had a red and black checkerboard pattern. Turner noted that it was the same color scheme as in Lenzati's master bedroom. All four walls were solid leather, two all black, two all red. The room had lush purple carpeting and soft pink, blue, and yellow lighting.

They walked through doors which led into other chambers with a variety of scenarios. One was a working dungeon, another was a jail cell, a third was a motel, a fourth a college dorm room. The room set up as a bar looked to be more than a stage set. The bottles behind the mahogany barrier were filled. Turner unscrewed the cap of one and sniffed. It was real liquor. Every single room was straight-from-the-furniture-store clean.

"This is about half the building," Turner said. They came to further barred doors in a bare unfurnished room, where they found smears that were almost certainly blood in front of the door. They had no key. Turner inspected the blood closely. It wasn't completely dry. They forced the door open.

Inside was a set of stairs leading up. The door at the top led to a room that seemed to stretch above all the others below. They found miles of cables leading from cameras to outlets in the wall. An entire wall was filled with shelves containing pornographic movies, some in professionally-made boxes, others with hand lettering on the sides. They decided to inspect the details of this room more fully later. First, they had to complete a quick walk-through to make sure there wasn't someone injured in the building.

The detectives went through a door into the next room. They found themselves on the second floor balcony of a room that seemed to stretch for the other half of the building. Unpainted gray struts and duct work filled the space above their heads. Along all four walls were computers, hundreds of them. There were monitors galore built into shelving on all four walls. In the center of the room were what looked to be two command centers. Facing each other were vast consoles with hundreds of buttons under giant screens with two massively comfy chairs in front of them.

In the middle of the room, sprawled backwards in one of the vast comfy chairs, they could see a man's body.

"If the last room was an El Dorado of clues," Fenwick said, "this is the whole fucking California gold rush."

They approached the body carefully. There were occasional smears of blood. The body itself had been stabbed at least as often as Lenzati's. The difference here was a stainless-steel knife had been left protruding from the center of the man's chest. It was a huge hunting knife with one serrated edge. This corpse's eyes were open. It glared unseeing at a computer screen which had a message in seventy-two point type. GOTCHA, YOU SON OF A BITCH.

"Who the hell is this?" Fenwick said.

Blood had splashed and gushed over every nearby surface. There was a stain on his pants below his waist—Turner smelled urine. The man wore dark blue jeans and the remnants of a gray sweatshirt. A black jacket lay on the floor. He was tall, skinny, blond—and dead.

With exquisite care, after donning his plastic gloves, Turner lifted a wallet out of the man's back pocket. He looked inside. He found a Social Security card but no driver's license. He said, "We're not going to have to worry about finding Eddie Homan to interview."

While they waited for the requisite murder scene personnel, they returned to what Turner thought of as a trophy room and examined it.

Turner pointed to a number of different pornographic box covers. "We didn't find nearly this many at Lenzati's house." Some showed only women, others men and women, and some only men. "We've got gay and straight ones here."

All the walls were lined with dressers. Turner opened the top drawer of one on the north end of the building. He found men's briefs and boxer shorts in freezer bags. He put on his plastic gloves before he touched any of them.

"Souvenirs," he said to Fenwick.

"Got to be," his partner replied.

"The results of their game," Turner said. "These are intimate reminders or proof they had."

The dressers on the south wall had jeans and jockey shorts in sealed plastic bags. Turner, still with his gloves on, opened one. The odor of urine poured out. He quickly resealed it. He said, "I think we've found the trophy case."

Fenwick said, "I've got a picture and mementos drawer." They also found the jockstraps and the baseball bat from the infielders in Iowa. Encased in white silk were the jockstrap and mouth protector which had the name of the hockey player Werberg had written about.

"Didn't he just retire?" Turner asked.

"I think so," Fenwick said.

Other items had dates and names; usually just first, sometimes only last names, and a few full names. They found hundreds of photos. They'd have to look through them thoroughly to see if there were any of the people they had interviewed.

"You know," Turner said, "I just don't see Werberg and Lenzati blackmailing these people. To get them into bed, maybe, but not after they'd had sex with them—there would be no point. Those guys didn't need money or a job; their companies weren't going broke. We've got no evidence they tried or wanted to do repeat business with any of these people. There was no boss to tattle to. They were the bosses."

Other dressers on the east walls were filled with male paraphernalia; besides underwear, there were used condoms, pairs of jeans, more photographs, T-shirts, socks, glasses with fingerprints on them, a few combs, toothbrushes—anything that a person might use that would retain some remnant of themselves.

Against the west wall the dressers were filled with feminine apparel. "Lenzati's trophy case," Turner said.

"Is this clue heaven or what?" Fenwick asked.

Turner inserted one of the tapes with hand lettering in one of the six video machines in the room. It began to whir. He found a remote control and pressed the on button. A small screen nearby leapt to life. The tape was obviously homemade in black and white. The lighting was alternately too light and too dark, creating vast shadows or turning everyone horror movie white. A man and a woman cavorted in a cell block, presumably the one below them. Turner ejected the tape. It was labeled by date. He checked their list.

"These are going to match." He spent several minutes walking along the wall. "There aren't any dates before the last few months. That's when they must have set up this place."

"I think this was their general pornography collection and the ones which they personally developed," Fenwick said.

"You're probably right."

"We're going to have to watch all of these?" Fenwick asked.

"You drooling or complaining?" Turner asked.

"Yes," Fenwick said.

"Where do the all these cables lead?" Turner asked. "There must be a taping room."

They found a largish booth with taping equipment, much of it looking new or little-used. There was no blood or destruction there.

Dylan Micetic showed up a few minutes after the ME. He set to work at the computer terminals after the crime lab technicians had dusted them for fingerprints.

An hour later the ME reported. "Obviously, somebody took that very large hunting knife and gutted him as if they were preparing to fillet him. He's been dead at least several hours, probably since sometime early this morning. The smears of blood on the outer door and at various points in the building could be his or not. We'll have to type them and then do DNA testing."

"He died after Werberg," Turner said.

The ME said, "He died in this room. He's got one big entrance wound in his back. That was probably the fatal blow. Then there's that mess from his balls to his sternum. Your killer swished that thing around inside of him."

"He was leaning over and looking at the computer when he was stabbed," Turner said.

"Very possibly," The ME said.

"Did you find evidence of sexual activity in Werberg or Lenzati?" Turner asked.

"Lenzati's was his own semen. Werberg's shorts had evidence of his own semen. It was dried. I can't say precisely when it would be from, certainly within hours, but not much more than that. In neither case did we find evidence that they had a partner. I can't say for sure if they were just beating off, or if their partners took their own body fluids with them."

Fenwick looked at the body. "Pretty hard to imagine any sexual activity here, but then I've seen killers do a lot of nutty stuff."

"We'll check. We always do." The ME left.

"Why is the body here?" Turner asked. "Was he living in some little cubbyhole we haven't found? Did he break in and get caught and stabbed? Did the killer bring him and why? Was Homan working at this location for Lenzati and Werberg?"

Turner said, "I don't see any evidence of him fighting back or struggling."

Fenwick said, "No sign of any damage either. The killer didn't try to break up the place. Lenzati was turned into a human pincushion, Werberg's place was smashed to smithereens, and this guy's practically gutted."

Turner suggested, "Maybe the killer was done. This was it. Just a final punctuation mark."

They searched the place thoroughly. There was no sign anywhere of permanent habitation.

"Of course," Fenwick said after they were finished looking, "someone could have just lived in a number of those different little scenarios."

Turner said, "Other than the souvenir room, we haven't found anything personal—a toothbrush, shampoo, a used razor, fingernail clippers—little things that you'd expect if a person actually lived here."

"Whoever got in was able to get past the card-swiping deals at the door," Fenwick said.

"Why didn't they have security cameras here?" Fenwick asked.

"Maybe the whole place was supposed to be secure," Turner said.

"None of the sexual contacts we talked to mentioned this place," Fenwick said. "Werberg entertained at his house."

"Maybe this place was built or put together since then, maybe just recently," Turner said. "Some of the VCRs and stuff are still in their boxes. This place could be pretty new."

Turner and Fenwick approached Micetic. "Wow," Micetic said.

"Wow what?" Fenwick asked.

"This is unbelievable. You know how they were working on security for all those companies?"

"Yeah," Turner said.

"They installed the programming in such a way that they could hack into any of the computers at any time they wanted."

"I'm not sure I if I prefer intellectually-gifted felons, or moronic gangbangers," Fenwick said.

"Other than a few IQ points," Turner said, "I'm not sure there is much difference, but that is extremely clever. The security people become the ultimate betrayers."

"There's more," Micetic said, "lots more. Because of what I've learned at their home computers, this is easier to break into. There are records of them hacking into companies before they bought them. They hacked into anything they wanted, whenever they wanted. Sometimes they waited years to use the knowledge they had. They stole ideas for everything—software, operating systems, everything. This is fantastic." He pointed and explained for ten minutes.

When he finished, Fenwick said, "They weren't geniuses on their own."

"They were smart enough to steal everybody else's ideas and not get caught," Micetic said. "I never heard of them even being suspected of this."

↘ 23 ↙

*I've made a couple of mistakes. I've missed a few. I've struck
too soon. No one has noticed the mistakes yet.*

They returned to Area Ten. There was another box of
chocolates.

Turner called the crime lab. No fingerprints on any of the
boxes. No identification of any kind. The white substance
from last night had been plain ordinary sugar, available at
thousands of stores in the metropolitan area. He sent the
new box over with no hope of obtaining any useful information from it.

He turned on his e-mail. The message this time simply
read, "Fear." He turned off the computer and made a note to
tell Micetic about the message the next time he saw him. He
choose not to unplug the computer. If the killer was commu-
nicating with him, better to leave it on and hope whoever
was doing it made a traceable mistake.

Turner's phone rang. It was Vinnie Girote sounding many

decibels below his usual bellow. "I want to apologize to you guys. I'm sorry. You won't be bothered by me again."

Turner asked, "Did you orchestrate the cover-up of the Korleski case?"

Girote revived a bit. "Don't press your luck," he snapped, then hung up.

Turner told Fenwick. "What the hell was that all about?" Turner asked.

"He got a conscience?" Fenwick asked.

"That's an oxymoron in a politician," Turner said.

"Did you just use that word correctly in that sentence?" Fenwick asked.

Turner said, "Besides being Mr. Wisdom, you do not get to be Mr. Grammar Person. I wonder." He picked up his phone and punched in Mrs. Talucci's number. He remembered her set lips and clenched jaw when they'd discussed Girote earlier. He said to her, "I just got an apology call from Vinnie Girote. You wouldn't happen to know anything about that."

Mrs. Talucci's rumored influence was legendary. When she made promises something would happen, it always did. She didn't promise often, but she always made good. Her contacts were beyond legendary.

Mrs. Talucci said, "I made a few calls, including to his mother. She owes me a favor or two. I explained what a nice boy you are. She saw reason." That's all she would tell him. Mrs. Talucci had never revealed her sources to Turner. He thought it best not to probe too deeply.

Randy Carruthers staggered to the top step of the third floor.

"He looks even more ghastly than usual," Fenwick commented.

Turner gazed in Carruthers' direction. He was pale and

trembling. Turner got up, went to him, held out a hand, and asked, "Are you all right, Randy?"

"Dwayne Smythe is dead."

"When did you hear this?" Turner asked.

"The guys on the admitting desk. I heard right. I'm not screwing up. They just got the news. Reporters are starting to gather downstairs. Dwayne was a friend of mine. I visited him just last night in the hospital. He looked like he was getting better, but they told me Dwayne was too messed up inside."

"How's the investigation going into his murder?" Turner asked.

"I don't know. I don't know. He was a friend. The only one I had around here." Tears started down Carruthers' cheeks. Turner would never tell him that behind his back, Smythe disparaged Carruthers as much as any of them. "He was nice to me. Jesus, I shouldn't be crying. People around here will never let me forget it."

"It's okay, Randy," Turner said. He placed a hand on Carruthers' shoulder. "It's okay. I know it's tough to lose someone you care about." He led Carruthers into the coffee room, and poured him a cup. "You gonna be okay?" Turner asked. He felt more sorry for Carruthers than he ever had before.

"Yeah, thanks," Carruthers said.

Turner rejoined Fenwick at their desks. He gave him the news.

"Is this the cop killing for Chicago?" Fenwick asked. "Does this mean we've met our quota?"

Turner said, "I don't know if I hope that's true or not." He called Area One and got hold of the detective on the case, Bryant Karnetis. Turner said, "You heard about Dwayne?"

"Just got the news a minute ago," Karnetis said.

"You got anything on the investigation?" Turner asked.

"We've got no conclusive forensic evidence. Right now, I think it was one of the brothers of the crippled kid. The whole family was furious at Dwayne. Supposedly, for twelve hours the night before the stabbing, they had a family pow-wow and things got pretty heated, but no one admits to doing anything violent."

"Nobody ever does," Turner said. "What about connecting it to the string of cop killings across the country?"

"I've got absolutely nothing on that," Karnetis said. "We have tried to match what we've got here to the pattern from the reporter. We could send you over our chart."

"Yeah. Do that. We'll send you what we've got. You also need to see if they can find any trace of piss on his clothes."

"You're kidding?" Karnetis said.

Turner told him about the connection with the cop killings around the country. Karnetis said he'd check it out.

If this were a cop show on television, they would be working on one case at a time. As it was, they were real cops, and murders piled on top of murders. They worked on as many as they could at one time, and most were unconnected to each other.

Turner hung up. "What do we know about Smythe and his murder?" He walked over to the spreadsheets on the other police murder cases. "Let's put what we've got so far up here as a possibility and see what it gets us. When we get Karnetis' chart, we'll add more. I don't think the attack on Smythe is connected to our case or the cop killings, but we have to rule that out for certain."

They filled in Smythe's age, birth date, marital status, number of children and their ages, data about the crime against him, and every other category that had already been posted that they had information about.

Turner examined their handiwork. "With Smythe up

here, the only things they all have in common are they were all cops with kids. That, and they were all breathing before they were killed. I don't think that last one is a clue. There's got to be a connection we're missing. Unless the killer is really angry about cops with kids, in which case we'd have more dead bodies than I ever care to think about."

Fenwick said, "We'll have to keep adding things as we find them out."

"What if we put up Lenzati, Werberg, and Homan on this?" Turner asked.

"They weren't cops. Doing that probably wouldn't tell us anything."

Turner said, "As soon as you say it won't, it usually does. What if there is some kind of inter-relation? I don't know what it could be, but we need to know about everything connected with these killings. What were the cops who were killed investigating? What kind of cases did they work on? Were other famous people killed in their cities before they were? We need all kinds of information."

Fenwick said, "In light of what we know now, we may have to call those places again."

While they waited for the workers from Lenzati and Werberg's business to show up, they examined the data on the cop killings, doing everything they could to see if there was a connection to Lenzati, Werberg, and Homan.

Turner printed out the spreadsheet data on the three murdered computer geniuses, and faxed it with their other data to Bryant Karnetis.

They called other cities, gathered information, and added it to the spreadsheets on the corkboard. They also included new columns for more comprehensive information as it came in. In less than an hour their grid had grown exponentially. They cross-referenced any kind of connection to each city.

Early on, Turner eyed the columns of data and said, "I feel like I'm playing an immense game of bingo. Filling in each little blank. Racing against death."

Fenwick said, "Let's hope we win."

The first person they interviewed late that afternoon was Terry Waldron, the man in command of the business end of Werberg and Lenzati's company.

He shook his head as he sat down next to their desks. "Last week at this time we were in perfect shape. Now it's all going to collapse."

"The business will go bust without them?" Fenwick asked.

"Oh, yes. They were the heart and soul of it. They really were creative, computer geniuses. Most of the rest of us simply did a lot of the basic work that led to the final product. Without them, there would be no product."

Fenwick said, "We heard they had some odd hiring practices."

"Oh?"

Fenwick said, "That they liked to play sexual games with people. We've got at least one job applicant who claims it happened to her."

"I don't know anything about that."

"You didn't hear about a sexual harassment suit?" Turner asked.

"No."

"For the past twelve years, they were playing a game of sexual conquest against each other."

"I'm not anybody's sexual conquest."

Fenwick said, "Your name wasn't on their list, but there are some anonymous entries. It is possible they had some history of sexual harassment when hiring."

"In this day and age? They'd get their asses sued faster than you could say equal opportunity."

"Who did you interview with?" Turner asked.

"Both of them."

"Neither one ever came on to you?" Turner asked.

"Certainly not. I would never have accepted a job from a firm where I had to sleep with someone to be hired."

"A lot of people said they were desperate to work for these guys. You weren't hot to get a job with them?"

"Of course I was. That doesn't mean I'm a moral cipher. They needed someone with a lot of brains who could add and subtract. They made lots of money, and they needed a watchdog. That's what I did. I never heard any mention of sex in the office. I never saw either man ever make an unwanted advance on anybody, ever."

"We'll need to go over Werberg's office at work," Turner said.

"That's fine with me. You'll find it's just like Craig's. Pretty barren."

"Still, we'll notify you when we need to inspect it. There should already be a guard posted at his office door." Turner had issued this order last night. "We'll bring the department's computer expert with us."

"Fine with me. I was in charge of the books. The books are in perfect order."

"We found a warehouse out on Grand Avenue."

Waldron looked blank.

"Lenzati and Werberg had immense offices there. Perhaps there was a good reason they didn't need spacious quarters at your location. They had something vast on Grand Avenue. They seemed to be doing a lot of illegal things from that spot."

"I know nothing about any warehouse, and certainly nothing about anything illegal."

Fenwick said, "Eddie Homan is dead. We found him murdered."

"I never met the man. I heard of him as a problem at the job. I know we had to take action against him as a cracker. That's all I know." He admitted to having been alone at all the significant moments when crimes were committed. He said, "I spent most of today playing chess with my computer."

Turner's phone rang and Waldron left. It was Bryant Karnetis, the detective from Area One. "I got something for you guys already. I've got a connection with your stuff and Smythe's. When Dwayne was first found, they discovered piss stains on his pants. It was assumed he'd pissed his pants. Nobody made an issue out of it. Nobody wanted to embarrass the guy. Now I think maybe it came from the killer."

"I don't see how he would have had the time," Turner said. "He didn't finish killing him. Why risk pissing if he's only half dead?"

"Maybe he thought he was dead," Karnetis suggested. "Or maybe it was more important for him to send a message, to feel powerful, or whatever sicko shit the killer was into."

"Or it could be Dwayne's," Turner said.

"Yeah," Karnetis said. "Whatever, it will have to be checked, if we saved his pants. Nobody figured it was important. He was the victim, and he was alive. We'll have to check his house and his hospital room. I doubt if they'd have them in the morgue or the evidence lockup."

"Better find out," Turner said. He reported all this to Fenwick. "Whatever you do, Buck, don't say this investigation is starting to piss you off."

"Why ever not?"

"There could be more than one dead cop in this city."

"I am offended. The thought crossed my mind, but I was holding back."

"You don't usually."

"I'm learning restraint."

Turner said, "That would probably be a bigger headline than Pat Robertson and Jerry Falwell naked, holding hands, and running down the middle of an expressway."

"That's disgusting."

"But accurate."

Fenwick said, "We have a killer or killers pissing on people. It's a start, but I want more connections—zillions of connections—or I want to know which of these killings is not connected to bodily functions."

24

I wish I was a knife. If I were, the moment I would enjoy the best would be the instant I entered a body. The millisecond when rushing through air changes to penetrating flesh, that's what I'd like to experience.

The phone on Turner's desk rang again. A voice said, "One down, and you're next." Then there was a dial tone. Turner immediately called the department's communications center. "Where did the call come from that I just received on this line?"

"Lemme check." The clerk didn't sound anywhere near as hurried and anxious as Turner wanted him to. Half a minute later the casual voice got back on the line. "Is this some kind of joke?" it asked.

"Where did it come from?" Turner demanded.

"The pay phone in the lobby of the police station you're in. Downstairs from where you are now."

Turner banged the phone down. He rushed for the stairs.

Fenwick called out as he followed his partner. "What the hell is going on?"

Halfway down the stairs, Turner stopped. Huffing and puffing, Fenwick pulled up beside him. Turner gazed at the large crush of reporters, along with the usual hangers-on, the people coming in to complain, the criminals being taken into custody, the cops on duty. He could see the pay phones. All three of them were in use: a woman who looked to be in her twenties, another woman in her fifties or sixties, and a teenage boy.

Turner said, "I got another threatening call. Communications said it originated from the pay phones in here."

"Urban legend time," Fenwick said. "The killer's in the house." He hummed a few notes from the "Twilight Zone" television theme.

Turner and Fenwick hurried through the mob. They waited for all three callers to finish. The older woman was in tears. They asked to speak to each of them in turn as they finished their conversations. None of the voices was remotely like the one Turner had heard.

"We got another pay phone in this dump?" Turner asked.

"Not that I know about," Fenwick said.

They asked everyone in the vicinity if they'd noticed anyone making a call in the past few minutes. The woman who was crying said, "I waited for a man in a dark outfit. I wasn't paying much attention to him. He was kind of muffled from the cold. I guess he was white. I'm not sure about much else. He was taller than me, but I'm not sure by how much. I didn't see where he went."

No one else reported seeing this man.

Turner and Fenwick went back upstairs. "That takes one hell of a nerve," Fenwick said.

"Download everything and print it," Turner said. "Print every goddamn thing you can find. Back it up to disks. Do whatever it takes. I'm not going to risk losing stuff like we lost that list of sex contacts on Lenzati's computer."

Fenwick said, "We've got to talk to all those computer people again and find out who knew about this place. I'm tired of racing around this city. I want people to come to me."

Micetic agreed to keep working on the computers and call them as soon as he found anything more.

Turner had a mixed feeling of dread and anticipation as he turned on his computer monitor. There was a new icon on his desktop: a red question mark.

"Am I going to click on this?" Turner asked.

"Get Micetic up here first," Fenwick advised. "Don't touch anything."

They sent for Micetic. They made more phone calls to the other cities with cop murders and caught up on paperwork. Since it was early Sunday evening, their calls were less successful than usual.

When Micetic arrived, he worked his magic and said, "There is a message connected with this question mark."

"What is it?" Turner asked.

Micetic pressed a couple of buttons.

In bright red, the message said, "More cops need to die." Turner called up his e-mail. A new note said, "More fear."

"Take the damn machine apart if you have to," Turner said. "Find out where the goddamn message came from."

"We may never know," Micetic said. "I know you don't want to hear that, but it's true."

Fenwick said, "I wish we had a computer shredder, just like we have paper shredders. I'd get great satisfaction out of watching the things die."

"It's not the computer's fault," Micetic said. "A human sent these notes. For some reason an electronic message on a screen seems more imposing than a simple hand-written note. I'll keep on it."

They adjourned to the conference room for the next few interviews. Rian Davis, the head of creativity at Lenzati and Werberg's company was next.

"This is hideous!" she said. "Hideous! I got into computers because it wasn't violent. I never had any of those stupid games that are all about shooting and dying. I just wanted to create new vistas and make the world easier to live in. This is just hideous. How can someone want these people to die?"

"We learned they had some odd hiring practices," Turner said.

"You mean that suit from Nancy Korleski?" Davis asked.

"Yes."

"It was bogus. I knew her from before when she and her husband were working on their little company. They had no business sense. They tried to take it public, but they made every mistake you possibly could when putting together a technology business. They were lucky the two of them didn't starve to death. They'd have both been hired if they were among the best. They weren't."

Turner said, "You mentioned Eddie Homan in our first interview."

"The rat," Davis grumbled.

"He's dead," Fenwick said.

"What?"

"Do you know anything about a work place Mr. Lenzati and Mr. Werberg had on Grand Avenue?"

"No. I've never heard of such a thing. Eddie is dead?"

"He was stabbed to death," Turner said. "We found evidence there that Lenzati and Werberg were engaged in significant criminal activity based from that location."

"I know nothing about that place."

"They never mentioned it?" Turner asked.

"Never."

"You talked about security and hackers and crackers," Turner said. "It seems that they were heavily engaged in hacking themselves."

"Whatever on earth for? They didn't need to."

"They had hacked into companies that were smaller, or

were possible rivals. They didn't necessarily ruin them or take them over when they hacked in. When a company bought the anti-hacker devices from your company, Lenzati and Werberg planted programs in them so that they could break into that company's computers any time they wanted."

"The cops were the crooks," Davis said.

"You knew nothing about any of this?" Fenwick asked.

"Most certainly not. I dealt with creativity. Security is not creativity."

"You and your husband's company fit the profile, a small firm they could have hacked into and ruined."

"I'm afraid we did that all by ourselves. Our incompetence needed no assistance."

The Davis's company had not been among those listed as broken into in the records.

She could account for her whereabouts at the time of the murders; spent with her husband, but uncorroborated by anyone else.

Turner stopped at his desk as the next person entered the third floor to be interviewed.

Micetic said, "You're not gonna like this."

"What?" Turner asked.

"You're getting inundated with e-mail."

Turner said, "Before this week, half the time the e-mail didn't even work."

"Well, it's working now. You're getting literally hundreds of these every second." Micetic pointed to the stark, black, seventy-two point size message: "YOU'RE NEXT."

"Shut it down," Turner said.

"It's probably going to crash in a few seconds anyway," Micetic said. "You've got too much data coming in. This thing is going to be overwhelmed." Before Micetic could press the escape button or close the computer down in any way, the screen completely froze.

Turner reached down and pulled the plug. He said, "Sometimes Fenwick has the right idea."

Nancy and Charley Korleski strode into the room. Mr. Korleski was short and thin, the type Werberg often seemed sexually interested in.

Turner ushered them into the conference room. He said, "You were known to harbor resentments against Mr. Lenzati."

Nancy Korleski said, "We filed a suit against Mr. Lenzati. If everyone who filed a suit was suspected of murder, there'd have to be even more lawyers than we have now."

"We were told you started rumors about them on the Internet," Turner said.

"We didn't need to start them," she said. "They were already there and well established."

"That maybe you yourselves were into hacking," Turner added.

"No way," Nancy Korleski said. "Never. No way." Her husband nodded agreement.

Turner said, "Eddie Homan is dead. Did you know him?"

"We knew of him. He's one of the most famous hackers in the world. He worked for Lenzati and Werberg. That's all we know. I never met him."

Turner said, "On our list of sexual conquests, we have you as well Mr. Korleski."

He said, "It was miserable."

"What happened?" Turner asked.

Charley Korleski said, "He made me do sexual stuff. Not much, really." Korleski described the same general pattern the other men had been asked to perform.

"We need to ask you about your business as well," Turner

said. "We have evidence that Lenzati and Werberg, possibly in league with Eddie Homan, set about destroying their competition."

"How?" Nancy Korleski asked.

"They were crackers of the first order. Sometimes they sold security programs to companies which contained bugs that allowed them to hack into companies whenever they wished. They could get huge jumps on the competition that way."

"Wouldn't someone have noticed a pattern of failures?" Nancy Korleski asked.

"As far as we can figure out," Turner said, "just because they had access didn't mean they used it. They didn't do any raids on products or services or programs or games that would lead directly back to them. Or they timed their attacks so there would be no suspicion aroused. Sometimes they altered other's work to increase frustration, sometimes to cause direct failure. On other occasions they just delayed the competition's product until they could get their own on the market. Were you aware of Lenzati and Werberg committing industrial sabotage to your business?"

"They ruined us," Charley Korleski said. "I knew we didn't fail just because we were inexperienced. I knew there was something behind it. We worked so hard, and they ruined us. Why? What shits they were."

After five minutes Turner interrupted their fulminating about Lenzati and Werberg. He asked the Korleskis to provide their whereabouts at the times of the murders. Their alibis were bland and unverifiable outside their two person unit; twice at home, this Sunday, at an afternoon movie.

25

What I'm really looking forward to is when they catch me. The moment I crave is the one where they parade me out of the station in front of the cameras. I've been practicing my superior smirk. They won't catch me for a while, though. I've got a lot of cops to kill.

While sitting in the conference room waiting for the next witness, Fenwick said, "I'm ready to go with a scenario where they all did it. We throw the lot of them in jail, and the computer age comes to an end."

"Would that it could be that easy."

"I'm the poet in this relationship," Fenwick snapped.

"For which I am grateful," Turner responded.

Molton marched into the conference room. "Your next interview is here, but I've got other news first. The detectives in Area One have the uncle of the kid Dwayne and Ashley shot in custody. They think he's going to be charged."

"No serial killer on Dwayne?" Fenwick asked.

"No."

Turner mentioned the new messages he'd been getting on his computer.

"That could be significant," Molton said, "but I'm getting reports that at least one detective in each squad in the city is getting similar crap. It seems that some loon has broken into the department's server. We're going to shut nonessential parts of the system down. After Micetic is done working with you, he'll join the team of experts that we've got working on it."

"We didn't buy our security from Lenzati and Werberg, did we?" Fenwick asked.

"I have no idea," Molton replied.

Turner explained the process by which Lenzati and Werberg sabotaged rivals, or at least discovered their secrets.

"Holy hell," Molton said, "and clever to boot. If Micetic knows about it, I'm sure he'll be taking that into account. I'll check to be sure." He left.

Fenwick repeated, "No serial killer for Dwayne."

Turner said, "I was feeling less vulnerable when I thought it might be him."

"Me too. I don't want to think about being vulnerable again." Fenwick might have a tough exterior but being blind to genuine fear was not one of his or Turner's faults.

Before the next interview, they were able to ascertain that a number of cops in three of the six previous cities got warnings, but it wasn't always the same cop that was eventually killed. Packages did come for some of the cops in all the squads of those who were killed. Anonymous packages that were not always sent to the victims.

"A random pattern," Turner commented. "This is a very clever and determined killer."

"Too good by half," Fenwick said.

Warren Fortesque, head engineer from Lenzati's and Werberg's company, was their next interview.

Turner asked, "Who was the engineer in charge of the anti-hacker and security devices at the company?"

"Mostly Lenzati and Werberg handled those accounts. I had a team that worked with them. I was in charge of developing the programs, usually after they designed them."

Turner said, "We have reason to believe they were using their security systems to break into other companies."

He gaped in astonishment. "You're kidding?"

"No," Turner said.

"I know nothing about that," Fortesque insisted.

"How could you not?" Fenwick asked. "You were in charge."

"Of a team of developers. I don't know about any sabotage. I tried to make sure companies were secure. I had nothing to do with breaking into anything."

Fenwick asked, "Were you ever in their offices at Damen and Grand Avenue?"

"Never."

"How could you not have been?" Fenwick asked. "Wasn't that where all the work was done on the security systems?"

Fortesque said, "That's where all the work must have been done on adding illegal or unwarranted changes."

"How would you not know about that?" Turner asked.

"Because nothing illegal was ever done at our offices. I would know about anything illegal at the main office. There wasn't anything. I ran a clean operation."

"How did you oversee everything?" Turner asked.

"Pardon me?"

"Did you analyze each system?" Turner asked. "Did you inspect every program that went out? How were these sold? Could a company go to a store and buy them?"

"No. You had to call us directly, and we designed a system tailor-made for your company. I made sure people met deadlines. I helped in development or worked on problem solving."

"Did you have to design a new system for every different customer?" Turner asked. "Isn't that kind of expensive, and sort of like reinventing the wheel each time?"

"Believe me, these people could pay. Often we used one basic program, but we adapted each one to fit a particular company's needs. In addition, we sold them guarantees that we would come and upgrade their service every three months for five years. We were the best. Those who wanted secure protection came to us. There were also weekly or monthly services for the ones who were more paranoid. Those were very expensive. Small companies could never afford them. There's a lot of competition in this industry and there's a lot of cutthroats out there. You need protection."

"But Lenzati and Werberg designed the special packages for each company?" Turner asked.

"Yeah, the vast majority of them. Then different engineers worked out all the specific details, and created the programs."

"How much did Lenzati and Werberg have to do with the final product for each of those companies?"

"They had as much or as little input as they wanted. If it was an especially big client or the problem a company was having was especially complicated, they liked to be directly involved."

"Very possibly, every single system your company sold was sabotaged," Fenwick said. "How could you not have noticed?"

"That's the third time you guys asked me that. I'm telling you, my job was to work on the systems that I was told to and do the part I was assigned. Craig and Brooks could take and alter them any time they wanted."

"I thought you were in charge," Fenwick said.

"I was."

"You don't sound very in charge," Fenwick said.

"I had no reason to kill anybody," Fortesque said.

Turner said, "If the sabotage is the reason for the killing, and you were in charge of that section, I would assume that you would be in as much danger as Lenzati, Werberg, and Homan. If we assume it, why wouldn't a person who was sabotaged assume it? If someone had hacked into your system and discovered what your company was doing, and they were bent on getting revenge, why wouldn't they kill all of you? How would they know which person worked on which program?"

"That would be difficult. We don't sign things."

"Then how does anyone know who worked on what?"

"Well, we know that."

"If you can know it," Turner said, "I assume there's a record of it, and if there's a record of it, then someone can break into that record."

"I could be in danger?"

"Very much so," Turner said. Turner saw the sweat on Fortesque's upper lip.

Fortesque said, "I need protection."

Turner asked him where he was at the time of the murders.

"Yesterday my wife and I left early to go antique shopping up in Wisconsin. She enjoys that. We spent the night in a bed and breakfast in Lake Geneva. We got back this afternoon, did a little grocery shopping, and went home."

His fear was palpable, but they got no further helpful information out of him.

Their last interview was Justin Franki, the surfer blond, the head of research and development. He said, "Once or twice, I had a niggling suspicion that something was going on. If you look at the companies that went broke and then at our hiring, sometimes it seemed kind of convenient."

"Why didn't you report that to someone?" Fenwick asked.

"To who? It was my job and my company. I certainly had no proof. I was never certain."

Turner said, "The pattern we've been able to discover does seem very random. Sometimes they seemed to cause the other company to go broke just as kind of a joke, a lark."

"They never did anything without a plan."

"Even getting killed?" Turner asked.

Franki said, "They were smart. They wouldn't do something stupid."

"Maybe somebody caught them at their own game," Turner said. "Maybe somebody hacked into their computers. Maybe they thought they were geniuses, smarter than everyone else—but maybe they weren't. Or maybe, somebody got lucky. They were doing something illegal and dangerous. Who in your company would be most likely to know what they were up to?"

"I think Fortesque must have known," Franki said. "How can he be head engineer of security development and not know?"

"Do you have any proof that he was aware of what they were doing?" Turner asked.

"Well, no."

Turner asked, "How did you get along with Mr. Fortesque?"

"He's a screamer. That's how he communicates. He gets all red in the face and goes ballistic. Usually, moments like that preceded flashes of genius on his part, so nobody really minded."

"You said you worked next to Eddie Homan."

"Yeah. So what?"

Turner made the announcement. "He's dead."

Franki looked from one cop to the other, licked his lips.

"Where were you this afternoon?" Turner asked.

"Working on some computer programs at home. I've got logs to prove I was there."

"I'd bet computer logs can be faked," Fenwick said.

"That's where I was. All weekend. I had no reason to kill any of these guys."

Turner said, "In our first interview, you mentioned constant glitches in the programs you were working on when you had your own company. We don't have all the data yet, but perhaps we're going to find that they hacked into your company. Maybe they deliberately ruined you."

"They hacked into my company?"

"We don't know for sure yet," Turner said, "but I think it's a safe assumption."

"That would explain it. I haven't had a bit of trouble since I started here. Only when I was with my own company. I thought it was flaws in my design. It was them. The shits."

Turner asked, "At the time you had no sense that anyone was tampering with your product?"

"No! I had no idea. Now that I know, if they were alive . . . those shits!"

His surprise and anger seemed genuine to Turner. He had as much of and as little of an alibi as the others.

After he left, Fenwick said, "How the hell are we going to get irrefutable evidence?"

"I have no idea," Turner said. "Maybe somebody hacked

into Lenzati and Werberg's system. That someone could have altered records. That someone could have hacked into a bunch of other businesses. Maybe a business rival was doing to Werberg and Lenzati what they had done to them."

Turner took all the data they'd gathered on Homan over to the corkboards. Fenwick followed him. "Why are you still adding to this thing?" Fenwick asked.

"I have no doubt that the three computer killings here are connected."

Fenwick agreed.

Turner said, "But we don't know about these others. We've got a lot of knife wounds and a lot of blood. And a lot of piss."

↖ 26 ↘

The thing I hate most about cops is the way they strut when they walk. It's an arrogance of the "in" group. It's power and the presumption of authority at all times. I hate the arrogance. I hate the presumption. When I see them dead at my feet, the hurt goes away for a little while.

Micetic joined them at the corkboard. "The message on your computer screen that froze everything else out came from the computers at Lenzati and Werberg's secret lab."

"They were dead," Fenwick said. "How could they be sending anyone messages?"

"Whoever killed them," Turner said. "It's only logical. The questions is, who would want to kill them and me?"

"I've got another possible scenario," Micetic said. "Once their computers were opened up to the Internet, they were vulnerable. It doesn't have to be their killer at all. They claimed they were geniuses without peer. Maybe there was somebody brighter than they were. Or at least maybe there was someone bright enough to break into their computers.

Or maybe someone simply managed to co-opt their computers like they did when they brought down Yahoo and those other companies last year. Someone used remote computers that they could break into and then send messages routed through them. A killer would know doing that would screw up the investigation. You've got several murders. You'd never know how they were connected. If they were or not, you'd have a slew of new data that would, at the very least, confuse you or cause you to ask more questions, endless questions. It would cost you hours of work to sort through the mess, and you'd never know which was connected to which. At the most, of course, you'd never solve the crime."

Turner said, "The killer was giving us millions of extra connections."

"Yes."

"We've got to sort them out," Turner said. "We need more charts. We need to get the name of every company that ever got security from Lenzati and Werberg. Let's get a profile of them based on all the data we can find. Then we'll take all our suspects, including the sexual contacts we've managed to unearth. We need to profile everything we know about them. Anything any of them ever had to do with a computer needs to be on there. Then we'll cross-reference all of that."

Several hours later the new charts filled more than half of the corkboard. Fenwick and Turner examined their handiwork.

"It looks great," Fenwick said. "I'm just not sure it's much help."

Fifteen minutes later Micetic, who'd been working at Fenwick's computer, announced, "I've got Eddie Homan's home address."

"How'd you get it?" Turner asked.

"We had his Social Security number. It doesn't take much once you've got that."

Eddie Homan lived in a apartment just south of the Stevenson Expressway. The McCormick Place complex dominated the view to the east and north. His one room apartment was a pig sty. Dirty clothes were stacked in one corner next to a purple futon. There was no dresser. Atop the sink, pizza delivery boxes containing half-eaten pizzas, several at the bottom beginning to mold, were piled fourteen deep. The refrigerator was crammed with cartons, most of them partially filled with what was possibly edible several lifetimes ago. Homan did have four unopened bottles of Samuel Adams beer.

"These are all of his clothes?" Fenwick asked.

"I haven't seen any others," Turner said.

"This must be rat heaven," Fenwick said.

Turner said, "I don't think even a self-respecting rat would live here." The toilet bowl was black with scum. There was no shower. The sink next to the commode was encrusted with rust.

Turner, Fenwick, and Micetic gathered at the only remotely clean spot in the room, the computer station. It took up a third of the space in the darkest corner farthest from any windows.

Micetic typed at the computer while Fenwick and Turner inspected the accumulated filth. Fifteen minutes later, under a pile of shredded paper Turner found a Palm Pilot. He handed it to Micetic.

The computer expert pointed at Homan's machine and said, "I've found records here of their security attacks. I'll print out copies in a few minutes." He took the Palm Pilot and connected it to the computer. In seconds the screen began revealing information. "I think this is Lenzati's," he said. "It's got names and addresses of people." He studied it for several minutes while Turner and Fenwick returned to inspecting the rest of the space. They found nothing that indicated who might have wanted to kill the three victims. They went back to Micetic. He said, "The Palm Pilot has anecdotal records of some of their sexual escapades. It also seems that Lenzati bragged a bit to Eddie Homan."

"The two of them were buddies?" Turner asked.

"From what this says, I think it was more he gave out hints like Werberg did to his sister. Homan was pretty bright. He must have found out about this thing's existence and gotten hold of it."

"Is there any way to print it out?" Turner asked.

"Sure. I'll print it with the other stuff. You're going to have hundreds of pages to go through. I think a lot of it matches what we found at the secret warehouse."

In seconds pages from the Palm Pilot began to emerge.

Turner grabbed the first sheet. "He kept records just like Werberg. I like a victim who keeps records of something that could lead to his killer." He and Fenwick examined more pages as they emerged. "These are only of the couples they seduced," Turner said, "what they did, and how he got proof to add them to the conquest list."

"Perfect," Fenwick said.

"How did Homan get it?" Turner asked.

Micetic said, "In the original encryption from Werberg, he talked about Lenzati's proof. This must have been what he was talking about. If Homan had Werberg's encrypted material, he could have glommed onto this as well."

"Maybe he was blackmailing them?" Fenwick said. "I was hoping we'd get blackmail in here somehow."

Turner said, "He knew what they had done. He got into their computers. He had the goods on both of them, but then somebody got to them and him. He couldn't have been killed before the two of them. The killer was after Homan too."

Fenwick pointed to the Palm Pilot. "Why? To get this thing? Why didn't the killer come here and retrieve it?"

Turner asked, "Maybe he or she didn't know it existed. Maybe he or she thought all records were somewhere on the computers at the secret warehouse and never found it. We wanted to find it, but we weren't frantic about it. We had no idea it would contain this much information. How would the killer know it would contain all this? He or she probably wouldn't."

It was nearly eleven when they got back to the station. Fenwick said, "I'm beat. I want to go home. I don't want you to check your computer anymore. I don't want any more phone messages."

"There's no chocolate on my desk."

Fenwick said, "Not every killer is perfect."

Turner walked up to the corkboard. "Let's at least put this information from Craig Lenzati's Palm Pilot up here." They spent fifteen minutes filling in as many blanks as they could. Micetic added the data he'd gotten so far from Homan's computer on the security fraud Lenzati and Werberg had been perpetuating.

Micetic and Turner met in front of Rian Davis's name. Micetic said, "She and her husband had a company that failed."

Turner said, "It's not listed on the printouts from the warehouse."

"But it is on Eddie Homan's," Micetic said.

"They didn't know about this backup file," Turner guessed. He checked the original sexual encryption they had downloaded. "There's no couple listed for three months before or after they failed."

"When was she hired?" Fenwick asked.

"Do we have records of that?" Turner asked.

"I'll check the Palm Pilot," Micetic said. He picked it up and began punching letters on the keyboard. Moments later he showed the results to the detectives.

Turner said, "Rian Davis, the head of the creativity division, had a business that failed and a husband who could have been part of a sex duo. The couple that filed the law suit also fits the bill. The Zengres didn't have a business. Who among those others was married?"

Fenwick said, "We haven't been able to find a lot of the married ones, and remember some didn't have names."

Micetic said, "It's here in the Palm Pilot. A month after the Davises business failed, Lenzati and Werberg made it with both a husband and wife. Lenzati refers to RPD."

Turner said, "Rian Porter Davis. Lenzati and Werberg wrecked their business. The Davises erased the records at the warehouse, but not at Eddie's. They didn't know about Eddie's."

Micetic added, "P is referred to as being a 'steady' with Werberg."

"Steady?" Fenwick asked.

"Yeah, Lenzati records that Werberg tried to add the number of times he made it with a guy to his proof profile. He refers to arguments they had about it. There were only a few repeats."

"Anybody else connected with this that has the initials RPD?" Fenwick asked.

Micetic searched the Palm Pilot. "Not that I can find."

27

I'm going to kill him. The next chance I get, he's going to be dead.

Turner and Fenwick found the home address for Porter and Rian Davis and drove over. It was just past midnight.

"I'm going to sleep for a week after this is over," Fenwick said.

"You and me both," Turner said.

They rang the doorbell for several minutes before it was answered. Rian Davis wore a sweater over blue jeans. Her husband, Porter, wore a sweatshirt and warm-up pants with a Stanford University logo on them.

"It's late," Rian said.

Porter Davis was short and thin—Werberg's type. He had short-cropped hair with a budding bald spot in the back.

"We found Eddie Homan's apartment," Turner announced.

"Where was the creep hiding?" Rian asked.

Turner said, "We found a lot of data on his computer that wasn't anywhere else."

Silence.

"We found evidence they attempted to ruin your company."

"What?" Rian asked.

"Big time sabotage. We have records that show they interfered with your company before it went broke. Eddie Homan had a record, although it wasn't in the files at the warehouse. Someone erased it from there. You didn't know about the files at his apartment, did you?"

More silence.

Turner said, "We also have a list of couples they had sex with."

"That's outrageous," Porter said. "Do you have any proof that we were among those couples?"

"Did either of you have sex with either of them?"

"I most certainly did not," Porter said.

"The whole concept is revolting," Rian said. "Are you telling us they ruined our business deliberately?"

"As far as we can tell, yes," Turner said. "Lenzati and Werberg caused your company to go bust. They got into your designs and altered them. You never discovered the flaws, so you couldn't fix them. They kept records of their triumphs."

Porter said, "I knew at the time we weren't all that bad."

"We were all that bad," Rian said. "They just nudged the inevitable on further and quicker."

"Maybe. But maybe we could have made it without their interference."

Turner said, "We also found Craig Lenzati's Palm Pilot."

"Oh," Porter Davis said. They were in the living room. The husband and wife sat on a lemon-yellow divan. Turner and Fenwick were in matching wing chairs.

282

Turner continued, "From data found in Lenzati's Palm Pilot, we believe they had sex with both of you. And Mr. Davis, we believe Mr. Werberg continued to have a sexual relationship with you."

"You did what!" Rian Davis said.

Porter Davis looked stricken. "I had to. He said if I didn't, they'd fire you."

Turner and Fenwick took the Davises down to the station and separated them. Rian was unwilling to speak to the detectives and demanded a lawyer. Porter, however, began to tell all.

"My wife and I found their scoring system. It took a while, but we broke the code. We erased all reference to ourselves. Or we thought we had. We didn't know Eddie Homan found or kept records at his home as well. We didn't know Lenzati kept a record on his Palm Pilot. We knew Brooks had anecdotal records. We found those and erased ourselves from them as well. They thought they were so damn smart about security. After we killed them, we erased everything that related to ourselves—including information about our company. That jerk Eddie still had a record."

"Why did you agree to have sex with them?"

"We were desperate for money."

"Why did you decide to kill them?"

"The sex stuff always rankled. Maybe we could have gotten over that. When we found out what they had done to our company, that was too much. Eddie Homan led us to that bit of information. We met him at a hacker's convention in Switzerland. We were eager to get revenge. He told us he was double-crossing them."

"Why kill Eddie?"

"He's the only one who knew what we had done—the

only one who had proof. We thought the warehouse was the whole operation. Eddie said it was. It was so complete. It turns out Eddie was double-crossing us as well. I should have known he'd keep a separate set of records. We never could discover where he lived. We even tried the IRS computers to get his address."

"You didn't try Social Security," Turner said.

"We could never find his number. He'd erased all of his employment records from the company. It was as if he didn't exist."

Turner asked, "How'd you get past the security system at Lenzati's?"

"My wife offered him sex. He was surprised to see her that morning. After she let me in, we killed him. When we were done, we simply took all the tapes from the previous week, just to be safe. We turned the whole security system off before we left."

To get into Werberg's house, Porter had used the ruse of going over for his monthly sexual encounter. "I got him to put off going to work after your interview that morning. He was always horny, even though he seldom did much. My wife didn't know I could get in because I'd been having sex. She thought Eddie and I had worked out a way to get past the security devices."

"Why didn't you tell her?"

"It was disgusting. I just didn't want to get into it."

"Why was he tied up?"

"For some reason, Werberg became suspicious. He must have figured out that Eddie was downstairs cutting off his escape. After he got suspicious, he fled to the computer room. He claimed he was going to the bathroom. I was tired of waiting so I went after him. I found him trying to send a message from his computer. We caught him before he could type more than a couple of words. We made him watch while we wrecked everything. It took both Eddie and me to pick him up and smash his head through the computer monitor. I never thought of myself as a violent person before I met these two fuckers. I guess I am. Maybe we all are. I know that doesn't excuse my guilt. I don't ever remember hearing a more satisfying sound, or seeing a more satisfying sight, than when his head first broke through. After he was dead, Eddie decided it would be a bit of bravado to use his own computer to announce his death. That was the deal with the chatroom announcement."

"But your wife was there?"

"She was there for all the killings. I did the initial stabbing. She finished them off. She did all the extra gore. She worked very hard and hated losing our company. She hated that she had to debase herself sexually. I hate violence, but it felt good—real good—to watch them die."

"How'd you find the warehouse and how did you get in?"

"Eddie told us about it a while ago. Ostensibly, we went there with him to try and salvage all the security hacking data they had done. We thought we might try to cash in on their hacking. Eddie knew how to get in."

"Why did you piss on them?" Fenwick asked.

"We both did. An appropriate farewell to some of the biggest pigs in town. On Lenzati it was more than just an afterthought. I was furious at them, but Rian went nuts. I thought she would never stop stabbing Lenzati. In the end I had to restrain her. She pissed on Lenzati. I did it on Werberg. We both did on Homan."

"Why send me messages?" Turner asked.

"We didn't send you any messages."

"Did you have anything to do with the detectives who died in different cities?" Turner asked.

"We hoped we could try and confuse our killings with theirs, but we didn't kill any cops. We had nothing to do with any cops. We can prove we weren't in those cities when it happened." He hung his head. "It's over. Finally, it's over. They've been stopped. We're going to have to pay, but those predators have been stopped." His hands trembled. "My life wasn't supposed to turn out like this. I want to close my eyes and make it all not have happened." He sighed deeply. "But I'm glad we killed them."

⊾ 28 ⊿

Watching them die. That's the best.

Turner and Fenwick worked long into the night finishing the paperwork involved with the arrests. They both had the next two days off.

The next morning Turner woke long enough to have breakfast with his family and to see his sons off to school and Ben off to work. He went back to bed and got up again around ten. He padded around the house in his stocking feet, faded blue jeans, and an old gray logo-less sweatshirt that belonged to his older son. He read the newspaper, drank some juice, did a little light cleaning, and threw in a load of laundry.

The house was startlingly silent, the weekday morning blessedly peaceful. The January thaw had eliminated all but the most tenacious mounds of gray-crusted snow. Just after twelve, he made himself a plate of left-over meatballs, sausage, and mozzarella. He nuked it hot then ate in the living room, a luxury he usually forwent so his sons would not demand the same privilege. After finishing half the meal, he sat down in front of the computer screen.

Turner had brought home all the research that had been connected with the killings of the detectives around the country. He inserted the disk with the spreadsheets into the super drive. The disk icon appeared, and he clicked on it. Then he opened the file with all the amassed data on the cop killings cross-referenced. He was desperate to find the one connection that would pull those cases together.

Turner read the information line by line on all the killings. The arrest and conviction records of the cops who'd been murdered was the most tedious of all the data to wade through. He began organizing all the arrests in a spread-sheet. He'd watched Micetic work with them over the past few days, and thought he had the hang of it. He'd been getting better at them. He took each convict and entered him by crime and time served. He also cross-checked each with Dwayne Smythe, Lenzati, Werberg, and Homan. He was aware that Porter Davis had said they had nothing to do with the cop killings, but Turner was determined to be thorough.

No one Lenzati, Werberg, or Homan knew was currently incarcerated. A former employee of Lenzati and Werberg had gone to jail in Chicago. He had died several years ago after having been raped repeatedly while locked up.

By the time he'd gone through the third cop's arrests records, he began to get an idea. Each of the detectives had a person who they had helped to convict die while in prison. Turner checked all the others. They had all had someone die in the past five years in prison.

Turner grabbed the phone. There was no answer at Buck's. He called Micetic. No one knew where he was. To the person who answered in the computer room at police head-quarters, he said, "I want the records on the following criminal cases in the following cities. These people all died in prison. I want the names of all the people they know, all their friends, relatives—anybody connected with them or their cases, no matter how remote. I want descriptions, current whereabouts, everything."

Within half an hour he had his first few answers. The third one was the charm. A man who had been convicted of computer hacking in Boston had been raped and brutally beaten in prison. He'd almost died. He had been released early, but his whereabouts were unknown. Turner read the physical description.

The doorbell rang. Andy Wycliff was on the front step. Turner didn't realize he'd been working so long at the computer. The cop car providing his protection was parked at the hydrant halfway down the block. He gave them a brief wave. Paul said, "I didn't think school was out yet."

"It's not. Can I wait for Brian here?"

Turner let him in. The boy slumped onto the couch and Turner returned to the computer screen. A second or two of looking at the latest data he'd pulled up, and he turned back to the teenager. He asked, "Andy, where are you from?"

Wycliff stood up and pulled a gun out of his jacket pocket.

Turner said, "I thought you just used a knife."

"I usually get the drop on someone or wait for the best opportunity. Here's the knife." He pulled a jagged-edged steel behemoth out of his coat pocket. Wycliff said, "I want to make this quick. You get to know why you are going to die, and then you die."

"None of the other cops fought back?"

"I didn't give them a chance. I researched the best places to stab on a person's body. The Internet is a marvel. But even better, in prison I learned how to fight with a knife. The very large Hispanic man who forced me to service him was a marvelous teacher. He taught me how to get revenge, exercise right, and kill someone with one quick thrust to exactly the right spot, or how to make someone suffer for at least a little while with a jab or two into vulnerable and valuable organs."

Turner said, "You're getting even with cops who put computer people in jail."

"You're close. It didn't have to be a computer person. No, these cops died if someone they put in prison was killed—especially a teenager, an innocent teenager, like me. I had to do a lot of research. I almost died in prison. I didn't do anything that serious, but they threw the book at me. I cracked into a few computer systems. Big deal. For that I almost got killed. Until I submitted to my protector, I was raped every night, sometimes by more than one guy. The innocent were made to pay in prison, so I figured the cops could pay when I got out. The murders of Lenzati, Werberg, and Homan were kind of a bonus. With that kind of carnage added to the mix, I found it easier to scare people."

"I don't know of anybody I arrested who died in prison."

"There you are very wrong. There are actually seven cops in the city of Chicago who have had young people die in prison. You were one of them. I watched each of you for a while. You were picked because I got to know you first. The only true connections in my vengeance spree were having an innocent person dead in prison, the cops had to have kids, and pissing on them after I killed them. I kind of played around with the other connections. I knew they'd try and make profiles. I enjoyed the *Tribune* article. The reporter made so many connections I never even thought of." He paused and used the sleeve of his jacket to wipe the sweat from his forehead.

"After I decided it would be you, I made my plans. Since it's easy for me to look like a teenager, I thought I'd try enrolling in your kid's school. Then I began hanging around the house. That got a little risky at times, but I enjoyed it. That was a heart-stopping few seconds the other night when the cops approached the van."

At least the guy could be scared. "You sent all the computer messages."

"Yes, and made the call from the station. Getting into the computers at Werberg and Lenzati's secret lab to send you a message from the machines there took a lot of doing. It's what took me so long to get around to killing you. I wish I had time to inspect what they did. Those guys were geniuses."

"Why the chocolate?"

"To make you uneasy, to make you scared. To make you suffer."

"I think I was more annoyed than scared." He wasn't about to tell the kid that at the moment he was plenty scared. Paul continued, "You didn't get the drop on me. I'm aware of you."

"I'm a better fighter. You might be a tough cop, but you've never been in prison. I kind of liked the transformation from neurotic computer dweeb, to buff, killing machine computer dweeb." He moved a step closer.

Paul saw that Wycliff was trembling. Both gun and knife wobbled almost uncontrollably.

Wycliff continued, "I've never talked to one of my victims. I've never gotten this close. This is perfect. More than perfect. I know who you are. I've spied on you. I've threatened you. I've seen you react. I know you're scared, and you're going to die."

"You're the one who's trembling," Paul pointed out.

For a second, Wycliff looked at his quivering hands.

Paul's son Brian walked in the door. Wycliff swung toward him, knife flashing. Paul surged forward. Brian fell to his knees. In two steps Paul was on Wycliff. Paul saw blood blossom on Brian's left wrist. With one hand he grabbed Wycliff's hair, yanked and twisted simultaneously, immediately bringing the kid to his knees. He took his palm and rammed it into the kid's nose. Wycliff dropped knife and gun. Paul slammed Wycliff's head against the wall. The young man dropped to the floor, gurgled unintelligibly for several seconds, then fell unconscious.

Kicking the gun and knife out of the way, Paul knelt over his son. Father and son looked at the cut on the outside of the wrist. "You all right?" Paul asked.

"It's not too bad," Brian said. He tried squeezing the deep, two-inch-long gash shut with his other hand. Blood continued to ooze. "What the hell is going on?"

"We caught a killer."

Turner called paramedics and backup cops. In minutes the street was flooded with rotating lights and official cars. Mrs. Talucci showed up in five minutes. Fenwick arrived half an hour later. Paul insisted that Brian get stitches. The visit to their family doctor's clinic office was mercifully short.

That night Brian, his wrist bandaged, sat with Jeff, Ben, and Paul around the kitchen table. Mrs. Talucci had brought over homemade raviolis for their dinner. She had insisted on not staying.

"I wish I'd have been here," Jeff said. "I'd have knocked him over with my wheelchair."

Paul told him, "I don't think this is about being tough and macho. We had a narrow escape today. I don't know about the rest of you, but I'm a little shook and a little tired." After dinner there was a requisite amount of homework and a little television watching. Paul helped Jeff with some math. Ben and Paul worked for a while in the basement on the water heater, which was malfunctioning. Paul knew they would need a new one soon.

Brian had been unusually quiet all night. After everyone else had gone to bed, Paul found Brian sitting in the darkened living room. He sat down next to his son. He said, "You don't have to go to school tomorrow, but you should try and get some sleep."

Brian said, "I brought a killer into the house."

Paul said, "I talked to the detectives dealing with the case while you were being stitched up. Andy Wycliff used the fact that he looked so young to help in his disguise. He was actually twenty-two. He'd planned well. He went to your school to establish an identity, a place in the city. When he called his parents for things, it was all play acting. He had his own apartment. To get into the school, he faked his records, which wasn't hard for him to do. The detectives found out he lived on computer work he did freelance."

"I feel stupid," Brian said. "I should have known."

"How could you have known?"

"Shouldn't I be able to sense these things?"

"I wasn't able to, and I'm supposed to be trained to do this kind of thing. I know it's a popular pastime to beat up on ourselves for not being able to predict the future, but you know we can't. As for insights into people, I've known a lot of people for a long time. They always surprise me."

"But usually, they don't surprise you with death."

"Some surprise you with love. You can't ever be sure what you're going to get. Go easy on yourself."

Paul put his hand on his son's shoulder. He saw a trickle of tears down the boy's right cheek. "We're going to be okay," Paul said.

"I know." His son wiped the tear with the back of his hand. "The danger's over."

"I was scared," his son said.

"It's done now," Paul said. He wished he had a way to make his son's fears disappear. He knew he didn't. It was late. They both needed sleep. Paul followed his son upstairs. In front of his door Brian turned, and they hugged silently. "Thanks Dad," he whispered.

In their room, Paul fell into Ben's arms.

"You're exhausted," Ben said.

"Cop work is tough, but reassuring a teenage boy is tougher." He told him what Brian had said.

After he finished, Ben said, "He loves you, I love you. We care."